REBEL SECRETS

DEVILS HOCKEY

STEPHANIE JULIAN

MOONLIT NIGHT PUBLISHING

REBEL SECRETS

DEVILS HOCKEY

CHAPTER ONE

FIVE MONTHS BEFORE THE WEDDING

ebel

"...so, to Rowdy and Tressy. Congrats on your engagement. Brother, you definitely don't deserve this special woman. But you're a lucky man because she agreed to marry you. And Tressy, when you get sick of him, I'll be here to kick his a— ah, but back into line."

From my left, I heard Krista, my soon-to-be niece, giggling. Turning, I gave her a wink. At almost eight and practically a resident at the arena, she'd heard much worse. But we were at my parents' house for the engagement dinner of my brother, Rowdy, and Krista's mom, Tressy. I knew better than to use that kind of language with my mom present. And in front of nearly half the town, including all of the women from my mom's various volunteer groups.

And even though the entire Devils team was here, I knew "ass" was out of the question, and "fuck" would get me a smack upside the head from either my mom or my sister, Rain. Probably both.

Dressed in a new suit my sister Rain had insisted I needed and that I loved more than I'd ever admit—I raised my glass of champagne and nodded my head at the couple beaming in front of the roaring fireplace.

Mom had managed to pull together this way-too-fancy affair in an incredibly short amount of time, but then my mom was amazing like that.

Rowdy had proposed to Tressy two weeks ago, on fucking Valentine's Day, if you can believe it. At the fucking Tea Room, the local bar, which I guess made sense, considering that's where they'd met a year and a half ago. Tressy had wound up stranded in St. David after her car had gotten a flat, and Rowdy fell hard and fast. Lucky for him, Tressy fell, too.

Good for them. I gave Rowdy a lot of shit, but he was a great guy, and Tressy was an amazing woman. They were good to each other, and their marriage would last. Rowdy didn't do shit half-assed.

Just the thought of getting married gave me the heebes. I barely had my own life figured out. How the hell was I supposed to deal with another person's shit at the same time?

With my duties as future best man complete, I could enjoy the rest of the night... as much as I enjoyed being forced to mingle with this many people. Rowdy called me antisocial. Rain called me grumpy. My younger brother, Rocky... well, he understood. We never really talked about it, but he and I shared more than just our love of hockey.

The crowd converged on the happy couple, and I gladly shifted away to the corner where most of the Devils were hanging out.

"Reb, nice speech. Almost didn't realize it was you. You actually sounded happy."

With my back to the room, I could safely give Kaden Felix the finger. I couldn't give him both because I couldn't drop my beer glass. The Devil's goalie laughed, raising his glass in a salute to me.

"Good to know the AHL hasn't civilized you."

Kaden and I had played together for years, at least until I'd gotten a contract with the Reading Redtails just a couple of months ago. This was the first time I'd been home since moving to a new league.

To say it'd been an adjustment was an understatement. But even as my anxiety rose, I throttled it back ruthlessly.

"Nothing'll civilize Reb. You're always going to be a pain in the ass, aren't you?"

My sister suddenly stood beside me, sticking her elbow in my side as she smiled up at me. I had to smile back.

"Always, Rainbow Brite. You learned from the master, after all."

She rolled her eyes at the childhood nickname, just like I knew she would, and shook her head. "You're a menace."

"You're a brat."

"And you're both too old to fight like children."

Our mom materialized at my side, wrapping her arm around my waist and giving me a little hug. Raffi Lawrence barely reached my shoulder, dressed like a more sophisticated flower child of the seventies and didn't look a day over forty. And she ruled our family with love…and an occasional iron fist. Covered by a velvet glove, of course.

"We're not fighting." I shrugged. "We're expressing our affection."

I got a laugh out of the only two women in my life who

mattered. Not bad for me. Usually I pissed everyone off. Of course, it was still early.

"I guess I should be glad you're behaving as well as you are," Mom glanced up at me. "Your speech was perfect, sweetheart."

That came with a gentle pat on my back and a smile just for me. My mom knew how much I hate public speaking, or public anything, unless it's playing hockey. After my family, hockey's the only thing I care about.

"Thanks."

"Now," Mom said, looking around the circle of huge, brawny hockey players she treated as an extension of our family, "we've got all this food. I expect you boys to make sure there are no leftovers."

Most of those "boys" had passed into adulthood several years ago, but, as if Mom had said the magic words, they said, "Yes, ma'am," and moved like someone had lit their asses on fire.

Leaving my sister and I alone for the first time tonight. She and her boyfriend, Brian, had been sticking close to Brian's sister Lindsey and her daughter, Maddy, most of the night. Lindsey, who'd moved to St. David with Maddy only a few weeks ago, was still getting acclimated to life in a small town. And the scrutiny that brings with it for newcomers.

So far, though, she seemed to be doing well. She'd gotten a job at the local coffee shop and would work part-time at the arena, where Maddy would have a community to watch over her. Maddy seemed to have fit into life in St. David just fine.

"So," Rain said, "Erin and I are coming to your game next week."

My head snapped around to look at my sister like she'd grown another head. "What? Why?"

If there was one of my sister's friends who I'd thought would never show up at one of my AHL games, it was Erin Wright.

Rain gave me a look that clearly expressed how ridiculous she considered that statement. My sister had definitely inherited that from Mom.

"I asked her to, and she's one of my best friends, so she said yes. Caity would've come, too, but the Angels have a dance competition that weekend."

I liked Caity. The mouthy redhead and I had once considered doing more than a casual thing, but I couldn't bring myself to commit. I didn't want to saddle anyone with my issues. And if I was honest, I didn't want to have to deal with anyone else's issues. I had enough of my own.

Erin… I winced just thinking about her. Perpetually cheerful. Always looking on the "bright side," whatever the fuck that was. I'd overheard her talking about "manifesting big changes" one day when I'd had to go to her bakery for coffee because my machine had broken, and it was like she was selling timeshares to gullible seniors.

Everything about her rubbed me the fucking wrong way. From her wavy red hair that she almost always had wrapped up in one of those messy buns on top of her head, and the chunky glasses she'd occasionally wore that made her eyes look even greener somehow. She always had flour on her clothing somewhere and usually on her face, that, yeah, was pretty if you liked women who looked like they'd climbed out of a children's fairytale.

And that wasn't an exaggeration. She loved dressing up as a fairy to go to the Pennsylvania Renaissance Fair. And I only knew that because she'd dragged Rain there every year since she'd moved to town. Rain had tried to get me to go one year, said I'd fit right in as a jouster with my messy hair and grumpy attitude. I took that as a compliment, but I'd never joined them, even though, yeah, I'd probably have fun. And I knew they made good beer there.

I'm pretty sure Erin felt the same about me. I'd overheard her ask Rain why I was so grumpy all the time, shortly after she'd moved here to help her granddad run the local newspaper and open her own bakery and coffeeshop.

When Rain had shrugged and said, "That's just Rebel," Erin had taken that as a personal challenge. She'd learned pretty quick she wasn't going to be the person to change my attitude.

So we usually kept out of each other's ways. But she was my sister's best friend and now business partner, so I couldn't just avoid her whenever I was home. Since I'd moved to Reading to play with the Redtails, that wasn't much of a problem because I didn't get home a lot.

And that was a whole other issue, wasn't it?

"Hello, earth to Rebel. Did you hear me? Will you get us tickets or do I need to order them myself?"

My turn to roll my eyes. "Of course I'll get you tickets, Rainy Day." Which meant I should make a note now on my phone or I'd forget. But of course, my sister knew me well.

"I'll text you Monday before you go to practice to remind you, and we'll see you Friday." Then she smiled so big, my lips curved as well. "I can't wait to see you play, Reb. I know you're still getting your feet under you in a new team, but you've already got a couple goals in just a few games. That's amazing for any defenseman."

I shored up my grin. My little sister could read people better than most people read books. And she especially could read her brothers like we were fucking billboards. It was annoying as all hell.

"Let's just say there's been a learning curve."

"Well, you don't have to learn how to play hockey. You were always great at that."

Rain was also her brothers' biggest cheerleader, as well as our biggest pest. And I loved her. I did. Sometimes, though…

"Erin's looking forward to coming to the game. She's never been to one other than the Devils, so I told her to be prepared because they're not as much fun." Her smile let me know she was kind of kidding. Mostly. "And we plan to take you out afterward, just for an hour or so. I know you have another game the next night. And you need your rest at your advanced age."

And there was the brat I knew and loved.

"I think I can manage to be civil for an hour." At least as long as Erin didn't open her mouth much.

"I'm gonna hold you to that."

I knew she would. I also knew five minutes into any conversation and Erin's gratingly cheerful presence would make me grit my teeth so hard, I'd get a headache. But I loved my sister.

"Hey, Reb. Rain told you I can't make it Saturday, right? Maddy's chorus concert is that night."

The man who stopped next to Rain and put his arm around her shoulders still occasionally looked at me like I might bite his hand off at any second. Brian Fiskers used to be one of my best friends. We'd fucked that up royally years ago, but his relationship with my sister had forced us to repair at least some of the damage. Not all.

"Yeah, no problem." I shrugged. "There'll be another game. Heard you had a few good games."

Brian looked at me as if he was trying to see the meaning behind my words, looking for the dig or the sarcasm.

Honestly, I could say there was nothing there. Brian must have realize that because he said, "I think I'm finally getting back into my stride."

"The Devils are lucky to have you." I meant every word.

"And we miss you."

Yeah, I still felt guilty about leaving in the middle of the season. Like I was abandoning the team I'd played with since I left college. My family's team. The team I'd always thought I'd live and breathe.

"The new guy's fitting in pretty well, so far." Rain was quick to fill the silence. "He's really young, though. And he's… a little rough."

When I'd left, the Devils had had to sign a new defenseman. Pop had found an eighteen-year-old kid from Michigan who'd been playing in the OHL. But he'd had some issues. Pop had a soft spot for troublemakers. Rowdy and I had given him lots of practice.

"I'm sure Rowdy'll get him in line."

Over Rain's shoulder, I saw a flash of rose-gold hair and dark green silk. For a second, my gaze caught Erin's. Her eyes widened before she made a made a sharp turn and headed in the opposite direction. Mentally, I rolled my eyes and sent up a little prayer for dodging a bullet. If I had to listen to her drone on about scones or cookies or—

"Reb? You still here?"

I shook my head, trying to throw off the bad mood Erin always put me in. Which wasn't completely fair. Most of the problem was mine, though I think she did go out of her way to be extra sunny and annoying around me since she knew I couldn't stand it.

"Yeah, sorry, just…"

Got distracted by my dislike of your best friend. Get your head out of your ass and pay attention.

"I don't think I've met the new kid yet. Is he here?"

Though I no longer played for my family's team, I still liked to know who everyone was. Our dad had made the announcement that he was retiring at the end of the season, and that Rowdy and Rain were going to be taking over operations. I still hadn't truly wrapped my head around those facts yet, and those subjects consumed a lot of my therapy time.

Rain's head turned, looking for the new kid, I assumed.

"Yeah, somewhere. Just…there he is. Oh. Maybe I should just…"

And then she walked away like someone had lit her ass on fire.

I looked at Brian with a WTF expression, and he glanced after Rain. He grinned a second later.

"I'm not sure which one she's going to save, but it looks like Erin and Dante are, uh, talking? Yeah, that's not gonna go well. She and the kid didn't hit it off exactly."

Well, then I really needed to meet this kid. He and I already had something in common. I turned to search for Rain, but of course, it was Erin's bright hair that caught my eye first. But she wasn't smiling now.

She had a look on her face I could only recall ever seeing when she talked to me. Her lips smashed together in a straight line, arms crossed over her chest and her body one long rigid line.

Jesus, what the hell had the kid said to put her in that state? Usually, I was the only one who could do that. I couldn't decide if I was impressed or jealous. As I watched, Erin's lips parted, but just before she could say anything, Rain put one hand on Erin's arm and one on the guy's shoulder, who was standing maybe just a little too close to Erin.

Not that I cared how close anyone stood to her. But if the guy was frightening her, that was something else entirely.

I switched my attention to the new guy. Tall, but not a lot of muscle. Like a St. Bernard puppy that was huge but didn't quite know how to control everything all at once. A head full of dark curls cut short and a face full of freckles. His light brown skin couldn't hide the flush on his cheeks. Whether from anger or embarrassment, I couldn't tell.

Been there, done that, kid.

With her back to me, I couldn't tell what Rain was saying, but her head swiveled side to side, addressing Erin and…

"What's the kid's name again?" I asked Brian. My memory was shit for names.

"Dante Cantagno."

"Where's he from?"

"Detroit originally. His parents moved a lot, so he played for a mess of leagues before he got drafted into the OHL for Erie. Good forward, got some real skill with the stick, but he's an ankle burner. Coach's been working with him, and he's made a lot of progress in a short period of time. He's hard on himself. Kinda reminds me of someone I know."

I gave Brian the finger but kept my attention on the situation on the other side of the room. I don't know if my sister recognized what was happening with Dante, but I certainly did. He wasn't angry. He'd just gotten himself into a situation he didn't know how to get out of. A situation he probably thought he'd created and didn't know how to fix.

Brian was right. That kid had a lot of me in him.

"Be back in a few," I said to Brian, then headed across the floor.

By the time I got there, Rain looked relieved, Erin's sunny smile was back, and she was talking a mile a minute, and the kid looked miserable. Which Erin, unsurprisingly, completely ignored.

I stopped between Rain and the new kid, who looked up at me like I was his savior. I stuck out my hand, which he took with a hard grip.

"Hey. I'm Rebel."

"I know. Good to meet you, sir."

Ouch. I wasn't that damn old. But I wasn't going to embarrass the kid more than he already seemed to be.

"Rain, Dante and I are gonna get something to drink."

I had ignored Erin until now. I didn't want Rain to complain later that I was mean to her friend. I wasn't being mean. I just didn't like her, so I kept my distance.

"Sure." Rain nodded, smiled, looking just slightly relieved. "Come on, Erin." Rain slipped her arm through her friend's, "let's get some of that yummy cake you made before the guys devour it all."

For a split second, my gaze caught Erin's again and, for another split second, I could appreciate the beauty of her green eyes and rounded curves of her face. And then she opened her mouth as if to speak, and I knew we needed to get out of there before she said anything and disturbed the calm I was trying to hold onto.

But Rain was already walking away, pulling Erin with her, and I heard the kid release a huge sigh as soon as they were out of hearing.

"Come on, let's get," I caught myself before I said beer, because he wasn't old enough to have one, "something to drink and find a quiet place for a few."

Again, I saw relief in his quiet exhale and the way his eyes closed for a second.

"Thanks. I… don't… um, crowds of people I don't know… Uh, yeah."

I smiled. "Yeah, me, too. Let's disappear."

———

"Five teams in three years. Damn, that's tough. A lot of guys would've quit."

Dante's left shoulder rose and fell, his gaze on the ground as we sat in the relative dark of a private sitting room in my parents' home. It'd been built as an inn in the 1800s, so this room was connected to a guest room no one was using right now. We could barely hear the party on the other side of the house.

"Didn't know any better. My dad sold medical equipment, but the company he worked for sent him all over the place. He traveled a lot, and he could work anywhere. He wasn't tied to an office anywhere particular. My mom liked to move. A lot. My sister and I… Well, we didn't get a vote so… Yeah, five teams in three years."

"How old were you?"

The kid and I had been talking for the past ten minutes or so. More like, we'd been exchanging facts in between long stretches of silence.

"Six, but my mom had me on skates before then. She signed me up for lessons. Wanted me to be a figure skater. But the hockey team had practice before the figure skaters, and I wanted to be one of them. I had a lot of, um, energy as a kid. Took my dad a little time to talk my mom into letting me play. He wanted me to play soccer." Another shrug. "I liked hockey."

I knew what he meant and what he wasn't saying. The skill. The speed. The physicality. Especially the physicality.

"Me, too."

Another silence.

"You like playing for the AHL?" he finally asked. "Is it…I mean, is it a lot different?"

I took a second to answer. I really had to think about it in a way that made sense. And was still honest.

"In some ways, yeah. There's more pressure to perform. To bring your A-game every night. I mean, it's not like you can't have an off night, but a three-game slump'll get you benched. You really gotta thrive on the pressure or you gotta be really good. Some guys are both. Those that aren't… they have to work harder."

When he didn't say anything, I asked, "Is that what you want? To play up?"

"That's the goal, yeah. I mean, I don't wanna play here all my life."

And then, like he realized he'd just insulted my family's honor, the kid looked horrified.

"I mean, I wanna play here. I like it here. The Devils are great and I'm so happy to have a spot and get to play and—"

I laughed, cutting him off. "Dante, seriously, it's okay. The Devils aren't like other teams. Our league's not like anything else. And that works for a lot of players. We're not a beer league, but we're not feeding the NHL on a regular basis."

"But you got picked up by the AHL."

Yeah, I had. And I'd never told anyone who fucking hard it had been to leave behind everything and everyone I knew to play for another team. How fucking amazing to get the call to play for the Redtails and how fucking terrifying. At least, for me.

"I got lucky. A whole hell of a lot of factors came together for that to happen. A few of them were out of my control. The only thing you can depend on is your game. Just keep working on yourself. And remember that you're actually being paid to play. Someone thinks you're good enough to give you money to play. My dad doesn't give out contracts to guys who can't. He's not in the business of charity. If he signed you, he knows you can do the job."

I didn't add that he also had a soft spot for hard cases. Like Dante. The kid was exactly the kind of player my dad signed for the Devils. He had issues. But he probably had massive talent, too. Sometimes, my dad was the only one who saw it.

"Sometimes it feels like it's too much."

Dante's voice had lowered so I could barely hear him. Maybe he hadn't wanted me to.

"Been there. Done that."

Dante shook his head but didn't say anything else. I understood that he didn't want to talk about his issues. Probably didn't realize I knew he had them. And that his issues were an awful lot like mine.

So we just sat there and drank our sodas.

And I waited for him to tell me he was ready to go back to the party.

I PAUSED in the hall outside the room where I heard the voices.

I felt so bad about Dante. I knew I talked way too much sometimes and occasionally got carried away. I didn't always realize it in time not to be a menace, but I knew tonight I'd gone a little over the line.

So much so that Rebel, of all people, had felt he had to rescue the kid.

That just frosted my cake so hard.

I wanted to apologize to Dante, *needed* to apologize to Dante before it consumed my every waking second. When I got in a shame loop, I needed to fix it. Immediately. And yes, I knew that was also part of the problem. Ugh.

But I couldn't do that now, since *he* was in there with the person I needed to talk to. And I couldn't go in when he was there. Because, well… Reasons, okay. There were reasons. So I stood there, caught in a trap of my own making. I needed to leave. But I also needed to know what Rebel was saying to Dante so I could choose my words carefully.

But what I heard was Rebel being…kind. Listening. Answering the kid's questions with what seemed like sincerity. I'm not sure I'd ever heard Rebel string together so many words at a time. Not even on the ice.

It made him almost human.

Almost.

Then they went silent.

Shit. I should really get the hell out of here and now. I didn't want to be caught eavesdropping on a private conversation. But I wanted to talk to Dante. Even though I knew I should probably let it go for tonight. And even though I knew my brain would chew at this until I apologized.

No, better to go and save the apology for another day. I'd make Rainy find out what Dante's favorite baked goodie is, and I'll give him a year's supply. Okay, maybe I'd start with a month.

I turned to head back to the party, but just as I was halfway down the hall, I heard Rebel say, "Erin."

I froze, exactly as if I were guilty of listening to a private conversation. Which I was. Shit. *Shit, shit, and shit.*

For fuck's sake, act your age. You're twenty-nine years old. Not five.

I took a deep breath and plastered on a smile, though I made sure to aim it at Dante. Who looked like a deer in the headlights.

Shit.

"I'm sorry. Really. I didn't mean to eavesdrop. I just wanted to say I'm sorry. And I've said it, so I'm going."

Dante blinked, his lips parting as if he wanted to say something. And I paused, waiting. And then he didn't say anything, and my gaze flashed to Rebel.

Bad move. The look on his face made me want to kick him in the shins. Hard. But not hard enough to actually hurt him. He played hockey, and I didn't want to do anything that would hurt his game but, oh, just one jab with the pointy tip of my shiny black pumps. Which were killing my feet, by the way, but they made my legs look amazing, if I did say so myself. Which I did. There was no one else in my life who would, except for maybe Rainy, but she was busy and—

"The party's that way."

Rebel crossed his arms over his chest and lifted his chin toward the event room. I would call it the ballroom, but Miss Raffi never called it that, and I wasn't sure if it would insult her if I did.

I wouldn't mind insulting Rebel, though. The man existed on this earth just to piss me off. I could swear he was sneering at me, even though he looked exactly like he had a minute ago.

Way too handsome for his own good and built like a hockey player. Broad chest, heavy muscles and a jawline that—

Well, never mind. That was a stupid thing to even think about. So he was handsome? All the Lawrence men were. It's just that Rebel—

Grr.

"I know where the party is."

Ugh, god, what's wrong with me. I sound like a toddler. Just walk away.

But I couldn't seem to drop his gaze. I couldn't help myself. He just made me want to throw things at him. Hard things. Not like my rolls or muffins or anything like that. No,

I wanted to throw really hard things. Which I know he would catch because, well, I just knew he would. He was good at things like that.

Walk away, you idiot.

With a huff, I forced myself to turn on my heel and go, even though I had so many more words on the tip of my tongue to say to him. Angry words. Frustrated words. None of which would make this situation any better and would just make Rebel even more convinced I was an idiot.

Amazingly, he said nothing behind my back as I tried not to escape. Which I wasn't doing. I was making a strategic retreat. I'd made a mess of things already and didn't want to make more of one.

And I was not going to cry, damn it. There was no reason. That man did not deserve my tears. Stress. That's all it was. I had so much going on right now. And I know that was my own fault. I always took on too much.

But I had all these ideas, and you only lived once, right? Unless the romances I read with ghosts and reincarnation actually were true. Anyway.

Just stop. You're spiraling.

I headed back out to the party, telling myself I could put this out of my head, just forget it ever happened. Of course, I knew I couldn't, but I had to try. Or I had to leave.

Leaving sounded good, actually. The toasts were made. I could eat at home. I mean, I didn't have much in the fridge because I'd forgotten to go to the store, but I could always make something and—

"Oh!"

I collided with another body, but where I bounced, they absorbed the impact like an oak withstood a car crash.

I looked up to see Kaden Felix gazing down at me, with a

smile I would've sold my eye teeth for at one time. I'd had a wicked crush on the guy for several months after I'd moved here, until I realized he'd never give me the time of day. He was into cool blondes who knew how to keep their mouths shut for more than two seconds. Like Sunny Yeakley. She and Kaden would be perfect together with his dark pirate vibe and her blonde goddess looks.

Except for the fact that he had absolutely no intention of ever settling down, and Sunny was looking for the love of her life. He'd told me flat out on our first and only date. I hadn't known whether I should admire his honesty or hubris.

"Hey, there. You okay, hon?"

I had the momentary urge to take offense to the "hon," but he really wasn't a dick. That was just Kaden. He had one hand on my shoulder to steady me, but it didn't feel creepy. Just comforting. The guy truly cared about people.

I forced a smile, which just made his eyes narrow as he looked around me to see if there was someone he needed to deal with. Like I said, decent guy. Except, he saw Rebel and got a knowing look on his face.

Kaden leaned a little closer, until his mouth was just above my ear. "Want me to punch him?"

I rolled my eyes. Did everyone in town know how much Rebel and I hated each other? It would be annoying if it wasn't so damn endearing. I loved my adopted town, but sometimes I longed for my hometown of New York City. It was easier to be less visible there. Honestly, sometimes it was hard to be the center of attention, especially when you were like me.

"Of course not. Everything's fine."

I had Kaden's full attention now, his gaze narrowed as he stared at me.

"You sure? I know you and Rebel…don't exactly get along. He can be kind of a dick."

My immediate reaction was to deny, that Rebel was just… what? Oh, who cares. But I also knew he'd never be intentionally mean to me.

"Nothing happened." My lips curved in a real smile now. Kaden apparently had the same hero complex as most of the Devils players. "Seriously, I'm just heading back to the party."

"Hey, me, too. Come on, I'll walk with you. They're just cutting the cake. Heard it's pretty damn good." He gave me another smile, which really should evoke more than a tiny flutter in my belly. Especially when Rebel—

Nope. Nope. Nope. Rebel did nothing to at all to my insides.

I turned just enough to the side that Rebel, still watching from several feet away, could see. Then I smiled.

"Thanks. I hope everyone loves it."

I'd made that cake. And the cupcakes. And the cookies. And all the rolls. My staff and I had prepped all week for this event. Everything had to be perfect. I really didn't want to miss the reaction to the cake.

"Then we should probably get a move on so we don't miss it."

I gave Kaden another smile, grateful to him for going out of his way to make me feel better. And for recognizing that I needed his kindness.

"Rowdy wanted chocolate and Tressy wanted strawberry, which isn't really a problem because they go together so well, but I knew Miss Raffi would want something sophisticated so I decided on a three-tier cake. But that top tier is special. It's for Krista."

As we walked down the hall, my mouth kept running, mostly to fill the silence. And since I didn't want Rebel to think he'd upset me. He hadn't.

Except, once again, he'd managed to get inside my head.

21

CHAPTER THREE

A LITTLE LESS THAN FOUR MONTHS TO THE WEDDING

*R*ebel

"DAMN, Reb, you never said your sisters were hot."

Stopped just outside the locker room in the Reading arena after the game, which we'd won, I glared at Ian Clark. But he wasn't looking at me. He was staring down the hall.

Glancing in the same direction, I saw Rain nodding her head and smiling as Erin babbled on, using her hands to talk like she always did.

"Only one's my sister. She's got dark hair. And don't even think about it. Her boyfriend'll rip you in two if you touch her. And then I'll get to work on what's left. Even your parents won't be able to identify you."

Ian's attention snapped back to me, wide-eyed and mouth open. Which made me want to smile. Good to know I could still keep the kids in line. I was new here, but I wasn't a rookie so that gave me some seniority over the younger guys. Not that I pulled rank. Ever.

I'd never say this to anyone, but the Redtails still didn't feel like my team. I gave my all every game, of course, but I still felt like an outsider. And it wasn't because the players treated me like one. They were great. This was all me.

So I ignored it like I did everything I didn't want to think about. So far, it'd been working to keep me on track.

"Dude, that might be most words I've heard you speak in a row."

I didn't bother to respond to that. The guys had learned quick that I didn't like to talk. And most of them accepted it as just who I was. Ian, who also happened to be my roommate, liked to talk, but he reminded me of my oldest brother, Rowdy. Good-natured, easy-going and generally in a decent mood.

Rowdy had rounded out my rough edges. Ian...Well, sometimes, he did stupid shit like tell me my sister was hot.

"So who's the other girl? She's pretty, too. She's not, like, a cousin or anything, right? Oh, wait? Is she your hometown sweetheart?" Ian's goofy smile made me roll my eyes. "She's not, right? You never talk about a girl."

Sighing, I shook my head. "She's my sister's best friend. And trust me, she's not anything to me."

"So are you gonna introduce me?"

"Yeah, sure. Come on." And then I had a brilliant idea. "You wanna come out with us? We're just gonna get something to eat. Won't be out late."

Ian's face lit up. "Sure! I can do that."

Okay, so I wasn't above using Ian as a buffer. If it was just gonna be me and Rainy, it'd be a different story. It'd just be me and her and a quiet dinner. Erin changed the equation. And though I'd never admit it, that pissed me off. We just didn't mesh.

"Come on, I'll introduce you."

With Ian bounding along beside me, I headed down the hall, my lips cracking a smile as Rain's face lit up when she saw me. She took a few skipping steps to meet me then threw her arms around my neck and hugged me tight.

"Hey, Reb. You played a great game tonight."

"Good to see you, Rainy." I gave her an extra squeeze. Despite the fact that I didn't talk about it, I missed my family. "Thanks for coming."

She pulled back to smile at me. "I'm just sorry I couldn't get here sooner. You looked good out there. For a rookie."

Her smile widened at the jab, which I took with the good nature I'm known for.

"Fuck you, Rainbow Brite."

"Ah, Jedi, I miss you."

At the mention of my Devils nickname, Ian's gaze bopped between Rain and me. The guy didn't miss a thing, which made him an amazing forward with the skill to be in the NHL. He just needed a little more seasoning to be truly great. And a break from the big club. Or to get traded to another team who needed a forward. That'd be a blow to the Redtails, though, who were having a pretty good season and were on track to be in the playoffs.

The team I still didn't quite consider my own yet.

I shook off the thought. My keen-eyed sister would read my mind, and I didn't want to have to deal with her empathetic anxiety. Plus, I knew she'd tell our parents and so far, I think I'd been able to keep them from realizing I was having regrets about leaving the Devils.

Yeah, it was stupid, but that's just how my brain worked.

Still, I couldn't resist hugging her tight again and feeling just a little closer to home.

Accidentally, my gaze slipped to Erin, who was watching us with eyes just as big as Ian's and an expression that fought between goofy emotion and nose-wrinkling disdain. And since disdain probably wasn't even a word in her vocabulary, it was the goofy emotion that won out. The smile on her lips softened and, when our eyes met, she actually looked happy to see me.

And I could honestly say, in that moment, I wasn't unhappy to see her. My therapist was going to have a field day with this at our next session.

Amazingly, Erin managed to rein in her impulse to blabber all over everyone, but I knew it wouldn't last. She just couldn't help herself. So I offered up Ian as sacrifice.

"This is my roommate, Ian." I put my hand on his shoulder and gave him a nudge forward, but he really didn't need any help. "My sister, Rainbow. And her best friend, Erin."

I managed not to grimace when I said her name, thought I sounded pretty normal as I introduced her. Maybe that's why she gave me a second look? Usually all of our interactions involved snark.

I wanted to say, "See, I can be a polite human," but I didn't. That would've negated the no-snark thing, so...

"Hi." Ian stuck his hand out to Rain first, who shook it with a smile, but when he turned to Erin, his expression just... Hell, I don't know. The guy looked like he'd just scored the game-winning shot in the playoffs.

I fought the urge to roll my eyes and tell him he didn't know what he was getting himself into. And when Erin smiled at him with that sunny look on her face, I wanted to tell him to run.

"Hi," Erin said. And didn't say another word.

Huh. That was different.

"So," Rain said into the silence, "why don't we go get something to eat?"

HALF AN HOUR LATER, I was still trying to figure out what the hell had happened to Erin.

She was actually tolerable during dinner. It helped that she spent most of the time talking to Ian, who seemed thrilled to have her attention. It left me more time to talk to Rain. Or rather, let Rain catch me up on all things Devils. And home.

"So Kat gets the puck and starts staking up the ice before the ref can blow the whistle. Everyone else is paired off because Rowdy said something stupid to Wilhelm, who took offence, which meant everyone started to go at it since there was, like, thirty seconds to go in the third. And the Stags had already pulled their goalie, so the net's wide open."

Since I can see where this is going, I'm shaking my head, my lips curved in a smirk. Rowdy is notorious for saying stupid things, usually with a smile on his face and a laugh that makes other teams wanna throw their gloves down and wipe away the grin.

"Now, I can see Body Johnson, who was reffing the game, catch sight of Kat weaving his way down the ice," Rain continued. "And I'm pretty damn sure he knew Kat had the puck, which is why he didn't blow his whistle."

I could see it all in my mind's eye. Kaden "the Kat" Felix, the Devil's goalie, gliding down the ice at a snail's pace, because he really wasn't a great skater. He was a decent goaltender, but wind sprints were his nemesis.

"I think the other team, at first, thought he was just getting out of the way of the fights. The game had been chippy from the start. You know Rowdy and Bonesaw have had this rivalry with Wilhelm and his brother, Johann, for years. I don't even think they know who started it anymore but—"

"Oh, they definitely know who started it. Remember that New Year's Eve game during our first season? Jo made a dick comment about dating you."

"Oh?" She got a look on her face that made me roll my eyes. "And why was that a dick comment? I wouldn't have been opposed to that."

"Yeah, well, your brothers were. They hit on any girl with a pulse back then. Before Wil met his wife."

"Ooh, you know I haven't talked to Katie for a while. I need to call her."

I could practically see the mental note my sister made to call Wil's wife and shook my head. Rain was the queen of multitasking, a skill that just wasn't in my DNA. It's why she and Rowdy would make a great team leading the Devils going forward.

I just wanted to play hockey.

Yep. And that's exactly what you're doing.

"I didn't know you kept in touch with Katie?"

Rain nodded, her smile bright. "I keep in touch with a lot of people. And I'd keep in touch with my brothers even more if they'd text me back once in a while."

I rolled my eyes but reached across the table to cover her hand with mine and squeeze for just a second. "I know. I suck. I'll try to be more responsive."

Rain's smile widened. "Good. I'd hate to have to track you down every couple of months and yank on your ear until you get back to me."

Her smile faded and her expression turned serious. And when she spoke, her voice was barely even loud enough for me to hear over the low hum of conversation from the rest of the restaurant.

"You're okay, right? I know leaving was hard for you."

I didn't blow her off because she was right. It had been. And anyone who knew me well knew how hard it had been.

Therapy helped. Having someone to talk to who wasn't my brothers or sister or parents had been one of the best decisions I'd made for myself after crashing out in college. That's been the lowest point in my life. Untreated depression and anxiety had cost me friendships and nearly cost me my hockey career. But my parents hadn't let me falter and I'd gotten help. And I still had it today.

"Most of the time…" I nodded. "I still miss home. I miss my family and my team." I grinned. "I even miss my nosy sister."

Rain grinned. "Good. Wouldn't want you to get a big head from all this newfound glory and forget all about us and go live somewhere and never let us know where you are."

"Never happen. I know you and Mom would track me down. I swear she installed tracking devices in us when we were babies."

Rain's laughter rang out over the quiet restaurant, drawing Ian and Erin's attention. Erin's automatic smile faded a little when she realized I was looking at her. Her gaze skipped back to Ian who looked more than happy to have her attention.

"Just a heads up, since Rowdy and I are in relationships, Mom's been a lot more interested in talking about you and what you're up to lately."

Shock gave me a jolt. "Seriously? Can you redirect her toward Rocky for me?"

Rain's smile got snarky. "Nope. She's on a mission, dude, and you're it."

Our mom on a mission was not something anyone wanted to dismiss. My mom was sweetness and light and an iron fist. And she loved her children. Full stop. I know I'd given her more than a few sleepless nights, probably more than my brothers and sister. And yeah, it'd sucked being the "problem child." My words, not hers. My mom would never use those words. And she'd never made me feel less than the others.

But I knew.

"When you get back, just tell her I'm fine. Hell, *I've* told her I'm fine. I'm not sure why she's so worried."

"Maybe because you ignore her texts and send her calls to voice mail."

My nose wrinkled. Guilty as charged. Some of the time.

"I pick up. When I can. My schedule's a little more…hectic here."

Rain's smile softened. "I get it. More games. More commitments. Rowdy said you're working with one of the local youth centers for at-risk kids. That's really cool."

It showed how scarily well my sister knew me that she lowered her voice to say that.

"Anyway, Rowdy and I have been talking about reviving the youth league. We know Dad tried when he first started the team, but he didn't really have the extra hands to give it a real chance. Rowdy and I think, with the growth in the area, that we can make it work this time."

"If you guys need help with that, you know I'll be home over the summer for a few months."

Unless the Redtails made a deep playoff run. Then I'd only be home for a month and a half at most. Unless my contract didn't get picked up. And if it did, was I going to take it?

One day at a time, Rebel. Don't get ahead of yourself.

I heard the voice of my therapist so clearly in my head, it was like he was sitting next to me. Mike, the Navy vet I'd started sessions with about three years ago, had become a fixture in my life. Honestly, I don't know what I'd do without him now.

"Oh, don't worry. I'm going to put you to work this summer. *After* Rowdy's wedding."

I breathed a silent sigh of relief that we'd moved on to topics that weren't centered on me. "How's that coming together?"

While Rain proceeded to tell me all about the plans Tressy and Rowdy were making and everything that had to be done before the end of June and the exact moment Tressy walked down the aisle in the backyard of our parents' home in St. David, my attention wandered. Straight to the woman sitting next to me. And I didn't mean my sister.

Erin was still talking to Ian, though she'd been weirdly subdued. It wasn't like I'd been listening in on their entire conversation. But I'd heard Ian talking more than her. The guy talked a hell of a lot more than I did, yeah, but Erin was usually a five-alarm fire when it came to conversation.

Weird.

"And you know you're going to need to dance naked along with all the other groomsmen at the reception."

My head snapped around. "What the hell are you talking about?"

Rain laughed. Cackled was probably the better word.

"So you were listening. Just checking." She leaned in and her voice lowered. "You seem awfully interested in the conversation on the other side of the table. Something I need to know about Ian?"

My face scrunched in a frown. "What? No. Why?"

"If there's something wrong with him, I need to warn Erin. Or do you want to tell me why you seem to be so out of it?"

Sighing, I shook my head. "I'm not out of it. I'm just… I've got a lot on my mind."

"You know you can talk to me, right?"

I met her gaze, saw the curiosity and concern. My sister was almost, but not quite, as good as my mom when it came to reading the men in our family. And I loved her with all my heart, but she could be worse than my mom when she sensed weakness. Or pain. Our mom had had our entire lives to figure out how to deal with us. Rain still didn't know when to stop pushing sometimes. She could get away with much more with Rowdy. He had the patience and the laidback personality to let her get away with it.

I didn't. But we were in public. Had to give my sister props for picking the time and place.

"I know. But it's not gonna be here and now."

Her smile made me shake my head.

"I know. I just want you to know you can call me. If you want. Anytime. I even promise to be quiet and listen."

I shook my head, but that left my brain unsupervised long enough to hear Erin say,

"—would love to, but I'm so busy right now. I just don't know when I'd have the time. And you must be busy with the team. And I really don't get to Reading a lot."

"How's the bookstore doing?"

I'd spoken loud enough to catch Erin and Ian's attention, and they turned back to Rain and me.

"I thought you owned a bakery?" Ian directed the question at Erin, but Rain jumped in, probably because she saw what I did—that Erin seemed to have met her match.

"She does, but Erin and I teamed up to open a bookstore in the same building."

Ian didn't see the look Erin gave Rain, but I did. Relief. But she was too nice a person to tell the guy she wasn't interested in him. Not that I cared. I didn't. But I didn't want her to be uncomfortable while she was here.

It's probably not Ian. It's you.

Except the look she flashed me wasn't filled with her usual disdain. She looked...confused.

She shouldn't be. My mom raised me better, and, contrary to popular opinion, I could be considerate. Most days.

"So you help your granddad run the newspaper and you own your own bakery and you run a bookstore. When do you sleep?"

Rain and Erin shared a look before Rain laughed and Erin just shook her head.

"That's a good question." Rain reached across to Erin and poked her in the arm. "I keep telling her she needs more downtime."

Erin shrugged, her lips twisting and her nose wrinkling.

"I like to keep busy."

"There's busy and then there's working yourself into the ground."

Our gazes connected and held. And held. I don't think I ever realized how bright her green eyes were. Or how pretty she was with a blush coloring her cheeks.

Then she blinked, and I shifted my gaze back to my sister. Who stared at me with arched brows. I returned her stare, otherwise she'd think something was up. And she'd be wrong. So very wrong.

CHAPTER FOUR

TWO MONTHS BEFORE THE WEDDING

rin

"Granddad, do you have that article on the fire at the Shaeffer farm?"

"Already laid out for Thursday's paper. Did you get that story about the runaway alpaca I sent you?"

Sitting across from each other in the office of the St. David Register, our desk backs pushed together, though we couldn't see each other over the large monitors we used to lay out the paper. Granddad was constantly complaining about his sore neck from having to twist his head to see around it. If it hadn't been for the printer demanding the paper move to digital layout five years ago, I'm pretty sure Granddad would've still been laying out the pages on boards.

My brain, which had been mulling over a list of books to order for the bookstore while I'd been designing pages for Thursday edition on autopilot, did a stutter stop.

33

"Alpaca story?"

My brain started paging through mental notes with all the panic of a college student going into a pop quiz without reading the material.

"Yeah, about that alpaca from the farm outside of Frogtown."

Frogtown. Was there really a place called Frogtown near here? How did I not know that?

"Um…"

Granddad leaned to the right, and I leaned to the left so we could see each other.

"The alpaca that took a walkabout and was gone for five days and showed up three counties away? That alpaca."

I blinked at my granddad for a few seconds while my brain processed that information, thought about it for a few more seconds, then mentally shrugged. Well, this was St. David.

"Um…"

"His name's Master Fluffy Jack."

"I assume you mean the alpaca."

Will Randolph looked over the top of his wire-frame glasses at me, his white brows arched over blue eyes only slightly less bright than they'd been for as long as I could remember. At eighty, Granddad was still as sharp as the day I'd been born, twenty-nine years ago.

The only thing that'd changed since that day was that I now worked for him. Though he still said I had him wrapped around my little finger. When he looked at me like that, I wasn't sure that was true.

"What have I taught you about making assumptions?"

I rolled my eyes, biting back a smile. "That they're correct sometimes?"

His mouth twitched, but his expression never changed.

Granddad had been a journalist for more than six decades. He'd gotten his start at the New York Times, after graduating from Hofstra, and had worked there for more than thirty years before my grandmom had died. Cancer. I don't remember her very well, but Granddad sometimes talks about her like she's still here.

My mom thinks it's strange. I don't mind.

"I think my training has been lacking with you."

"I didn't realize I was in training."

Granddad gave me the look. The one most people in this town had learned to respect. Or fear, if you had something to hide. You'd be surprised how many people had something to hide in a small town. Take Sir Fluffy Jack.

"Which just means I'm better at this than I thought I was."

He gave me a wink, and I dissolved into laughter. This was one of my most happiest places. This dusty, musty, dimly lit space with its wood-plank floors that creaked with every step and the plaster walls that had started to crack again and needed to be fixed.

It looked straight out of a movie from the fifties, like that one set in a newsroom that Granddad and I had watched a few years ago. When I'd first moved here and hadn't known anyone and had thought I'd only be here a few weeks to help him wind down the paper and sell the building.

"So…Sir Fluffy? Where did he end up?"

Granddad's mouth twitched into a smile. "An alpaca farm outside of Reading. No one's sure exactly how he got there, but foul play is suspected."

"Someone kidnapped Sir Fluffy and then released him at another farm? Was it a prank?"

"Farmer swears the damn alpaca walked off by himself. I

need you to get in touch with the farmer in Berks County and get some detail to go with what our farmer told me."

Shaking my head, I took down the number he recited.

"Thanks, Care Bear." He pushed away from the desk. "Now, I'm going to head over to the diner for coffee."

I waved him off, not bothering to mention the fact that I owned a bakery in the next building, and he could drink his coffee for free there. The coffee wasn't the point. He was going to get the latest gossip from the retired people who hung around the diner all day. He called it investigative reporting. We both knew it was totally for the gossip.

But that gossip sometimes led to a juicy story. This was not exactly a juicy story. Not like the news I'd been sitting on for months.

Colonel Lawrence was going to retire at the end of the season.

Now, a few people in this town wouldn't give a crap. Not everyone idolized the Lawrence family. Maybe idolized wasn't the right word.

Admired was better. People admired the Lawrences for what they'd done for the town. They'd brought the downtown back to life with the addition of the arena and the hockey team. I mean, St. Lawrence wasn't a thriving metropolis to begin with, but there were still people here who remembered when it'd been more than just another small town with a dying Main Street, decimated by manufacturing closures.

St. David had managed to avoid becoming a ghost town simply through the sheer force of will of the townspeople. And when the Lawrences had arrived with big plans and a large bank account, they hadn't immediately been accepted.

This town still considered anyone whose grandparents hadn't been born here visitors. Like me and Granddad. We were still considered outsiders, even though Granddad had moved St. David almost ten years ago and owned the local newspaper.

I don't think some people even knew my name yet, and I'd been here for almost five years. Then I told myself the people who mattered knew my name. And most of them even liked me.

The first time I'd met Rain, I'd thought, *She's nice, too bad I'm leaving in a few weeks and won't have time to get to know her.*

Of course, I hadn't left. I'd discovered the place I belonged. And caused a huge rift in my family. Every time I talked to my mom or dad they wanted to know when I was coming home "where I belonged." My sister thought I was hiding from my broken engagement, and my brother barely talked to me.

I blew out a breath, tamping down my rising anxiety. My mom had never understood how I could be so outgoing and have so much anxiety over everything. Just another one of those things we didn't see eye-to-eye on. Along with everything else.

Since hyper-focusing on something else usually helped when I started to spiral, I called the number Granddad had left for me on my desk. By the time I got off the phone half an hour later, my face hurt from smiling.

"You look like you're having a good day."

The voice from behind me belonged to Tressy, and I jumped up from my chair to give her a hug.

"Hey, what are you doing here? Wait, do we have a meeting? I don't think I have anything on my calen—"

"No, no, we're good. I just stopped at the bakery to get Krista those cookies she loves, and I got Rowdy some, too. The man loves your butter cookies. If he ever leaves me, I'll know it's because I don't bake."

"That man loves you too much to ever leave you, even if your baking...needs some encouragement."

Tressy threw back her head and laughed. "That was very diplomatic of you." Then she shook her head. "I did come here with one delicate situation I wanted to talk to you about."

"Oh, is something wrong? Do we need to change anything for the wedding? Is someone allergic to something? What—"

"No, no, no." She shook her head, her lips twisting in a rueful smile. "Nothing like that. It's kind of a favor. Well, no, it's a definite favor."

"For the wedding? Of course, anything."

"Hear me out before you say yes. You may tell me to take a flying leap off the water tower."

"Why would I do that?"

She paused for a breath. "I'd like you to dance with Rebel at the reception. During the wedding party dance. I know it should be my sister since she's my maid of honor, but she begged me to let her dance with Rocky. I think Rebel frightens her a little. And my sister can be a little, um, flaky? Rain will be dancing with Brian so...

My brain stuttered a little at that. And then it just kind of shut down for a second while it rebooted. Tressy bit her lip before continuing.

"I know it's a lot to ask. You two aren't exactly, um, friends?"

That was an understatement. Still... "Not exactly true. We did manage to have dinner together with Rainbow, and we didn't even get into a staring contest."

"Well, that's good to hear. If you think it's going to be too awkward—"

"NO! No, of course not. It's one dance."

Tressy's nose wrinkled. "And a couple of practices. Miss

Raffi put her foot down on this one thing. She wants her children to be presentable on the dance floor. Personally, I think she's been on a crusade for most of her life to get her kids to take dance lessons. Now she's finally getting her shot, and she's taking it."

"And Rowdy agreed?"

"He did when I said I'd really appreciate it, and it would make me happy."

"You have that man wrapped around your finger." I couldn't stifle my sigh soon enough. "Must be nice."

"Are you sure you don't want to add a plus one to the wedding? I know all the guys will be there, but are you sure—"

"Trust me." I held up a hand. "I'm sure. You said it yourself. All the guys from the team will be there. If I want to dance, I'm sure I can find a partner."

Not that I would want to. When I danced anything that wasn't a structured ballroom dance, I looked like a chicken with its head cut off. Which I'd accidentally witnessed one day when I went to a local farm to interview the owners for an article. It'd been horrifying, but I still eat chicken so...

Ugh. Stop. You can do this.

Of course, I could.

"I won't have a problem with Rebel." And if I did, I'd step on his toes with my pointy heels.

Tressy lit up like I'd given her free chocolate cake for life. "Thank you, thank you, thank you! This makes my life so much easier. I know you and Rebel don't have the best of relationships but—"

"Geez, you make it sound like we're mortal enemies. We're adults. We'll deal."

Tressy gave me a quick squeeze. "Thank you. I love my

sister, but she can be a bit of a drama queen, and it'll just be easier—"

"Tressy." I put my hand on her arm and squeezed. "Stop. You shouldn't have to worry about any of this. Rebel and I will be fine. It'll all be fine."

Of course it would be. No problem at all.

Then why did I suddenly feel like I had a boulder sitting on my chest?

CHAPTER FIVE

SIX WEEKS BEFORE THE WEDDING

ebel

"You want me to what? And with who?"

"I want you to dance with Erin during the wedding party dance, and Mom wants us all to take lessons. I already told her we would."

I was sitting in my apartment shoving food down my throat before the Redtails' next game. We were two games into the last round of playoffs and up two games on our opposition.

And I'd never felt this kind of pressure in my life. It was a great position to be in. The Redtails were winning. Yeah, the level of play was higher than the Devils', and it was fucking hard every fucking day. But every day it got a little easier, too. I gelled more with my teammates. I'd picked up the hockey system pretty quickly. Coach had been surprised by that, I think.

Hell, I'd even made a few friends.

"I told Mom this wouldn't be problem."

I heard the question in Rowdy's voice, directed straight at me. He'd clearly just asked me if I was going to be the problem.

"I know you and Erin don't get along but—"

Suck it up. "That's not going to affect your wedding. Whatever else you're thinking, don't. I'm not gonna fuck this day up for you."

"Reb, that's not what I'm saying at all. I know you wouldn't. Never even crossed my mind. I just need to know you're gonna be comfortable enough to do it. If you're not, we'll figure something else out."

And right there was why my brother was a "golden retriever," according to my sister. The guy couldn't help himself. He needed to make sure everyone around him was okay. Rowdy had a spine—and he was definitely no pushover—but sometimes that spine wiggled like he had a fucking tail.

Okay, that didn't make complete sense, but you got the picture. Rowdy wanted people to be happy. And it worked on his last nerve that I was such a miserable SOB most of the time. I was working on that.

"It'll be fine."

"You sure?"

"Ask me again, and I'll make sure Erin and I look better on the dance floor than you and Tressy."

My brother's laugh made me wince a little, it was so loud.

"Not gonna happen, dude. Tressy and I have natural rhythm, on and off—"

"Say another word, and I'll make you limp down the aisle."

More laughter because he knew I'd never do anything to sabotage Tressy's big day. I loved that woman like a sister.

And she was the perfect woman for Rowdy. Which still didn't prove that there was someone out there for everyone. Even if Rain and Brian were pretty good together, too.

"So you're still coming stag to the wedding?" Rowdy asked when he stopped laughing.

"When the hell do I have time to date, much less meet anyone? Especially now."

"Yeah, I gotta say you're making us all proud as hell of the way you're playing, Reb. You're kicking ass."

The praise made my chest tight, damn him. "Thanks." And since I really didn't want to touch that subject right now, I deflected. "Hey, that book you suggested is pretty great."

I wondered if he'd let me get away with it and, luckily for me, he did.

"I knew you'd like it." The guy sounded practically giddy. "I mean, come on, who doesn't love dragons."

"It's got a good story. The dragons are a bonus."

"Yeah, the dragons aren't the reason I told you to read it. I knew you'd connect with the heroine."

And he was right. Of course.

The female lead character had issues, and I identified with a lot of them. No, I wasn't female, and I didn't live in a world filled with mythical creatures and magic and enchanted libraries. But she dealt with a lot of the same issues I did. Anxiety, panic, depression. The trifecta of my dysfunction. So yeah, I identified.

And surprisingly, I'd recently discovered a love of reading, which I'd confessed to Rowdy one night back in September. I'd texted him when I couldn't sleep. The next morning he'd told me to read a book, and I'd be asleep in minutes. I thought he'd been joking, but I'd been desperate. I didn't want to take meds. They'd make me slow on the ice. I couldn't risk it. Been there, done that. It was bullshit. But I also knew if I didn't get enough sleep, I'd have other issues. So I'd asked him for a recommendation. And after a few minutes, he'd given me the title of a fantasy book with fairies and vampires and werewolves.

It'd kind of reminded me of the movie Underworld, which I fucking loved. Who couldn't appreciate Kate Beckinsale with fangs in a black shiny skinsuit. But that book had had a hell of a lot more sex. And I discovered I didn't actually hate that part of the book as much as I thought I might.

And so, our little book club had begun.

"And you were right. As always."

Rebel snorted. "According to our sister, I'm never right."

My turn to laugh. "What's she on your ass about now?"

"She says we're not moving fast enough on the youth program."

"Are you?"

"Dude! You're supposed to be backing me up." He paused. "But she's not wrong. We're running into a few more obstacles than I thought there'd be."

"Yeah, like what?"

"Red tape from the city council."

"Why are they giving you a hassle? You'd think they'd be all over this shit."

"They're not giving me a hassle. It's more me learning to deal with this shit. Pop just made this all look so easy."

I heard something in Rowdy's voice I didn't hear much. Doubt. "Pop knew what he was doing handing the reins over to you. I know that for a fact. I also know he wouldn't have done it if he didn't think you could do it."

A pause. "Yeah, well some days I just want to throw in the towel and tell Rain she's on her own."

Since I knew that wouldn't happen, I just smirked.

"Shit. Sorry. Didn't mean to dump this on you," he said. "But if this keeps up, I might need the number for your therapist. How's that going anyway? You still keep in touch with that guy?"

"Yeah. We talk once a week. Actually, a few of the guys have sports psychologists, so it's not that unusual."

"Good. I'm glad you feel it's helping. And you know you can always talk to me too, right?"

I rolled my eyes, knowing he couldn't see me, but I knew he meant every word. Because he was Rowdy.

"I know. And I appreciate it."

"Good. And you should. All right, I know you've got a game tonight so I don't wanna hold you up any longer. And Reb?"

"Yeah?"

"I appreciate you being good with this."

"Of course."

"Talk to you."

The call disconnected, and I set the phone on the table next to my plate. While I finished my food, I debated making another call. It'd be the right thing to do. It'd be the decent thing to do.

And still I sat there staring at my phone.

"Damn, what'd that phone do to you?"

Ian walked out of his bedroom in sweats and a t-shirt, running a hand through his hair like he was trying to flatten it. Wasn't working worth a damn.

"It asked me stupid questions before I finished eating."

Ian stared at me, his mouth hanging open a little and his eyes squinty, for several seconds before his face scrunched, and he barked out a laugh.

"Okay, maybe I deserved that." He walked over to the fridge and began to pull out food container after food container. "But, dude, you look pissed."

I shook my head. "I'm not. Just thinking about something I've gotta do."

"According to your face, you don't wanna do it."

While he put his meal together, I mulled that over. What the hell was wrong with me that I didn't even want to call Erin? It's not like we're mortal enemies. She was just too damn…happy. It was suspicious as fuck. I mean, no one could be that happy all the time. It just wasn't natural.

Be a fucking adult.

Yep. I got up and put my empty plate in the dishwasher, grabbed my phone off the table and ruffled Ian's hair on my way to my bedroom to make this call. He waved his hands around his head like he was chasing away a bat.

"Dude, I'm not twelve. Jeez."

No, but he reminded me of Rocky. Ian was a couple of years older than my younger brother, but he still brought out the old man in me.

"I need to make a call. You wanna catch a ride with me to the arena?"

"Okay, yeah, thanks."

Ian's beat-up pickup needed major work before I'd ever get in that death trap, so I always offered to take him with me on game nights.

"Leaving in half hour."

I heard him mumble "Okay" as I closed the door behind me. Sinking onto the edge of the bed, I pulled out my phone and pulled up Rain's message chain. I know she'd texted me Erin's number at some point and for some reason I couldn't remember.

I finally found it after scrolling for at least fifteen seconds. My thumb hovered over the number for longer than I cared to admit before I pressed it. And when it began to ring, I got hot around the collar. Which was just fucking ridiculous. I needed to get over whatever the hell this reaction was to her. I wasn't going to fuck up Rowdy's wedding because I couldn't not be a decent human for a couple of days.

But when the call went to voice mail, I breathed out a sigh of relief, like I'd dodged a bullet. At least for now.

"Hey, Erin. It's Rebel. Just talked to Rowdy about the dance lessons. Just checking in to…" What? Why the fuck had I called in the first place? "Just thought we should touch base beforehand. Give me a call back. I've got a game tonight, but I'll be around all day tomorrow."

I hung up and started getting dressed for the game.

CHAPTER SIX

THREE WEEKS BEFORE THE WEDDING

rin

"Hey Erin, did we get that monster romance in for Mitzi? I can't find it in the pile."

The bookshop's part-timer, Abigail Kantrell, called from the checkout counter in the front as I headed toward the area set aside for the book clubs. Since the romance book club generally drew pretty well, we'd added a few more chairs to the romance nook along the far side of the store. The table for the snacks and drinks had to be crammed into the corner between the bookshelves.

I'd just finished cleaning the kitchen after a busy day in the bakery, but I was running late and book club would start in less than an hour.

"Yeah, sorry, it came in yesterday, but I haven't had time to unpack the boxes yet."

"She said she'll pick it up tonight. Here, let me help you with that."

Taking one of the trays I had balanced precariously on top of the other, Abby shook light brown hair out of her eyes, dark-frame glasses perched on her nose. She was only a year younger than me, but she dressed like a ninety-year-old on her way to a church potluck. Baggy tops and sweaters and skirts that covered her from her waist to just above her ankles.

When we'd met at her interview for the job, I'd thought maybe she dressed that way because of her religion. It didn't make any difference to me what she wore, just that she could do the job. Which she handled spectacularly well. She loved to talk books and read voraciously.

But then I'd met her husband, and I realized why Abby hid behind her clothing. Just thinking about Dale made me want to spike his daily coffee with castor oil. I always made sure to schedule Abby late on book club nights so she had an excuse to tell Dale she was staying. Otherwise, he'd have some reason for her to be home.

"Thanks. The bakery was a madhouse today. We were mobbed from open to close. Good thing I made the treats for book club yesterday."

"Everything looks great, as always." Abby put the tray on the table and took the other one out of my hands. "Ooh, you made the chocolate cake. I really shouldn't have that, but I'm going to be bad tonight."

It took everything in me to bite my tongue. I made that cake specifically for Abby. But for some reason she thought she shouldn't eat sweets. And I knew exactly why. Because fucking Dale thought she "could stand to lose a few pounds."

He'd actually said those words when he'd come to pick her up one night after work.

Asshole.

And I'd thought of the perfect way to stick it to Dale. "You given any thought to coming to work for me full time?"

I really could use the help. Business had started to pick up at the bakery and I couldn't spend as much time in the bookshop as I should. Why the hell had I thought it'd be a good idea to run two businesses?

In my defense, at the time, the bakery had been kind of slogging along, breaking even but only just. And when I'd opened the bookstore, it'd been a little slow, not even breaking even the first three months.

Granddad had warned me that the locals were slow to give their business to "out-of-towners." And even though Granddad had lived here for more than ten years, and the townspeople finally, grudgingly, considered him local, I still wasn't.

Which is why I went out of my way to kill everyone with kindness. But that was a boundary I needed to figure out another day. I did need someone full-time to help me run the store. And if Abby couldn't, or wouldn't, take the job, then I needed to find someone else.

"Actually," Abby said, drawing my focus back to her, "I think…yes, I'd like to."

I blinked, a little stunned. That was totally not the answer I'd been expecting.

"Really? Abby, that'd be great!"

Her round cheeks turned a pretty shade of pink, set off by the fringe of straight-brown hair around her face, and her wide smile made her face kind of extraordinary. Abby was shorter than me by a few inches and had curves I envied, though I knew she didn't appreciate them. Probably because Asshole Dale thought she should "lose a few."

I really don't know how I'd managed to keep my mouth shut about that dick, considering I usually couldn't keep my mouth shut about anything.

"Yeah, I think…I think I need this. Dale's been, um, working a lot lately, and I keeping busy will be good for me."

Okay, I was no psychologist, but I'm pretty sure there was something else going on behind the scenes with Dale and Abby. And while I would never say anything to Abby about her dickwad of a spouse—unless she said something to me first—I would not be sad to see Abby get rid of the dead-weight. Which wasn't exactly fair to Dale. The guy did have a decent job working on a local dairy farm but—

He was still an asshole.

"This is great! I'm so happy you're going to be here all the time."

Especially with Rowdy and Tressy's wedding in just a little over a month. Miss Raffi and I had been double-teaming the details the past couple of weeks. She was handling the catering of the plated meal, and I was handling everything else from the bakery, from appetizers to rolls to desserts and the cake.

It was almost too much for me to handle, but with the help of Rain and my staff and most of the Angels Dance Team, we were making it work. No, we were doing better than that. Tressy and Rowdy deserved it for their big day.

"I really appreciate you giving me the chance. I haven't had a full-time job since Dale and I got together, and I'm looking forward to feeling useful again."

My brain glitched for a second as I tried to understand why this smart, sweet woman would think she wasn't useful.

And the only reason I could come up with was...Asshole Dale.

A smile wasn't hard to conjure up for Abby, but it was almost impossible for me to swallow down the words I wanted to say about her significant other. I would gladly put tiny bits of glass on that man's morning donut. Just saying.

"You have been the most useful person in this place since I hired you." And I wasn't even blowing smoke up her ass. I meant every single word. "I'm grateful you took the job. Rain and I couldn't have kept this place running without you. I can only do so much, and Rain's been spreading herself thin between the team and trying to help out here. I should be thanking you for giving us your time."

Abby lit up, her gray-green eyes bright. "You know I love working here. I was so excited when I found out an actual bookstore was opening in town. I mean, I love the library, and I read so much that I would blow a fortune on books if I had to buy all the ones I want to read. And," she rolled her eyes, "Dale used to have a fit when I spent money on something that wasn't food or stuff for the house. Now that I have a discount, he doesn't say as much about the books I bring home. And I just mix them in with the library books and he never knows the difference. And now I feel like I'm actually using my degree, at least a little bit."

Abby had told me she'd graduated with a BA from Penn State, but she and Dale had gotten married right out of college so she'd never really had a chance to create her own space in the world and fend for herself.

Fucking Dale.

And I really needed to stop thinking about him like that or one of these day's I was going to slip and call him that to his face.

Unclenching my jaw, I nodded and reached for her hand.

"I'm really glad you said yes."

"I know how busy the next few weeks are going to be for you, with the wedding prep and all. And Rain told me you have dance lessons coming up for the wedding."

Shit, I'd almost forgotten. But just like that, the realization that I was going to be dancing with Rebel in just a couple of weeks hit me. I'd be standing in front of him, putting my hands all over him. Well, at least on his shoulders. Our bodies pressed together—

Dammit, had it gotten hot in here?

Forcing a smile, I turned away to start arranging the treats on the table.

"It's no big deal. It's just one dance, but Miss Raffi wants us to look good doing it."

Abby snorted out a laugh. "And what Miss Raffi wants…"

"Miss Raffi gets," I finished, grinning over my shoulder at her. "I guess she doesn't trust her boys not to embarrass her on the dance floor."

"I don't think those boys would ever embarrass anyone. Rowdy's such a great guy and the few times I've met Rocky, he seemed like a real sweetheart. And Rebel… well, I don't really know him, but he seems…nice?"

I huffed out a laugh at her diplomacy.

"I mean, I've never really spent much time with him," she hurried on, "so I don't really—"

"Abby, it's okay, really. Rebel's—

"A pain in my ass most of the time, and he can be kind of a bitch," Rain said from almost directly behind us. We both turned to see Rain hurrying through the store, carrying a cardboard box.

"Sorry, I'm late. I had to pick up a few extra bottles. Found out we're having a couple special guests tonight."

I'd left a space for the drinks in the center of the table, and Rain plopped the box there with a little huff. This was already our largest book club meeting, if everyone who'd responded showed up. The book had been popular. I'd even had time to read it. The fact that it was a romance had helped. Not the kind I usually read, with cowboys or billionaires, but one with magic and elves and a grumpy heroine who failed a lot.

Actually, Rowdy had been the one to suggest the book, which had shocked the hell out of me. Not the fact that he read, which I knew he did, voraciously. But because this book was out of his normal genre. He usually went for mysteries, thrillers and the occasional space opera.

This fantasy had a female protagonist with mental health issues who slowly worked on her issues to become a warrior for her people. I'd loved it. It spoke to me.

"Oh yeah? Who's coming? We're going to need more chairs."

Rethinking the whole arrangement of the table, I began to move things around, then realized I needed to get another table. And chairs.

"Yeah, about that," Rain said.

I knew that tone. I looked up from the table, where I was mentally moving things around, eyes widening when I saw the look on her face. Who could possibly be coming to book club to put that look on her face?

"So, you know how Rebel got home a couple of days ago?"

My mind went blank. Actually, I hadn't known. I'd been underwater the past few weeks with the paper and the bakery and the bookstore. In the weeds. *Drowning.*

No, not drowning. I was managing. Maybe I'd bit off a little too much more than I could chew in the past few weeks, but things were looking up. Abby had agreed to work full-time, and the wedding craziness would be over in three weeks. I just needed to keep swimming, and I'd be able to take a breath soon.

"Oh?"

Rain crinkled her nose a little and her mouth did a little quirky twist.

"Yeah," she drew out the word to about five syllables. "So, he'll be here tonight."

My eyes widened so fast, I must have looked like one of those cartoon characters whose eyes pop out of their face in surprise.

"What? Why?"

"Well, from what I understand from Rowdy, he read the book and really liked it, and I quote, 'the guy needs to get the fuck out of his head for a little.'"

"Wh—Oh, yeah."

The team he'd been playing for had lost their championship game. I only knew because Rain had come into the bakery last week, mope-faced and needing a chocolate muffin. Then she'd told me Rebel's team had lost, he was coming home, and her car needed a complete overhaul.

At the time, I'd been working on…oh hell, I don't even remember what I'd been working on. Sample apps for the wedding, I think. And since I tended to just gloss over all things Rebel, it didn't really register.

"He's been home for a few days, getting settled back in his place and scarfing up my mom's homemade food like he hasn't eaten in weeks. But yeah, he'll be here tonight, and I wanted to give you a heads up before he walked through the door, and you made a beeline for the kitchen and stayed there all night."

"Hey, it's not like I hate your brother, you know." I shrugged. "We just have opposite personalities."

"You know that old saying, right?"

I gave Rain the look. "If you say opposites attract, I'm going to throw this cupcake at your face."

I picked up the closest one from the tray and held it up, truly ready to fling it if she said one more word. Behind me, Abby snickered, which in itself was a worth the dramatics. She was a few years older than Rain and me, but sometimes I forgot that. She just seemed so shy a lot of the time, that I always thought she was younger.

Rain laughed. "Oh, please no. Don't throw the cupcake. Just hand it over, and I'll eat it."

I stuck my tongue out at her and put the cupcake back on the tray. "Just for that, you don't get any."

"Aw, don't be mean. You know I love your cupcakes. They're the best."

"If I had known Rebel was coming, I would've made more. Guys always eat more."

"You always make more than enough," Abby said. "They'll be plenty."

But of course, now I was worried about running out of food. And, yeah, knowing Rebel was going to be here made my stomach curl into a little ball.

No time for that.

I left Rain and Abby to set up the table and headed for the glass door that separated the café from the bookstore when it was closed. I planned to pull a few of the chairs from the café into the bookstore and was just walking past the front door when it opened.

Of course, I wasn't looking, so when the door swung inward, it startled me.

I let out a little yelp and grabbed the door before it could hit me, which just made the person on the other side say, "Shit," and push harder. Stumbling backward, I released the door, tripped over my feet and would've ended up on my ass on the floor if someone hadn't caught me.

Strong arms wrapped around my back and hips, dragging me close to a warm body that smelled like spicy mint and vanilla. A warm, hard body with huge hands that molded into my skin.

And were connected to Rebel.

"Oh—"

"Shit—"

We froze, staring at each other like deer in headlights, not saying a word. I couldn't unstick my tongue from the roof of my mouth. I stared into his eyes like I'd never seen them before. And I hadn't. At least, not this close. I'd known they were dark, but not such a deep, velvety brown. And had his lips always been so…lickable?

Oh my god! Was I insane? Had I hit my head against the door while I was falling? This was Rebel. Not some random guy off the street I could lust over. I didn't lust over Rebel.

Nope. Ick. Absolutely no.

A split second later, he pulled me to my feet and took a step back, pulling his hands away like he'd touched a hot stove. Or was standing a little too close. To me.

"Sorry—"

"Sorry—"

"Hey, you're blocking the door. Everything okay?"

Rowdy had stopped just behind Rebel, holding the door open so it didn't swing shut and smack us.

"Yep" I threw a smile at Rowdy. "Everything's fine. Just need to get a few from chairs from the café."

"Hey, Reb, why don't you give her a hand so I can bring in the extra bottles we brought."

Only I saw Rebel's slight hesitation and the tightening of his lips before he nodded.

"Sure."

I went into default mode. Smile and babble. And what made it worse was that I knew Rebel couldn't stand that.

"Thanks, but I'm fine. If you just want to—"

"Erin. Just open the door."

His voice did something to my brain, I swear. Rebel's voice was deeper than Rowdy's and had a little bit of a smoky quality. Not raspy but like he was thinking dirty thoughts all the time. My mom would call it a bedroom voice.

I definitely knew Rebel was not thinking about me and a bedroom at the same time. No way in hell. I'm pretty sure that was exasperation in his voice when he'd basically ordered me to open the door. And of course I wasn't going to give him the satisfaction of following that order.

I pasted on my finest fake smile and watched his eyes narrow and his gaze drop to look at my lips. Now, why did that make me feel tingly in my stomach? Probably indigestion from eating way too many cookies today. I'd been way too busy to eat anything else. (Ha! said my inner Mom voice.)

"I'm certain I can manage—"

"You know we'd be done already, right? We can both get two chairs and won't have to make another trip."

Since I couldn't argue with his logic, even though I really, really wanted to, I bit my tongue and turned to the bakery door, pulling the master key from my pocket. Slotting it in, I turned abruptly, determined not to let him think he'd won anything—

And found him checking out my ass. I mean, I think that's what he'd been looking at. It was such a foreign concept, I knew I had to be dreaming. There was no way Rebel had been checking out my ass. So naturally, I looked down to see if I had something stuck to my butt.

"Do I have…I mean, is there something…"

I looked up to find an expression on his face I'd never seen there before. I could almost swear he was embarrassed. Was he embarrassed to get caught looking at my butt? I had to be wrong. Rebel would never be caught dead checking me out.

"Erin. Let's just get the chairs."

I could take a hint. Sometimes it took a sledgehammer over the head, but eventually I got what people meant. Rebel wanted to put some space between us. As fast as possible. I turned back to the door, but before I did, my gaze caught on the t-shirt he was wearing. Okay, what it actually got caught on was the way it stretched across his broad chest. And the way it accentuated the muscles there. The very muscley muscles.

Oh my god, now I was eyeing Rebel like a side of beef. I quickly refocused my attention on getting the door open and walked into the dark bakery without turning on a light. I knew exactly where I was going, and I figured there was enough light from the bookstore that Rebel would be able to see. But I'd figured wrong.

I heard a thwack and then Rebel cursing.

"Do you think we could have a little light so I don't kill myself before my brother's wedding. I don't think my mom would be very happy if I can't stand up for my brother."

"Sorry, sorry. I know this place like the back of my hand. I wasn't thinking."

Hurrying to the counter, I flipped the switch and light flooded the room, banishing the shadows.

"Are you okay?"

I hurried back over to find Rebel bent over, rubbing his shin.

"Do you need ice?"

I think I actually saw Rebel roll his eyes. "One chair leg to the shin isn't going to do me in."

"Oh, that's right. You're a big, strong hockey player. Nothing hurts you."

I don't know where the words came from. Usually I'm not that sassy with Rebel. He's so damn prickly.

Prickly and Sassy. My inner voice snorted.

Our porn movie name.

Oh, for fuck's sake. Where the hell had that come from? I was watching too many reruns of Brooklyn Nine-Nine.

Releasing a huge sigh, I gave him the look. The one that usually makes men cross streets to avoid me, either because they think I want something or because I want to talk to them. Either is enough for them to turn tail and pretend they don't hear me or see me.

Honestly, you would think I was subjecting them to torture.

Straightening to his full height, Rebel crossed his arms over that broad chest I couldn't seem to stop looking at. I swear the man had filled out since his time with the Redtails. He definitely had more muscle. Not that he hadn't had a great body before he'd left. Not that I checked the guy out or anything. He was just hard to miss, you know? And the fact that I was besties with his sister meant he was always around.

"Maybe a slapshot to the face."

He said it so deadpan, my mouth dropped open. I never really expected him to respond to my teasing. He just never paid me enough attention to care. Or at least, that's what I thought. And then I immediately wanted to know more.

"Have you taken a slapshot to the face?"

"A few times, yeah. Hurts like a motherfucker."

"I bet."

"You take a few of those, you tend to rethink your career choice. Which chairs do you want me to grab?"

My brain got a little bit of whiplash. I heard something in his voice I wasn't used to hearing when he talked to me. Seriousness. And suddenly, I wanted to hear more. I wanted to know everything.

"*Are* you rethinking your career choice?"

Was he talking about moving to the Redtails or hockey in general? He didn't say anything right away, and I had a bit of a surreal moment when I actually thought he might open up to me, say something meaningful. And I found I wanted him to. Despite our frenemy status, I didn't want to curse the guy or anything like that. I mean, he wasn't a bad guy. We just weren't—

"I'm gonna take these chairs over. You coming?"

Obviously, we were *not* having a meaningful conversation tonight. Not that I really expected us to.

Grabbing the two closest chairs, he headed back to the door, opened it, then waited for me. I picked up another two chairs and literally bit my tongue so I didn't say anything else.

And made very sure I didn't actually bump into him as I passed by.

ebel

As Erin passed by me, my jaw locked into place against the words that wanted to push past.

What the fuck was wrong with me?

Erin and I didn't do heartfelt conversations, but for a few seconds there, I'd almost confessed something I hadn't even talked to Rowdy or Rain or my parents about.

I wasn't sure I was going back to the Redtails.

And it wasn't because I'd played like shit. I hadn't it was just…

Damn it, this was part of why I was here tonight. To get out of my head. I spent way too much time in it lately. But the conversation in the bookstore was a lot louder than I'd been expecting. There were a lot more people here than I thought there'd be.

Silently following Erin across the room, I set the chairs

next to the ones she'd brought in and when she turned her to smile at me, her gaze didn't meet mine.

"Thanks. I'm just gonna…"

Then she turned and scurried in the opposite direction. Like she wanted to be far away from me.

Shit.

"Hey, Reb. It's good to see you, man. The Redtails played a hell of a season. You guys should be proud."

Bobby "Bonesaw" Brassard had come up behind me while I watched Erin walk away. I turned to see him stop at my side with a huge smile on his broad face. Towering over me, he grabbed my hand for a shake before he wrapped an arm around my shoulders and squeezed me so tight, I swore I heard my bones creak.

He was one of the few people who wasn't afraid to get into my personal space. His face only inches from mine, he put his hands on my shoulders and gave me a little shake.

Now thirty-three, Bobby had always said he wouldn't quit playing hockey until he couldn't bend over to tie his skates. He loved the game, but the game had been hard on him. He'd broken his nose more than a couple of times, had broken several bones in various parts of his body and had what could've been career-ending ligament surgery. It's the last one that'd put the coffin nail in his NHL career, at least publicly. Privately, it'd been the cocaine.

Bobby had been with the Devils since the moment he stepped out of rehab. My pop made contact and signed him. And he'd never left.

"Thanks. That last one was a tough series."

"Yeah, but you got there, and you kicked ass. You made us all proud, man."

That knot in my gut got tighter with every word, but I kept the smile on my face.

"Thanks. Appreciate it."

"The Redtails went on a really good run. Too damn bad they didn't make is all the way to the end," goalie Kaden Felix added.

I was surprised to see Kaden, but the shocker was Reid Wellar. The young hothead didn't strike me as a reader, but then some people would say the same about me. I know Erin had been surprised to see me, though she'd tried to hide it.

While the guys discussed hockey and the upcoming Stanley Cup finals, my gaze kept being drawn to Erin. The woman never seemed to stop.

After we'd brought the chairs in, she'd hightailed it over to Rain's side, probably giving her an earful about not warning her I was coming. Hell, I hadn't known until about an hour ago, when Rowdy

had shown up at my door with a couple six packs of beer. I'd thought we would spend a couple hours shooting the shit and drinking, but he'd told me to get the hell in the car, we were going to book club. I'd thought he was kidding at first.

Now I was wondering if he'd given me that book just for this reason. So he could drag me here.

I'd only gotten home a few days ago. Our season had ended about a week and a half ago, but I'd taken my time coming home. It'd only taken two days to pack up, but I'd spent an extra few days with Ian, who hadn't seemed in a hurry to leave. He didn't really talk about his family much, and I hadn't been able to figure out if there was a problem there or what.

But when I'd told him to give me a call when he got home and maybe he could come spend some time with me before the season started, he'd been all for that. Which led me to believe the kid didn't want to go home.

When I had gotten home, I'd spent the first two days putting my home on my parents' property into shape. It was still a work in progress, unlike Rowdy's place, which was built for a family. And now he had one.

As the guys talked around me, my attention wandered to my brother, who was standing with Tressy, Rain and Erin on the other side of the circle of chairs. I couldn't hear their conversation, but everyone had a smile and Rowdy laughed a few times, making Tressy smack her hand on his chest.

A few seconds later, Erin left their little group and joined the three women gathered near the bookshelves. Mitzi, the owner of the Tea Room, was holding a conversation with Brian's sister, Lindsey, and a woman I didn't recognize. She looked younger than me, but I couldn't get a good look at her. She was turned to the side, brown hair hiding most of her face.

Erin put her arm around the woman, excitedly telling the group something that made the other woman's head fall back with laughter and a bright blush flood her cheeks, as the other women congratulated her for some reason.

"You checking out Abby? Don't bother, dude. She's married. To an asshole."

Bobby's voice broke through the intense focus I seemed to have on Erin tonight, which was just weird.

"Not interested, just don't recognize her."

"She and her husband moved to town a few months ago so he could manage the Eisenbrown's dairy farm. He's a distant cousin or something. The Eisenbrowns' kids don't want to work on the farm or are at college or some such shit. Abby and her douchebag dick live on a house out there, but she works here at the bookstore. Rain said they just hired her to work fulltime at the bookstore."

"Seems like you know a lot about her."

I slid Bobby a glance but only for a second. My gaze went right back to Erin. I don't know why. Whatever the reason, I had to stop. But now she was talking to another group of women, who looked to be more my age. I recognized Sunny, one of the Devil's Angels, and the others were familiar, but I couldn't come up with their names.

Which didn't matter. I hadn't come to find a date. I was here because Rowdy had told me I was coming and practically dragged me out of my house.

"Not a lot." And then under his breath, he said, "Not like I'd like to."

Huh. Bobby had a crush on a married woman. That never ended well.

"So, what're you planning to do this summer, anyway? Just gonna golf and kick back like the pros do?"

Erin saved me from answering by announcing that book club was about to start.

"Get a drink if you want one and take a seat and let's talk about our book."

I was going to kill Rowdy.

———

TWO HOURS LATER, I stuffed a second cherry almond scone in my mouth and reconsidered murdering my brother.

I'd actually had a good time. I'd even considered adding to the conversation once or twice, though that wasn't like me. I really hated public speaking, even among friends. And somehow Erin seemed to know that.

She'd been the perfect host. She kept the conversation moving, always having another question ready when the conversation lagged, and somehow managing not to dominate the discussion. I'd learned a few things about the book I hadn't known, which made me want to go back and read it again. Everyone else here seemed to have loved it just as much as I had.

The big surprise, though, had been Reid. The guy talked like a fucking English lit teacher, about themes and journeys and character arcs. Rowdy didn't look surprised, but Bobby and I had exchanged raised eyebrows. We'd grill the kid later. Apparently, he had hidden depths.

At the moment, everyone else was gathered in little groups again, talking. And I was hanging in a corner, letting my people battery recharge with some peace and quiet. Until a few seconds later, when the hair on my arms rose.

"Everything okay over here?"

Erin had finally made her way around the room to me. I'd been watching her approach out of the corner of my eye, muscles tightening as she came closer. It wasn't like I was afraid of her. She posed absolutely no threat to me. The top of her head was barely level with my eyes, and she didn't look like she spent time doing reps. That's not to say she was overweight. She had slight curves, which I usually like on women, when I could get past the insane awkwardness I felt around most of them.

Most people thought I was just a grump with a chip on my shoulder. Very few people knew that it'd taken me a hell of a long time to come to terms with the fact that I just didn't feel comfortable around people I didn't know. That it took me a fucking long time to make friends who weren't teammates.

And there was just something about Erin...

I nodded in response to her question, as she approached me with uncertainty in her eyes and her teeth in her bottom lip. I stifled a sigh. I knew this was all my fault, this awkwardness between us, and I needed to do better. At least until the wedding was over, and I figured out what the fuck I was going to do next season.

"Good." She paused. "Did you have a good time? Did you like the book? You didn't really say anything during the talk, so I wasn't sure if you did or not. Or if Rowdy just dragged you along. Although I can't imagine anyone being able to make you do anything you don't want to do." She blinked. "I mean—"

"Yes, I had a good time."

I realized at that moment that Erin rambled when she was uncomfortable. I made her uncomfortable.

Join the club.

She blinked a few times, making me notice how her eyes weren't just green, which is what I'd always assumed because they matched the whole redhead-with-green-eyes theme. They were swirled with pale blue. Unusual. Kind of mesmerizing, actually.

"I'm glad."

Then we stood there and stared at each other for a few seconds before I swore I could see the gears of her brain fire up due to too much silence. Her lips curved in a smile that made the tightness return to my muscles, which just pissed me off.

"Well," she said, "I'm just gonna—"

"I think we should probably have lunch sometime next week. Before we're shoved into each other's personal space for this dance at the wedding."

Apparently, I'd struck her dumb with my brilliance. Or

maybe she thought I'd been taken over by aliens, since I was the last person she'd expect to ask her to lunch. And honestly, maybe I had been.

"I'm not sure I can. Lunch is the busiest time of day for me and I'm not—."

"Shit, I totally forgot the bakery's only open for breakfast and lunch." And before I realized what I was going to say, the words were out of my mouth. "Then how about dinner?"

Her eyes widened, as if she were considering the aliens thing again. And maybe that the aliens were here to cause mass destruction.

"Dinner?"

"Yeah." Then my brain started spinning in circles because it had caught up with my mouth and now it was trying to figure out what the hell I'd gotten it into. Dinner was a whole universe away from lunch.

Lunch was all bright light and busy people rushing around to get something to eat before heading back to work. Lunch was a finite period of time.

Dinner… Well, dinner was dark lighting and way too much time to sit and fuck up a conversation.

"Dinner would be…good. Sure. Dinner is fine. Is there a night that's better for you? I have another book club next week for the teens on Thursday. Oh, and Tuesday we're having a painting class. We're going to paint bricks to look like books to decorate a garden. I'm really kind of excited about that one. I only have a little garden, but it definitely could use some work. Oh wait, Wednesday's out too—"

"How about Monday? Paolo's work for you?"

Paolo's was the local pizzeria. Bright lights, families with kids, groups of teenagers. Lots of noise and laughter and talking. Enough distraction to keep him from stressing too much about who he was with.

"Sure. That works."

"You want to meet there around six-thirty?"

"Sure. That—That's good. I'll see you there." Then she looked over her shoulder like she was desperate for an exit. "I should get back to—"

"Yeah, no problem. And Erin?"

"Yeah?"

"Book club was good."

rin

"YOU AND REBEL? ON A DATE?"

"It's not a date. He didn't ask me out on a date. It's more like a get-used-to-each-other dinner before we have to dance at the wedding."

Rain and I were stocking shelves Sunday after closing. We'd been mobbed this weekend. Lots of people getting their reading material for the pool or vacation. Or it'd been a big release week, and we had a lot of new inventory.

Whatever, it'd been a busy day, and I was more than ready to head home with some Chinese takeout. I'd baked all week and had absolutely no desire to be in a kitchen tonight, and the next couple episodes of Wynonna Earp. Linny's daughter, Maddy, had turned me onto the show, and I was hooked.

"Are you sure you two can be trusted in a public space together for more than five minutes alone? I mean, I'm sure

Vic would like his restaurant to still be standing after you two leave."

"I'm sure he'll be on his best behavior."

Rain's grin held mischief. "He's not the only one I'm talking about."

Rolling my eyes, I shoved a book in an open space and ignored her smirk.

"Fine," I shoved another book in an open slot then realized the latest Preston and Childs book did not belong in romance. Sighing, I grabbed it back and stalked across the store to the mystery and thriller section. "I'll be on my best behavior. I promise."

Rain followed behind me with the cart. "You know I'm just yanking your chain. But seriously, I can't believe he asked you out. And I can't believe you agreed."

I shrugged, slotting the book where it was supposed to go. "It's just dinner. I'm sure we'll manage not to stab each other with forks at the table."

While Rain laughed, my phone vibrated in the back pocket of my jeans. I pulled it out to check the number.

"Shit."

"Something wrong?"

Sighing, I continued to stare at my phone. "It's Mom."

She'd texted, which I knew from experience, if I didn't answer, she'd call next. And I had to think about when our last call was. And when I realized it'd been more than two weeks ago, I knew I had to be a fucking adult and talk to my mother.

"I can finish this," Rain said. "Unless you don't want to talk to her now."

I glanced over my shoulder and curved my lips in a closed mouth smile. "No, better now than later."

Later, I could drown my feelings in chocolate cake and alcohol.

"I'm just gonna go in the office."

Rain nodded slowly, her expression sympathetic as I headed for the small office at the back of the store. It was more of a storeroom than an office. If we had any business, we did it more comfortably in the bakery at one of the tables there. Not in the dark, tight room where we stored the books and where Connie Troutman, who owned the nail salon down the block, said someone had died. She wasn't sure who and she didn't remember when, but she knew the police had taken a body out of there in the '50s.

Connie had been said it so matter-of-factly, I had no reason to doubt her, and the lights were prone to flickering at weird times.

Perfect place to talk to my mom.

My inner rational adult rolled her eyes, but my overdramatic inner teenager thought it was fitting. At least in here, no one could hear me scream after I hung up.

Pulling up her contact number, I hesitated for just two seconds before I hit the little phone icon. Then I took a deep breath and blew it out.

"Hello Erin. How are you?"

"Hi, Mom. I'm fine."

And then I went into my typical roundup of how great everything was going. Books sales were doing well, prep for the wedding was ramping up, and Miss Raffi and Tressy had loved the sample appetizers. Normally, I wouldn't have mentioned the newspaper, but the devil on my shoulder told her about the article I did on Sir Fluffy Jack, the alpaca who'd gone on walkabout.

"Well, that all sounds…interesting," Mom said. "You seem to be keeping busy."

Busy. That's what my mom thought about my livelihood. That it was "busy" work. My jaw clenched so hard, I swore the bones fractured.

"Yes, I've been busy," I added a little emphasis on the word and tried not to sound too pissy. "So, what's up, Mom?"

My mom didn't call unless she had news or wanted something. Or both.

I heard my mom sigh, very faintly. "I wanted to remind you of the McNamara wedding in August. The invitation was for the family, of course. And your cousin is looking forward to seeing you. We need to order you a dress by the end of the month, if we're going to get something decent."

And that right there was exactly how my mother operated. A little nudge. A little guilt. Outright force when necessary. And when that didn't work… The cold shoulder.

The McNamaras were cousins on my mom's side. Amanda McNamara, who was just out of college, had bagged herself the rich heir to a cosmetics empire.

And I was being a total bitch. Amanda and I had attended the same boarding school, prep and college. That's what McNamara-Wrights did. We had traditions.

Amanda had been a few years behind me, so we didn't exactly mingle, but she'd seemed sweet. I had no idea what she was like as an adult. I hadn't seen her in a few years. This wedding, unlike Tressy and Rowdy's, was a command performance for me. And since I didn't want to argue with my mom, I swallowed down the bitterness and said, "Sure, Mom. Just send me a few links, and I'll take a look."

A pause from the other end. "I thought maybe you could

meet me in the city one day next week, and we could choose your dress together."

My eyes closed as the guilt crept it. I usually managed to keep it at bay when I talked to my mom, but right now it was kicking my ass. I knew she actually did want to see me. And it had been a while since I'd been home.

And I knew, between Abby agreeing to work full time and the staff at the bakery, I could afford to take off Tuesday. But I had that date with Rebel—

Wait. No. Not a date. Definitely not a date. It was just dinner so we could talk.

"Would Tuesday work for you?"

"That's perfect, Erin. I'll make a few appointments. Any place in particular you want to go?"

"I'll leave that up to you, Mom. I trust your judgement."

For the next few minutes, my mom listed places I either didn't remember or never went to with her. And I'd gone to a lot of boutiques with my mom over the years. Until I'd escaped.

Okay, maybe that was a little overdramatic, but at the time, I'd felt like I had.

When my parents had asked me to come help Granddad shut down the paper five years ago, I felt like I'd been thrown a lifeline. I'd been drowning in New York City after college, trying to be the good daughter and care about the family business. My dad's family owned a real-estate business. An empire, really. One that sold multimillion-dollar homes to the rich and famous.

My older brother had joined right after college, jumping in with both feet. He enjoyed the cutthroat mentality needed to become a top moneymaker. My sister loved it, too, though she worked with families...who had huge amounts of money to spend on Penthouses and townhomes on the Upper West Side.

I hadn't seen a place for myself there. I'd hated all the entertaining my parents did at their home, where I was expected to be the perfect McNamara-Wright daughter. And I tried. I conformed as much as I could. Even my college degree hadn't even been my idea. My mom had suggested pre-law and I'd thought, "Why not?" She'd actually been half-right. I had enjoyed the history and civics classes, but I'd loved my electives even more. Latin and English literature and feminist studies.

But I knew after I'd graduated that I wasn't going to law school. And then there'd been my failed engagement. But I didn't talk about that. I didn't even like to think about it.

Finally, my mom said, "I'll have a full itinerary sent to you tomorrow. It'll be nice to see you, sweetheart. It's been...a while."

Ugh, the guilt. My heart raced and my stomach twisted. All because my mom said it'd be nice to see me. I was a horrible daughter.

"I'm sorry to cut this short, but we're just closing the store for the night and I—"

"How's it going? The store? I talked to your grandfather the other day. He said you're doing well. Both the bakery and the bookstore."

Granddad hadn't mentioned that Mom had called.

He knew it would do this to you.

"They keep me busy."

And there that word again. Ugh.

Another pause, like my mom didn't know what to say to that. The woman who could speak to every single person in a crowded room about anything at all didn't know what to say to me about my livelihood.

"And Granddad? How's he?"

Was that what this was all about? "He's fine, Mom. He's doing really well."

"That's good to hear. I've been thinking about coming out for a visit, before we go to the Hamptons for the wedding. I have a trip I need to make to Pittsburgh, and I could stop in St. David on my way."

"Well, there's a big wedding in town in a few weeks, and I'll be really busy heading up to that. I'm handling a lot of the food and—"

"Why don't you send me the dates for that, and we can work around it?"

Which meant Mom had already made up her mind about coming. Goody.

Since Mom had gotten what she wanted, we hung up a minute later. I sat there, feeling all the shit I felt after I talked to my mom. Then I made myself get up and walk back out to the store.

"Everything okay?" Rain's question held no inflection.

I nodded as I went to pick up the tray. "My presence has been requested. A command performance."

Rain watched me with a steady gaze. "Would you like an emotional support friend to accompany you to wherever you've been commanded?"

I put the tray back down and took the hug Rain was offering. It loosened my jaw just enough that it wasn't threatening to crack anymore.

"My cousin's getting married. Mom's taking me shopping for the appropriate dress."

"That doesn't sound too bad?"

Flopping down into one of the armchairs we'd pulled into the circle, I sighed and let my head fall back against the cushioned back.

"It's not. It's just…"

Rain took the seat opposite me, her steady gaze grounding me as I tried to stop from spiraling. I took a few deep breaths and blew them out, like I was in yoga. Definitely not skipping class tomorrow morning.

"I hate when I get like this. She's not a bad person. She loves me and I love her. It's just…I feel so bad that I can't be the daughter she wants me to be."

"You are who you are, Erin. You and your mom are different people."

"I know that in here," I tapped my head, "but there's still that little girl in here," now I tapped my chest, "that just wanted to go to public school and play soccer and, yeah, I know how pitiful this sounds. I'm twenty-nine fucking years old. I need to get over it."

Rain nodded. "Yeah, you do. But we all want our parents to love us for who we are and not who they want us to be. Maybe you just need to show yours who you really are."

ebel

"NAMASTE, everyone. Be gentle with yourselves today and every day. Be mindful. Be kind. Go now and have a good day."

Pushing up off the floor, I rolled up my mat and headed for the wall to my water bottle.

When Kaden had told me about the yoga classes in town, I'd told him to go fuck himself, I wasn't falling for that prank.

"Seriously, man. Every Monday, Wednesday and Friday morning, Missy Jane holds classes at seven in the all-purpose room at the church on Main. A few of the guys and I went to a couple classes because Rain and Erin begged us to support the class so that Missy Jane would keep holding them. The whole damn team showed up. You know how persuasive your sister is. And Erin just wears you down until you give in."

"Who the hell's Missy Jane?"

"Oh yeah, forgot you've been gone. She's the dentist who took over Doc Swisher's practice."

I hadn't been expecting much when I showed up this morning. I'd started taking classes in Reading when Coach had suggested it to help with conditioning, and it'd become part of my morning routine. Roll out of bed and do a three-mile jog then another twenty minutes of yoga to keep loose.

When I'd left St. David last year, no one had been teaching yoga. In Reading, several members of the Redtails actually paid a local instructor to lead a class once a week for us.

Since I found it helpful to have an instructor to follow, I was happy to hear about the local classes. But there were a hell of a lot more people here than I'd expected. Half the team, a good amount of the Angels Dance Team, several older women I recognized from some of my mom's clubs. And a couple of younger women I didn't recognize who smiled at Kaden and I as they walked out the door.

For a second, I'd held my breath, hoping they wouldn't approach. I didn't want to talk to anyone this early in the morning, much less make small talk with women I didn't know. And be a decent human about it.

Of course, my sister didn't give a shit about my personal boundaries.

With Erin following in her wake, Rain stopped at my side, stuck her finger in my waist and smiled at me.

"Hey, I didn't know you'd be here."

"I didn't know I had to give you my schedule for the week."

Rain's nose wrinkled just before she stuck her tongue out at me. Which of course meant I had to pull her ponytail. Some things you just had to do.

Rolling her eyes, she slipped her arm through mine as we started walking toward the exit.

"Saw the new girls eyeing you up. You want an introduction?"

Out of the corner of my eye, I saw Erin's face scrunch, though I couldn't tell if she was trying to hide a laugh or a grimace.

"I think I've got enough on my plate before the wedding, thanks."

"True. Plus, you'll be leaving in August anyway. You two wanna come with us to get coffee. You don't mind if I bring these two dull skates, do you, Erin?"

"Oh, course not."

I had to sneak a glance at Erin to make sure she'd actually spoken. It been so...not Erin.

"And I can finally fix that leaky faucet in the kitchen for you," Kaden said, "if you make me a pot of that amazing chocolate coconut pie coffee."

Now she laughed, the sound snaking into my ears and down my spine, like a chill. Except I wasn't cold. I was overheating. From class, of course.

"You'll do anything for that coffee, won't you?"

"It's my one vice, what can I say?"

I rolled my eyes and could resist needling Kade. "Yeah, that's bullshit. You've got way more than one."

"Hey, man, I gotta have some secrets."

Kade's dark eyes narrowed as he grinned my way. I expected Erin to be staring at Kaden, mesmerized by the guy's smile, like most of the women in this town. The guy was a serial dater, though he'd been engaged to be married when he'd come to the Devils.

Kade didn't talk much about what happened, but a few months later, someone asked when he was getting married, and he said never, and he didn't want to talk about it, and he never had.

Grinning, he slipped around me and opened the door with a flourish. Rolling my eyes, I waved Rain and Erin by then slipped through the door before Kade could shut it on me. His face clearly expressed his intention to do so.

Turning so the girls couldn't see me, I flipped him the finger, which made him laugh.

"I don't know what you two are doing but it's probably not appropriate for adults, so stop."

My sister sounded so much like my mom that Kade and I stopped and stared at her for second.

"Damn, you heard it too, right?" Kade said.

My sister frowned so hard, her forehead creases had creases as she stopped in the parking lot, one hand on her hip. "What?"

Kade and I smirked at each other and then I caught Erin's gaze, and the smirk became a smile. Our gazes met and held. And held.

Until Rain smacked my chest with her hand.

"Hey!" I rubbed the spot she'd hit. "Why are you attacking me?"

"I'm sure you deserve it for something. Why are you all laughing at me?"

My smirk was back. "We're just gonna call you Miss Rain from now on."

It took her a second to get the joke, though it wasn't really a joke. She had sounded exactly like our mom.

She stuck her nose in the air. "I consider that a compliment. And I'm gonna tell Mom on you."

That made everyone laugh, including Rain. But all I heard was Erin.

Since the coffee shop was only a couple of blocks from

the church, we decided to walk, Kade and Rain keeping up much of the conversation. I fell into step behind the other three but found my gaze falling on Erin more than anyone else.

She had her hair woven into a loose braid that waved down her spine to the middle of her back. It was a beautiful color, so many shades of copper and auburn and gold all mixed together. And then my gaze slipped to her perfect ass.

Fuck.

I yanked my gaze up and over her shoulder, staring straight ahead. What the fuck was I doing checking out Erin's ass? Seriously?

When we reached the café, Erin opened the front door and ushered us all in, locking the door behind her. Monday was the one day of the week the bakery and the bookstore were closed.

"I'll put a couple of pots on," Erin called over her shoulder as she headed for the kitchen at the back. "Guys, help yourself to anything."

Rain opened a refrigerated case behind the counter, and Kade and I took out the stacked trays. Muffins, scones, lemon pound cake, banana walnut bread, all sorts of other pastries.

It'd been a running joke when Erin had moved here that she'd burned down the kitchen the first time she'd used it. That wasn't completely true—yeah, the fire department had to be called—but it hadn't been all her fault. The ovens had been faulty.

That had been almost five years ago, and now she was providing everything that wasn't the main meal for the biggest wedding this town had seen in decades. We weren't the best of friends, but the least I could do was admit that the woman made the cherry almond scones I'd ever eaten.

"Maybe that'll sweeten you up a little." Rain elbowed me with a little snort of laughter as I took two scones.

"Then maybe you should have some."

"Brian thinks I'm sweet enough already. And Mom loves me more."

I burst out laughing. Only Rain could get me to laugh like this and the grin she got when I did was worth it. Wrapping an arm around her shoulders, I pulled her in tight for a hug.

"Admit it," she said. "You missed me while you were gone."

Yeah, goddammit, I had. I missed spending time with my family and friends. Missed having breakfast on a random Monday morning with one of my best friends and my sister. And Erin.

A week ago, just the thought would've made me want to run in the opposite direction.

Yeah, and now you're checking out her ass.

My gaze snapped in her direction as she returned from the kitchen carrying two carafes.

"Ah, the love of my life," Kade said, making Erin give him a look.

"I know you're talking about the coffee." She held out her left hand. "This one's for you and me." She set it on the counter in front of Kade. "And this one is for the blackhearts over here."

She smiled at Rain, who thanked her profusely and poured the two of us steaming mugs of nectar of the gods.

Perfect. Bitter and strong. Just the way I loved it.

"Thanks."

She blinked, looking almost like a deer in the headlights.

Then her lips curved in a slight smile, and she nodded before turning to talk to Rain. Leaving me to study her profile. How had I never noticed how pretty she was before? And why was I noticing now?

Probably not something I wanted to dwell on.

Except we were going to dinner tonight. Together. Just the two of us.

And I might actually be looking forward to it.

———

I SPENT way too long deciding what to wear, and I was already running late.

I'd lost track of time working in the yard after I'd gotten home from breakfast at the café, and now I was fucking around figuring out what I should wear to a dinner that was not a date.

Not even close. More like a working dinner. Yeah, let's go with that.

"Fuck this," I grumbled and grabbed a pair of khaki shorts and a plain t-shirt in a color that didn't clash.

By the time I got to the restaurant, I was a minute late, and Erin was nowhere in sight.

"Rebel! It's nice to see you. We miss making all the food for you. Rosie's thrilled to cook for you again. Rosie, Rebel's here!"

Trying not to wince at the volume of his voice, I had a genuine smile. "Hey, Mr. Mike, you're looking good."

"It's that Mediterranean diet everybody's talking about." Mike Benanti patted his round belly, his dark hair gone completely white now and barely enough to circle his head. He only stood five-foot-five, but he filled the room with his personality. If the windows were open in their home down on Steel Street, the neighbors sometimes heard him singing.

Most said they actually turned off their TV to listen. "I'm Mediterranean. I eat. Guess that's all there is to that."

"There he is. Handsome boy. You look like you've lost weight while you've been away. Come on, let's get you something to eat."

When someone said "Italian grandmother," what picture comes to mind? Rosie Benanti was what you'd get. Dark hair peppered with silver, dark eyes, round everywhere and about five foot-nothing.

Mike and Rosie had been running Paolo's restaurant for longer than I'd been alive. Their food was amazing, and they'd even been featured on a national television show about Italian restaurants in Pennsylvania not to miss.

They'd kept the Devils players in carbs for as long as the team had been around.

"Mama Rosie, you're as beautiful as ever."

Her smile widened as she grabbed me around the waist and squeezed hard enough to make my bones creak.

"And you're still a charmer."

Mike had to be pushing eighty, but he still worked the floor every night. He knew everyone in town by name and knew everyone's favorite dish. And Rosie ran the kitchen, though now she had their son, daughter and son-in-law in there with her.

Rosie pulled back to look me up and down. "Mike's right. We need to get some food in you. Sit down, sweetheart, and I'll get you some lasagna to start."

"Thanks, but I'm meeting someone so I'm gonna wait for her."

I think a bomb exploding might have gotten more attention. Maybe.

Mama Rosie got a big smile, and Mike patted me on the

back like was a kid who'd just passed a major test with flying colors.

"It's not a date."

And just that fast, their faces collapsed.

"Well, that's okay." Mike assured me. "I'm sure you'll find some nice girl soon."

If my parents had said that, I'd have told them that wasn't going to happen. But this couple ranked as honorary grandparents. There was no way I was going to tell them I wasn't even looking. Until Rosie got a look in her eye as she glanced at Mike.

"Doesn't your niece Dani have a daughter about Rebel's age? I should have thought of that before."

Mike frowned. "Which one is that? Dani with an 'I' or Dana with an 'a'?"

Oh shit. This was not good.

"Guys, I'm really not—"

"Hi! Sorry I'm late, I got caught up a new recipe I'm trying and then I realized I had to take a shower because I was covered in flour and—"

Erin stopped talking as if she'd flipped a switch. You could practically see her brain connect with her mouth and tell it to shut. Then she realized everyone had turned to stare at her. Her cheeks flushed bright red, which made the freckles scattered across her cheeks stand out. If I tried, I could count each one, they were so distinct. Not sure I ever really noticed them before. But then why would I? We'd spent the last few years studiously avoiding each other. She made me crazy.

Right?

"Erin!" Rosie wrapped Erin in a big hug, one that Erin returned wholeheartedly and without hesitation. And as naturally as if she were family. "How are you? You look like you could use a good meal. Are you here by yourself?"

The blush on her cheeks darkened. "Um, no, actually, I'm here to meet, um, Rebel."

The expressions on Rosie and Mike's faces were almost comically dumbfounded.

Probably should've picked another place to eat. Outside of town.

Everyone in town knew Erin and I weren't exactly besties, as Brian's niece, Maddy, would say. Which was why Mike and Rosie looked at us like they were caught between two stray cats fighting over turf. And that was just ridiculous. Where the fuck was my brain right now?

Still trying to figure out why I'd never noticed how adorable those freckles made her look.

Shit.

Finally, I shook my tongue loose. "We're going over some stuff for the wedding."

And that apparently made everything right in the world again.

Rosie nodded as if, of course, that was the reason, and Mike slapped me on the back.

"Coming up soon, yeah? Rosie and Raffi have been working on the rehearsal dinner with Tressy's mom for weeks. You two must have a lot to talk about so we'll get out of your way. Rosie, let's feed these kids. Come on, you two, I reserved your regular table in the back, Reb. Should be quiet enough for you to talk."

Considering tonight's crowd, that would be a good thing. I'd thought the restaurant wouldn't be so crowded on a Monday night, but I'd thought wrong.

"It's family night, so we get a bigger crowd, but you should be able to hold a conversation back here."

Mike led us through the restaurant, Erin trailing behind me. Of course, she had to stop and say hi to someone every couple of tables, which made the walk across the room take twice as long.

Another night that might've annoyed me. Tonight, it gave me a little time to chill. The few people I knew by name I waved at but didn't stop. Most did a double take when they saw Erin trailing behind me.

We lived in a too-fucking-small town. By tomorrow, the book club and the garden club members would all know Erin and I had had dinner together. Which meant I'd get a call from my mom tomorrow morning. And Rain would either call or just knock on my door and demand to know why I'd forced her best friend to go out with me.

Mike finally showed me to the table at the back of the small connecting dining room. The building had previously been a duplex home that the Benantis had converted into the restaurant by cutting two archways in the wall to create one large kitchen at the back and several separate dining areas.

We were in the only room that didn't have anyone else in it tonight.

"How's this for you? Quiet enough to talk, yeah?"

I nodded and forced my lips into a smile for Mike. "This is great. Thanks."

He slapped me on the back again, his smile genuine. "Good to see you, kid. You'll have to tell me how the big boys are treating you another night."

After I promised Mike I would absolutely be back another night, he left, and I waited for Erin to finish making her rounds. Through the widened doorway, I saw her talking to a family with a couple of kids, one of which she picked up when the little girl held out her hands.

Leaning back in my chair, I watched her listen intently to whatever the little girl was saying then respond with an animated smile. When the little girl clapped her hands, Erin threw her head back and laughed then set her back into her seat, waving goodbye.

She looked happy. And when she caught me watching her, for a split second, she smiled at me the same way, wide and uninhibited. She lost it a second later. Too bad. It was a really nice smile.

And it was my fault. As my sister said, I had resting grump face, whatever the fuck that was. Rain had told me I should work on that. I hadn't felt any need to. Until this second.

Now, Erin picked up the pace to get to the table.

"Sorry, I just had to say hi to Caroline. She's the sweetest, and she hasn't been feeling well. The doctors don't know what's wrong and—"

"Erin. It's not a problem. Seriously, you don't need to apologize to me for anything."

"Oh." She slid into her chair, her quick smile a ghost of the one she'd had for the baby. "Anyway, sorry to keep you waiting. I'm sure you want to get this out of the way as quickly as possible."

My brows rose as that flush burned her cheeks again. "Sorry. That didn't come out right. I didn't mean—I don't mean to imply—Just forget I said that."

"I think I'm the one who should be apologizing."

Now her gaze met mine head on, eyes wide and her lips parted slightly. She had a really nice mouth. Something else I'd never noticed about her before. And shouldn't be noticing now.

"I know I can be..." I considered using grumpy but knew that wasn't the right word, "difficult and hard to talk to. I don't want that to affect my brother's wedding. And you and Rain are practically attached at the hip. I don't want you think of me as the enemy."

Her eyes widened even more. "I don't feel that way about you."

"Good."

"Good."

And then we sat there and stared at each other for a few seconds.

"Hey, Reb. Nice to have you back. Andy'll wanna know when you're coming over for beers. What can I get you guys to drink? Erin, you want a Cherry Coke?"

One of Mike and Rosie's granddaughters, Luna, stood by the tableside, pad in hand ready to take our order. She and her husband, Andy, and I had graduated high school together. We'd been pretty close back then. Easy-going Andy had smoothed over my rough spots in our friends' group. He and I had played on the same high school team. I'd majored in hockey in high school. Andy had gone to tech school and majored in cars.

He'd been a damn good hockey player back then. Probably could've made a career of it. Instead, he'd gotten married and went to work in a relative's garage.

"Thanks, Luna, sounds good," Erin said, her tone subdued, which got a side-eye from Luna.

"Your brother still mixing the sangria?"

Luna's dark eyes flashed, and her mouth quirked up on one side. My mom always said Luna was her grandmother's doppelganger. To which I always replied, "Mike did good." Luna was a beauty.

"Frankie doesn't let anyone else mess with the sangria, you know that."

"Then I'll have a glass of that."

"You got it. Be right back."

Luna walked out, dark hair swinging down her back, making me remember when I had the biggest crush on her.

"Did you used to date?"

My attention snapped back to Erin.

"What?"

"You and Luna? Did you date in high school?

I huffed out a laugh. "Mike would've broken my arms and legs. Maybe my hands, too. No, we were good friends in high school. I don't get to see them much now that we're old."

Erin snorted, her eyes rolling. "You're not exactly ancient."

True, but... "Sometimes I feel like it."

"Since you're only a year older than me, I'm going to ignore that. If I don't, that makes me old, too. And I refuse to consider myself old at twenty-nine."

We sat for a second in silence, gazes locked, while I told myself she looked a hell of a lot younger than twenty-nine.

Then she cleared her throat, looked down at the table, then her gaze lifted to somewhere over my shoulder.

"So, what are we doing here, Rebel?"

Good question. Right now, I didn't have an answer, except the one I'd given her before.

"I think if we get to know each other a little better..."

"You wouldn't think I was so annoying."

My lips twitched, wanting to smile at her sass. "I don't think you're annoying."

She hmphed, arms crossing over her chest. "Oh, please. You practically run in the other direction when you see me coming."

My turn to roll my eyes. "I'm not afraid of you, Erin."

"Then why do you avoid me?"

Shit. How truthful did she want me to be? How much truth was too much? And how much did I really want her to know? I wasn't used to talking about my issues with anyone except my therapist. Didn't think anyone else needed to know.

But she was right. I'd invited her.

I rubbed a hand across the back of my neck, rethinking my entire strategy for this dinner. I'd thought we'd manage small talk for ninety minutes then go our separate ways. And at the wedding, I'd be a little less likely to want to spend most of the wedding on the other side of the room from her.

Now, she watched me like she was expecting me to bare my deepest secrets, her expression more than a little stubborn. I'd almost call her cute, but I'd never say that out loud to a woman. My mom didn't raise an idiot. And I didn't think she was cute. Cute was for kittens and toddlers.

"I'm not good with people I don't know. And it takes me a while to warm up to strangers."

And I hated exposing my jugular to anyone.

Erin's expression softened with every word, which made me stiffen. I always hated to be pitied. Luckily, Luna returned with our drinks and took our order. Apparently, Erin came here often, as well, and knew the menu. When Luna disappeared again, another silence fell. This one was worse. I knew she was judging me.

But what she said next surprised the hell out of me.

"I know I can come on strong. I'm sorry I make you uncomfortable."

Now she looked uncomfortable, and I wanted to bang my head on the table. Damn it, it was not my intention to make this woman feel bad. Her gaze had fallen to the table and her hands had folded into a knot in front of her. Jesus, she looked like I'd kicked her puppy.

"Erin, this isn't about you. It's about me. You're not at fault."

She nodded, and her lips curled into a false smile.

"Good to know."

Oh, for fuck's sake. "Erin. It's not you, it's me."

I thought I might get a smile out of her, but once again, I got it wrong.

Her lips twisted into a grimace. "Not the first time I've heard that. My former fiancé said the exact same thing before he called off our wedding."

My brain hit rewind. "Your fiancé? You were engaged?"

"What, you don't think anyone would want to marry me?"

"NO! That's not what I meant. Jesus—"

Her lips twisted and finally curved into a true smile.

"I'm kidding, Rebel. Take it easy. Yeah, I was engaged. It ended." She shrugged. "End of story."

It didn't exactly sound like the end of the story. In fact, I was pretty sure there was a hell of a lot more to the story. But I knew she wasn't going to spill it to me. And it's not like I needed to know. We were just here to get used to each other. But I found myself wanting to know more.

"Did it end before you came here?"

"Yes."

"Did you end it?"

"No."

Okay, now I knew why my sister got pissed at me for one-word answers.

I sat back in my chair and considered what to say next. Erin stared back, looking a little more wary than she had a few minutes ago.

You're not here to interrogate her.

No, but I found I wanted to know more about her.

"So, you're from New York City, right? You grew up there?"

She nodded, eyeing me like I was trying to pry state secrets out of her.

"I did." Her teeth lodged in her bottom lip like she was trying not to say anything more, but then it was almost like she couldn't help herself. "Upper West Side."

"Your family has money."

It wasn't a question. It took money to live well on the Upper West Side. And it wasn't a dig. My family had money. My great-grandparents had built a small-time whiskey business into an empire. A small one, but still enough that my parents had been able to build the Northeast Professional Hockey League into a viable business when so many other leagues had failed through the years.

Erin had been chewing over her response for several long seconds, until she finally nodded. It wasn't like it was a big secret. Everyone knew her grandfather was loaded. The guy had outright bought the local newspaper and the building from the former owners and had kept everyone on the payroll until they had either moved on or retired.

Which was how Erin had come to be here.

"Did you always want to work in journalism?"

She blinked, as if her brain was trying to compute the change in conversation.

"No, not at all. I studied pre-law in college because I really didn't know what I wanted to do with my life. My dad's family is into real estate, and I thought I'd work there after law school, but I never went." She shrugged, her gaze falling away for a few seconds. "I worked for the company for a while until Mom asked me to come help Granddad close down the paper."

"But you ended up staying, and St. David still has a newspaper."

Her left shoulder twitched. "Things changed."

"That have anything to do with your broken engagement?"

She stiffened, her gaze flitting around the room, as if she were looking for something or someone to save her. She got lucky. Luna returned with her our salads. But it was only a brief reprieve. I found myself wanting more, wanting to know more about her.

"Have you ever been in long-term relationship that ended…badly?" she asked after a few bites of her salad.

Payback time. "Yeah. One."

Her eyes widened. She hadn't been expecting that.

"Really?"

I didn't know whether to be amused or offended. "Yeah. In college."

"I'm not sure I knew you went to college."

My turn to shrug. "I wasn't going to. I was just going to join the team. All I wanted to do was play hockey."

"What changed?"

"Have you met my pop?"

Her spontaneous laughter seeped into my bloodstream and made it heat. A slow burn that felt almost uncomfortable, like an itch under the skin I couldn't scratch.

"I have."

"He told me it was either college or service." Then I told her something I'd never told anyone else. And I had no idea why. "There are times I wish I'd enlisted."

Her eyes widened. "Really? Why?"

I nodded. "I wanted to follow in my dad's footsteps. But I'm not my dad."

Her smile softened. "That's not a bad thing, Rebel."

"I know. Which is why I didn't enlist."

"What did you study?"

"Business, but I majored in hockey."

"Ah. Did you get good grades?"

"Do you think my parents would accept anything less?"

Her lips quirked. "Of course not."

For the first time in a long time, I wanted to talk about what had happened during my senior year. I hadn't spoken about it since I'd unloaded on Brian last year. Not a lot of people knew that I'd nearly ruined my life because I'd been too afraid to ask for the help I desperately needed.

And it made no sense that I wanted to tell her. So, I didn't say anything.

We spent the next few minutes focusing on eating, our meals following the salads minutes later. We managed to keep up small talk through dinner, but afterward, I caught her looking at her watch. And I found myself not wanting to leave.

When Luna brought the bill, Erin wanted to pay half of it, but the look I gave her must have convinced her not to try. We left shortly after that, and I walked with her the couple of blocks to the newspaper building, where her apartment was on the third floor.

"So," she said, "do you think we'll be able to spend the night together?"

My lips quirked in a smile, her eyes widening as she realized what she'd said.

"Oh, my god, I didn't mean—I mean, that's not—"

My laughter echoed around us, cutting off her words. "I

know what you meant, Erin. And yeah, I think we'll be okay for the wedding."

Her lips curved and, again, that heat curled in my gut. Must be indigestion.

"Me, too."

Several seconds passed before she blinked and took a step back toward the building.

"Thanks for dinner, Rebel."

"Night, Erin."

I waited until she opened the door and disappeared inside the building before I headed for my car.

CHAPTER TEN

Erin

"Wow." Rain stood in front of the dress my mom had bought for me. "That is absolutely stunning."

I sighed, laying across my bed. I'd driven home from New York yesterday with that dress in a bag in the back seat of my car, loving it and hating it at the same time. I'd known it was the one the second I saw it. The problem was, so had my mom. We'd instantly agreed.

"It is. I love Chanel."

Rain looked over her shoulder at me, brows raised. "But…"

Shrugging, I rolled over to look at the ceiling.

"But my mom chose it."

"Ah."

"Yeah."

Rain flopped next to me on the bed, staring up at the ceiling with me.

"Is she really that bad?"

I sighed like a hormonal teenager. "No, she's not. Of course, she's not. We actually had a nice day."

"So, what's the problem?"

The problem was I hadn't been able to stop thinking about Rebel since our not-date Monday night. And that was a major problem. I'd seen another side of him. The non-grumpy side. So what? I was sure he'd be back to his same grumpy self the next time I saw him.

"I feel like I'm still twelve when I'm with her. But that's a 'me' problem."

"You wanna talk about it? Or do you wanna go have some wine and whine?"

I glanced over at Rain, who had a goofy smile on her face but was clearly pleased with her wordplay. I grinned and shook my head.

"No on both. I'm on a self-imposed alcohol freeze until the wedding. I don't want to have to worry about fitting into my dress. And I've got a therapist for whining."

"Did you decide to go to your cousin's wedding stag?"

My nose curled. "I hate that word. It seems so…male centric."

"Would you rather I ask if you're going alone?"

"That sounds pathetic."

Rain rolled her eyes. "Are you taking anyone with you? Jeez, I should know better than to fight with verbally spar with a writer."

"Except I'm not really a writer."

"Sounds like something your mom said yesterday."

"She's not wrong. I wasn't trained as a writer. Actually, I wasn't really trained to do anything except take tests and do very, very well on them."

Rain's expression hardened. "You went to college for four years and didn't learn anything other than how to read textbooks? I call bullshit. You write articles for the newspaper, articles that make people laugh. You're really good at those, you know. And you run two businesses. Well, three if you count how much you do for your granddad at the paper."

Rolling onto my side, I bent my arm and propped my head on my hand. "You're a really good friend. Will you marry me? Ooh, or you could come to the wedding with me."

"You know I would except Brian and I are going to the shore that week."

"Shit. I forgot." I really hadn't but I could hope something had changed. "I just…really don't want to go alone. My sister will be there with her perfect husband, and my brother will be there with his flavor of the week, and she'll be some beautiful woman with an amazing career.

"And all night, I'll have to fend off questions about how I'm such a good person to give up everything to help my elderly grandfather manage his affairs. Like he's on his deathbed, and I'm just waiting for him to die so I can collect his money."

"Your family reunions must be loads of fun."

"We don't have reunions. We have board meetings, and no, they're not fun."

"Wow. Your family drama sounds made for TV."

"I swear my parents' staff leaks info to the tabloids. It's a nightmare."

"Did you just say your parents have staff? Like, 'maids and butlers' staff?"

Rain and I had been friends since the moment we met in the Tea Room where Granddad and I had had dinner the first night I'd arrived. He'd introduced us and, when she hadn't run from my initial obnoxious, anxiety-ridden verbal assault, I'd immediately realized she was a keeper.

But even though I'd told her a lot about me, I hadn't exactly told her a lot about my family. I mean, sure I bitched about my mom like a normal person, and I'd told her a little about my dad, though that was a touchier subject. I didn't feel like I had a real relationship with him.

And of course, I always complained about my perfect siblings. My sister was Type-A on steroids, and my brother made playboys look like philanthropists. But the more cringey stuff, like the wealth and the lifestyle...I never really talked about it.

Her family was wealthy, yes, but mine was a level above wealthy. And it made me uncomfortable to talk about it.

"Yes," I drew the word out to about five syllables. "I mean, I just assumed you knew."

Not true, but hell, everyone could Google. All she had to do was a simple search. And I'm sure she had.

"Well, sure, I knew you came from a rich family. I guess I just never thought about it being mega-yacht and second-mansion-in-the-Hamptons rich."

"Replace the yacht for a villa in Tuscany, and you'd be close."

Rain's eyes widened. "Damn. I mean, my parents are loaded, but yours are on another level, aren't they?"

And this is why I didn't tell people about my family. They looked at me differently.

I just shrugged. She knew the answer to her question just by the look on my face.

"Shit." She made a face that was both amused and resigned. "There is such a thing as too much money, huh?"

"My parents' wedding was more of a business merger. My

granddad's not poor, obviously," I waved a hand around at the building I lived in, which he'd bought on a whim because he'd always wanted to run his own newspaper, "but my dad's family…yeah."

"So, how'd you turn out so normal?"

This is why I loved Rain. She was the sister I'd never had. My actual sister and I had never really been close. I'd blame the age gap of eight years, but really, we just didn't have anything in common.

And now my eyes started to tear up.

"There are a few people around who would say I'm not."

Rain rolled her eyes. "And they're assholes, so ignore them. Seriously, you're the least snotty rich person I know."

"I mean, you know I went to prep school. I was pretty much an outcast there, although I did make a few fellow outcast friends. We kept each other grounded, you know?"

Nodding, Rain pushed herself up to sit on the bed cross-legged. "Yep. I get it. I know you told me you stayed because you love it here, but I'm beginning to think there's more to it."

In all the time I'd been in St. David, I'd never mentioned my fiancé to Rain. I didn't like to talk about him. I *never* wanted to talk about him, but my mom and sister would always manage to work it into the conversation. I should be over it by now.

And I was over him. Had been for a while. I didn't even really think about Michael anymore.

Except, I'd never told Rain about him. I didn't ever talk about him, except to my therapist. And even then, not as often as we had six years ago when it was fresh and it'd hurt like I'd been shot in the heart.

"I guess, maybe, it might have something to do with my failed engagement."

Rain blinked. "Say what now?"

I shrugged, like it wasn't really a big deal, even as I couldn't hold her gaze. "It was a long time ago. A couple of years before I moved here. We were engaged in our senior year of college. It ended after four years."

"You were engaged for *four* years? Did he cheat on you?"

"Not physically. Emotionally…" Another shrug. "He fell in love with someone else."

Rain reached across and squeezed my hand. "That sucks. I'm sorry."

"I know it was for the best now. We weren't right for each other."

Except that's not what I'd thought at the time. I'd thought we were perfect. And he hadn't.

"Well, I say you dodged a bullet."

Except everyone in my family thought I'd been the one at fault. Everyone except Granddad.

"I know that now. I should've known it when he got engaged to a friend of ours six weeks later."

"Oh, he is a total dick."

"Actually, he's not. He runs an international charity for children, and he and his wife have adopted three kids."

"Well, damn. Now I really hate him."

I burst out laughing. "I know, right? It's like the plot of a bad romcom, except I'm the sad side character who disappears into the background after the main characters get married and live happily ever after."

"You're not a side character, Erin. I really hope you don't think that."

"I did, for a while. That's part of the reason I came here to help Granddad. Part of it was I wasn't happy with myself or my life, and I needed a change."

"Is that why you haven't really dated? Because of the douchebag?"

I loved Rain for making me laugh. "No. Yes. Maybe a little. I mean, I have dated."

She gave me a look. "When was the last time you went out with a guy?"

Monday night. With her brother.

"Oh wait." Rain's eyes narrowed. "I heard a rumor you and Rebel had dinner. But I can't believe that. You would have told me if you were going out with my brother."

"It wasn't a date. It was just dinner."

Rain's brows couldn't get any higher. "Why do you sound a little defensive?"

"I'm not. Rebel thought it would help us get rid of some our awkwardness during the wedding dance."

"Huh. Okay. I'm kind of amazed to say my brother might have had a good idea. But don't tell him I said that. So, did it? Help?"

I didn't have to think about the answer. "Yeah. I think… Yeah. We know each other a little better now. I think we'll be able to smile convincingly for the cameras on wedding day."

"I don't think anyone was worried you'd ruin the day, you know that, right?"

"I know. Rebel and I just don't have the best track record."

"And that's his fault, not yours."

I knew that wasn't completely true. "I can be a little… extra."

Rain huffed. "I wish you could see yourself the way I do. You're only extra in the best ways. You're kind to a fault. You genuinely love to talk to people, and you like to take care of them. That's how I see you."

I blinked, feeling the sting of tears.

"It's nice that you do. But there are a lot of other people in town who still look at me like an outsider. And a weird one."

"Stop that. You're not weird. And if anyone out there thinks you are, that just makes them dicks."

"Thanks, Rainy. I appreciate it."

"Yeah, but you don't believe me, do you?"

"I know you mean well, but I also know myself. It's something I've been working on with my therapist for years. Learning to accept myself the way I am."

"The way you are is what makes you who you are. I wouldn't want you to be any other way. And Rebel and all those other people can go screw themselves sideways."

Laughing, I fell back onto the bed again. "Your brother's not that bad, you know."

"I know. He's got things he needs to work through, but he's working on himself, too. Guys just take longer to develop critical thinking skills. Some of them anyway." Rain got off the bed to pick up the Chanel and hold it against herself, standing in front of the full-length standing mirror that at one time had belonged to the original owners of the building and should probably be in a museum somewhere. "So, you and Rebel are good?"

"Yeah, I think so."

"Good. I really think you and I need to go on a shopping trip to New York City. I gotta get me one of these. I think Brian would definitely like to see me in something like this."

And for a brief second, I wondered what Rebel would think of me in that dress.

*ebel*

"So, um, hey, Rebel."

"Ian?"

"Yeah. Hi. It's me. How's it going?"

I put down the rake I was using to weed the garden bed in front of my home. Living in the woods was great, away from nosy neighbors in town who watched your every move from their windows. Until you realized the woods didn't give a fuck if you had a little stone wall around your beds to keep the forest out. That meant yardwork, which I didn't hate. It got me out of the house doing something physical. I didn't sit well.

I'd taken my phone outside with me, expecting a call from Brian about Rowdy's bachelor party this weekend, so I'd answered without looking at the screen. It took my brain a second to make the switch from the expected to the unexpected. But when I did, I heard something in Ian's voice that made my brain snap to attention.

"Ian, what's wrong?"

I was pretty sure I heard him sigh.

"Um, so… Well, nothing's wrong. It's just…um…"

I waited, knowing him well enough to know he'd spit it out eventually. If you interrupted, it just took him that much longer to get out what he wanted to say.

"Well, my place for the summer fell through, and I need somewhere to stay for a while. Just a week or two, just until—"

"Sure. When are you coming? Do you need a ride?"

Silence from the other end.

"Ian? You still there?"

"Yeah. I just… I didn't… Really? You don't mind?"

Okay, this didn't sound like Ian.

"No, I don't mind. I'll text you my address unless you need a ride. I can come get you. I could be there in an hour or so."

Another silence.

"Ian?"

"Yeah, no. I mean. Nah, I'm good. I'm all packed."

Behind me, I heard wheels on gravel, which meant someone was pulling into my driveway. I turned to see who it was as I pulled the phone away from my ear and put it on speaker.

"I'm gonna text you my address and some directions. Let me know when you leave, and I'll make sure I'm home when you get here."

"I don't wanna be any trouble."

My dad stopped his golf cart a few feet away and shut it off. I lifted my chin in greeting.

"You're not any trouble, Ian. Just leave already. I'll see you when you get here."

Another pause. "Thanks, Reb. I really... Yeah, I really appreciate this."

"No problem. See you then."

I hung up before the kid could start thanking me again.

Pop's raised eyebrows asked the question.

"My roommate needs a place to stay for a while."

My dad had been in the hockey business for more years than I'd been alive. And while he'd never played, he knew hockey players inside and out. They had their plans for the offseason set before the end of the season.

"How old?"

"Just turned twenty-two."

"Can't go home or doesn't want to?"

I didn't know much about Ian's parents. He didn't talk about them a lot, but I got the feeling there was some tension there. "Little of both, I think."

Pop nodded, gaze sliding to the beds I'd been working on. His brain always had about five browser windows open at the same time.

"You better get that purslane outta there now or you'll never get ahead of it." He pointed at something in the garden bed before he paused for a second. "I don't think this is the plus one your mom was hoping for."

He said it so deadpan, it took a second for my brain to catch up. But when it did, I nearly choked on a laugh.

"Not sure he's gonna be here that long, but, damn, Pop, you do have a sense of humor."

"Only when it's called for."

We grinned at each other, knowing we were thinking the exact same thing.

Rowdy had inherited Pop's ability to schmooze. Rain had inherited his business sense. Rocky… Well, Rocky seemed to have gotten more than his share of intelligence from both of our parents.

Pop and I were a lot alike when it came to what we considered funny. Most people thought we didn't have a sense of humor. Totally untrue. Most people just never understood how dry it was.

"So, what's up?"

Rowdy, Rain and I were used to Mom checking in randomly. We joked among ourselves that it was to make sure we hadn't secretly moved away, but Pop had never made a habit of it. Which meant he had something on his mind now.

"You know your sister's been on me about getting this youth program up and running, and with the wedding, we're not going to be able to manage it this year. But I just got a call from the high school team's coach. They always run a two-week camp in July at the arena, but he's having surgery he didn't expect, and the assistant coach's wife is pregnant and due around that time.

"Coach asked if we had someone willing to the run the camp. A few of our guys usually volunteer for a day or two, but most of them have jobs over the summer and can't take the time off." Pop's lips quirked. "And I wouldn't trust most of them to run the camp by themselves."

And since he was standing here, I knew who he was nominating to run the camp.

"Pop—"

"I think it'll be good for you."

I didn't say anything else. I knew it wouldn't do any good. Pop had made up his mind. It wasn't open for debate.

"Camp doesn't start 'til the week after the wedding. You can run drills with the kids with your eyes closed."

Yeah, I could. And it would get my mind off—

"You wanna tell me what you've got on your mind, son?"

Damn, maybe my mom wasn't the only one who read minds. "Nothing, Pop."

"Bullshit. I know my kids. Something's up with you. I know you haven't signed your contract yet. Got something to do with that?"

Jesus. "How do you know that?"

His brows arched for a split second. "You just told me. What I don't know is why."

Shaking my head, I turned back to the garden bed.

"Damn it, Pop. I hate when you do that."

"If you weren't so much like me and opened your mouth more, I wouldn't have to."

We shared a grin that probably would've looked identical to anyone watching us.

"So." He crossed his arms over his chest. "You wanna tell me why?"

I shrugged. "Just haven't."

"You plan to?"

I huffed out a sigh. "Honestly, I don't know yet."

Pop nodded, his expression way more low-key than I expected. "Okay. I just want you to know I'm here if you need to talk it out. And you know Rowdy—"

"Has enough on his plate right now. The guy's getting married in a few weeks. I'm not putting anything more on his shoulders right now."

"Fair enough," Pop said. "Well, I'll let you get back to your weeding."

He headed back to the golf cart but stopped a few feet away and pointed at something in the grass.

"Better get that ground ivy outta there before it takes over the whole yard." He settled himself into the seat, a little slower than normal. The thought made my gut knot.

"And Reb? The kids'll think you're a god. An actual AHL hockey player teaching them hockey. Let me know if you're up for it."

———

"SO BASICALLY, he guilted you into it?"

Sitting at my dining room table about an hour later, I scratched my neck, which I'm pretty sure was sunburned, and sighed. Brian was on the other end of the line. He'd called to finalize plans for Rowdy's bachelor party and, when we had, I told him about my dad's scheme.

"Not quite. I think I can still say no. But...they're gonna have to cancel if no one steps up. I remember going to hockey camp when I was their age. I looked forward to it all fucking year."

"Guess I should call you coach now?"

An undercurrent of amusement ran through Brian's tone, and I gave him the finger even though I knew he couldn't see it.

"It's not like I had anything else to do this summer."

"I figured you'd be flying off to spend a few weeks with your teammates somewhere warm."

"Pretty sure St. David is hot enough for me."

"Okay, then somewhere beachier."

"Nah. You know me. I'd be bored as fuck laying around all day. Besides, I needed to be here for the wedding."

And I'd rather be here.

Brian's huff of amusement came through loud and clear. "Guess you can be grumpy here just as well as anywhere else."

"You've been talking to my sister too much."

"Rain says you spend too much time alone."

"Well, that's the one thing I won't be doing for the time being. My roommate needs a place to stay for a while. He'll be here in a few."

"Oh yeah? That planned?"

"No. He's younger. Only twenty-two. Said his plans fell through."

"He have family?"

"Yeah, but he doesn't talk about them much. Never met them, either. Guess he wasn't planning to go home and whatever else he had lined up isn't gonna happen."

"Guess you will have a date to the wedding."

"Jesus, everyone's a comedian today. Dad said practically the same thing."

Brian's bark of laughter made me grin. "Don't tell your sister that. She and Erin were doing some stupid online quiz about your perfect partner the other night, and one of the questions was something about your mate reminding you of your father. Man, I am *not* like your dad. I mean the Colonel's a great guy, but… I ain't him."

"What'd Erin say about hers?"

Why the hell had I asked that question? It's like my brain momentarily disconnected from sanity. I didn't want to know what Erin said about her dad. None of my business.

"Not much. She never talks about anyone but her granddad. Never really thought about it before, but now I wonder if she even has parents."

"She does. I don't think they're too happy she moved here."

From outside, I heard tires on gravel and a mistuned engine.

"Hey, I gotta go." I looked out the window. "Got company."

———

"You wanna talk about it?"

Ian sat across from me at the Tea Room, pushing around the remains of his meal. The place wasn't busy. Yet. But it was only six-thirty. The Wednesday night crowd would be here after eight.

The kid had been quiet through most of dinner, which wasn't like him. I hadn't pushed. I knew when I didn't want to talk about something, people asking me what was wrong was a sure way to make me shut up. I'd been waiting for him to open up. Usually Ian couldn't keep his mouth shut. Today, I couldn't get him to open it. All I got now was a shrug, which made him look at least ten years younger.

I tried not to worry about that shrug, because that wasn't me. I wasn't the guy who patted the younger guys on the back and encouraged them to become their better selves. That was Rowdy's job. I was the guy who bought them a beer and sat and listened when they wanted to bitch and complain before they moved on to someone like Rowdy who could tell them what to do.

"So that's a no. Okay, I can deal with that. You wanna hear about my day weeding the garden beds or –"

"Hey, you must be Ian. I'm Rowdy."

My brother stood by our table, welcoming grin on his face and hand outstretched. I couldn't believe I hadn't seen him coming, but I'd been so focused on Ian. The kid looked up at my brother, blinking. After a short hesitation, he took

Rowdy's hand. And since Rowdy missed nothing, he slid me a quick glance, his smile never dimming.

"Um, yeah, hi."

"Nice to meet you." Rowdy's smile didn't waver, even though I knew Rowdy had clocked about nine different things that seemed off about Ian. I could sometimes miss things that were right in front of my face, but Rowdy missed nothing, even though he came off as a clueless, smiley golden retriever. "Reb said you'll be around for a while."

While Ian's brain tried to come up with a suitable response, Rowdy released Ian's hand and turned his attention to me.

"So, Pop said you're gonna take the camp coach position."

I rolled my eyes and sighed heavily, though it was mostly for show. "He forgot to tell you I didn't agree yet."

"Yeah, we both know that's just a formality. You're gonna do it. And seriously, the kids'll love you. Just wanted to stop and say hi before Tressy sees you and forces you to come sit with us. Now I can tell her you told me to fuck off and leave you alone."

I smirked at Rowdy as I gave him the finger, Ian looking between us with his mouth hanging open.

"Now you can tell her the truth. And I still haven't told Pop yes."

Rowdy's grin widened. "You know you're going to do it. Don't know why you think you're not."

And like the tornado Rowdy was, he turned and headed in the opposite direction, where I saw Tressy and Krista waiting by the entrance. Tressy did a little finger wave, but it was Krista's happy arm-waving that made me grin and wave back, before turning my attention back to Ian.

"Sorry about that. Rowdy can be a lot, even in small doses."

Ian shrugged. "No problem. I know I came at a bad time. You've got a lot going on—"

"Ian." I leaned forward, just a little, making sure to hold Ian's gaze. "You don't wanna tell me what's going on, that's fine. You wanna talk, that's fine too. You're welcome here for as long as you fucking want to be here. Got it? My place is more than big enough for the two of us." And I just had a brilliant idea. "If you're up for it, I might even have a job for you."

Ian perked up at that. "A job? Seriously? Doing what? I had a job, but it fell through… when everything went to hell."

I paused for a second, considering what I wanted to say. "You in trouble? You need—"

"No!" Ian sounded like he'd dropped back into his pre-teen years. "No, I'm not. I just…" He sighed hard, and I knew I had to drop it.

Something had happened, and I hated that he didn't feel comfortable enough to tell me what was going on. Then again, my face didn't exactly coax people into confiding in me. And usually, I didn't want to know. But Ian was a friend. And he had a problem. And yeah, maybe I had more of my dad in me than I cared to admit.

"So, this job," I said. "I'm not sure you're gonna want it, but I got…" *roped into* "an offer I couldn't turn down. And it turns out, I'm gonna need help."

Ian finally looked me in the eyes, missing a little bit of the guilt and, yeah, despair, he'd had before. And I knew this was the right thing. For both of us.

"You know my brother's getting married in a couple weeks, right? And then they're going on their honeymoon for a couple of weeks. Turns out the local hockey club needs a coach for their two-week camp. Usually, this is something Rowdy would do but—"

"How come?"

"How come what?"

"Why would Rowdy do it and not you?" Ian looked genuinely confused. "I mean, you're a fucking awesome player. No offense to your brother and all, but you got an AHL position without coming through the system. That's fucking awesome."

I'd heard that before. Someone people had said it straight to my face with a sneer, like I must have bought my way in. Those were players I mopped the ice with during games. They didn't open their mouths again. Some players, like Ian, had been better about it. Most everybody had an opinion, though. Which meant a lot more attention than I was used to. And that had sucked.

Now, the absolute sincerity on Ian's face made me smile. Which is what I was doing when a flash of rose-gold hair caught my eye from across the room. I caught Erin's gaze and the surprise on her face turned my smile into a grin. Which made her mouth drop open in shock. That girl would get fleeced in any poker game she ever played.

My grin quickly turned into a frown when I realized who she was with. What the hell was she doing here with Kade? And why the hell did it matter?

What the fuck, dude?

Kade followed Erin's gaze and grinned when he saw me. Then I noticed Brian and Rain behind them, and—

We should've stayed home and ordered pizza.

"Is that Erin?"

Ian had followed my gaze, his expression lightening and a smile emerging.

"Yep, that's Erin."

"Cool. Can we say hi?"

I didn't really have to answer that. Kade was already on his way across the room, Rain and Brian close behind. And Erin trailing along behind them, biting her lip as her gaze met mine before hers slid away again. Her smile emerged only when she caught sight of Ian.

My sister didn't even bother to say hi to me. She was all about Ian, introducing Brian and Kade and never asking him what he was doing here. Brian must have gotten the word around. Good. That was good.

Ian seemed most excited to see Erin, who was all smiles for him. I sat back and let Rain and Erin handle the conversation as Kade and Brian pulled another table over to ours. And in some weird twist of fate, Erin ended up next to me.

I trusted Rain to keep everyone else from overwhelming Ian for the time being. My brain had decided it was more interested in whatever Erin was doing. Which wasn't much. She sat quietly, fidgeting a little but not enough to be noticeable to anyone else. But her silence would be. And that was because of me.

I turned to look at her just as she turned to me.

"I think we—"

"I heard you—"

We both broke off.

"What were you going—"

"Sorry, go ahead and—"

I tried not to roll my eyes. I really did. But I knew I'd lost the battle when she huffed out a sigh. I held up my hand, and she pursed her lips.

"Ladies first."

Her brows rose and her lips twisted into a semi-smile. And again, I wondered why I'd never noticed how pretty she was.

You always thought she was annoying.

Always talking, always in motion. Always busy. Just being near her made me want to tear my hair out. Except right now...

"Rain said you're going to run the team camp this summer. I just wanted to let you know I'll be providing the lunches this year."

"I didn't realize that was part of the program."

"It wasn't until a couple years ago. Have you run the camp before?"

I huffed out a laugh. "I haven't even agreed to do it yet."

She looked confused. "Why? I think you'd be perfect for the job."

My brows rose as her cheeks flushed. It made her eyes greener. Something I shouldn't have noticed.

"Why does everyone keep telling me that?"

She didn't even stop to think about her answer. "Because you're so still."

She said it like it was obvious. And I had no idea what she meant.

Frowning, I shook my head. "Still?"

"Quiet." She shrugged. "I think kids respond to that better than...other ways. The only coaches I ever had were intense."

Interesting. "What sport did you play?"

Her nose wrinkled. "Tennis."

"You didn't like it."

Her left shoulder lifted slightly. "I love to play. I don't like competing."

"Couldn't you just play the game and not compete?"

She paused, and I saw the calculations going on in her head. What should she tell me? How much did she want to reveal? How much did she trust me? It pissed me off that she didn't trust me enough to tell me this small piece of herself. And yeah, I knew it didn't make any sense.

Fuck it.

"That's not how it worked in my family," she finally said.

Okay, that gave me a little better picture.

"Parents had high expectations, huh?"

"Just a little, yeah?"

She said it with a smile, as if she really didn't care, but I saw hurt in that way too expressive face of hers. And it pissed me off even more. Not *at* her. For her. But from the way she was staring at me, I could tell she thought I was coming down on her. Shit.

She pulled away mentally. Shut down. I saw it in the flat lines of her face. She didn't do that with anyone else but me. Made me feel like shit, honestly.

Holding her gaze, I leaned forward, her eyes growing larger every centimeter I got closer. At the moment, no one else was paying attention to us. I knew because I checked. They were all engrossed in their own conversations.

"You know you don't need to live up to anyone's expectations but your own, right?"

Her lips parted and her eyes widened like I'd told her I wanted to strip her right here and now and lay her out on the table so I could kiss her from that adorable nose to the tips of her toes.

The thought flickered through my brain at lightning speed, too fast for me to be able to tear it apart. So I pushed it to the back of my brain and focused on watching her.

"I do. But it's hard when it's your parents. I mean, your parents are amazing. They're so supportive and loving and—"

"Yeah, they are. But that doesn't mean they don't have

expectations. And trust me, I haven't always lived up to theirs."

Her head ticked to the side as she thought about my words. Then that little smile came out again, and I knew our conversation had reached its limit. For her, at least.

"No parents are perfect, I guess."

That right there was her exit ramp to this conversation. The problem was, I didn't want to give it to her.

"And some are worse than others."

She held my gaze for a few seconds.

"My parents aren't monsters."

"Didn't say that."

She huffed. "Then what are you saying?"

"I'm just saying sometimes parents aren't always right about what their kids need."

Her teeth latched onto her bottom lip, digging in until the skin turned white before she released it. My hand curled into a fist under the table, resisting the urge to press my thumb there and make sure she didn't hurt herself. It pissed me off that she might.

"Is that why you moved here?" I nudged at her just a little more.

"Because my parents thought I should win more tennis matches?"

Sarcasm coated her voice, which didn't suit her at all. And it pissed me off. Took a little bit of work to keep my expression neutral, but I think I managed. She didn't run screaming, anyway.

"You wanted to be where you could be yourself."

Now she looked at me like I had two heads and a tail. Finally, after a few quiet seconds, she shook her head, and her gaze slid away.

"So anyway, about camp. I usually bring lunch around 11:30 so I have time to set up. Everything's ready by noon for the kids to eat. You won't have to do anything. I do cleanup, too."

I didn't say anything right away. "Seems like we're going to be seeing each other a lot more than we anticipated."

"And are you okay with that?"

She said it with a little more of her natural sass and something inside me settled.

"Guess I am."

And part of me wasn't unhappy about that.

CHAPTER TWELVE

TWO-ISH WEEKS BEFORE THE WEDDING

"I'M REALLY NOT sure this is a good idea."

Standing in a corner of the great room in the Lawrence house with Rain, I couldn't understand why I felt like I wanted to jump out of my skin.

"What? Dancing lessons? Trust me, you want Reb to have lessons. The man might not look like he weighs a lot, but he's solid. You do not want him to step on your feet. Besides, I thought you were getting along better since you spent time together."

Rain didn't look at me when she said that, but I knew she was asking for details. She had her eyes on Brian, who stood across the room talking to Rebel. I'd been studiously avoiding looking at Rebel. I was afraid if I started, I wouldn't want to stop. Which was ridiculous.

Except I didn't know what to tell Rain that wouldn't make

her give me that look. The one that expected even more answers than I was ready to give. Or really had any idea how to give. Rebel seemed to have gotten over his dislike of me, but that had brought up some weird reactions. Like my brain telling me Rebel was hot.

Which was the worst thing for me to think. First, no, that wasn't happening. Second, he was Rain's brother. And third, he didn't like me.

Except, maybe he did now? Ugh, who knew with Rebel. The guy was so damn hard to read. Although, he had smiled at me…

I grimaced. "Sorry. I've just got a lot on my mind. I don't even know why I said that. Just ignore me."

Of course, that meant Rain did the opposite. She turned to look at me, gaze narrowed and brain running at full speed.

"Did something happen between you and Reb?"

"No!" *Whoa, take it down a notch.* "No, nothing happened. There are just a lot of moving parts happening right now. I want everything to be wonderful for Tressy, and I don't want to let anyone down."

"Are you worried about not having enough help? You know the Angels will be more than happy—"

"I know. And so many of them are already pitching in. No, it's just me being me."

Rain tapped me on the arm. "Well, stop. Worrying, I mean. Not being you. You're fine. Seriously. And I have a feeling you're going to show us all up on the dance floor."

I had made the mistake of telling Rain I'd had ballroom dance lessons in prep. And I'd told her I'd enjoyed them. At the time, I had. It'd been an easy gym credit, and I hadn't had to compete. I'd just had to move. And yeah, I'd been good at it.

"I haven't danced in years, so I don't think I'm going to be that good."

"Well, you'll be better than that crew," she pointed across the floor at her brothers and Brian, who were standing in a circle across the floor. We were waiting for Tressy and her sister and Tressy's business partner Jen to arrive. Tressy had let us know they were running a little late. Jen had hit traffic on her drive from New York City, where she and their other partner, Leon, ran their talent agency.

"You're telling me none of them can dance? I've seen Brian on the ice. The man has moves."

Rain laughed, her smile widening and her gaze going back to her boyfriend. "That's true. But my brothers... not so much."

My attention caught on Rebel again. He had one shoulder propped against the wall, his mouth curved in what passed for a smile from him. He wasn't speaking at the moment, his gaze focused on Rowdy and then Rocky, the youngest of the Lawrences. I'd met Rocky a few times, but he'd been at college for most of the time I'd lived here. He returned for a few weeks in the summer, but he mainly stayed at his parents' place.

He looked a lot like Rowdy, with the same eyes and mouth, but his hair was dark and cut shorter. He still looked like a kid, and since he was barely twenty-one, I guess he was. He wasn't as broad as Rebel, but he had Rebel's build, which made him a little taller than Rowdy. Standing together like they were, there was no way you could mistake those guys for anyone other than brothers.

But it was Rebel who held my attention. He always seemed just a little more put together than the rest. He was wearing pants instead of jeans. His dark hair was a little longer than normal, but still not as long as any of the other guys. He must get it cut every other week to keep it perfect like that. And it did suit him perfectly.

Even his stubble was perfectly trimmed.

It just wasn't fair.

Right now, I felt like an absolute mess. I'd had to hurry over here from the bakery and, since it was warm outside, I was flushed and a little sweaty in places I didn't want to be sweaty. I'd stopped off at my apartment to take a quick shower so I didn't embarrass myself, but my hair had decided today was the day humidity had won the battle.

I'd braided it, but individual strands had escaped and were reaching for the sky like seedlings in search of the sun.

Ooh, Granddad would slash that out of a story with a red pen so fast. And why had I thought a sundress would be a good idea? Yes, it was hot outside, but now I was a little cool, and I hadn't thought to bring a little sweater and—

"Oh, good." Rain sighed. "Tressy's here. I thought I was going to have to break into my parents' liquor cabinet to keep the guys from revolting. And that would not have been a good thing. Let's go say hi."

Rain headed for the other side of the room to greet her soon-to-be-sisters-in-law. Did Tressy's sister count as a sister-in-law to Rain? Or just in-law? Not that it would matter. The Lawrence's considered everyone family.

Raffi was hugging Bebe, Tressy's mom, while Tressy's sister, Tiffany, hugged Rain then Rowdy then Raffi and Rocky. Except where was—

"You look like you wanna run."

I gasped and my head swiveled to find Rebel standing next to me, staring across the room at all the commotion.

"What the hell, Rebel? Where did you come from?"

He didn't answer either of my questions. "I'll make a distraction if you want to save yourself."

It took me a second to realize he was teasing because there wasn't a hint of humor on his face, and he still wasn't looking at me. My lips twitched, after I got over the shock, but I was determined not to break first. Even though I had to bite my tongue for a second.

"We could both slip out the back," I said. "I wouldn't want you to suffer in my place. Besides, I'm not the one dreading this."

My nose scrunched. Maybe that came out a little too sharp. He turned to look at me.

"Why do you think I'm dreading this?"

His steady gaze made my temperature spike. Definitely not feeling that chill at all anymore. I'm sure my cheeks had turned bright red. His gaze dropped for several seconds before rising back to meet mine. And while his expression hadn't changed, I swore his eyes got darker. They were already a velvety brown, but now they seemed like liquid dark chocolate. My mouth dried, and my skin prickled like I was close to a lightning strike.

Except he was the lightning.

No, no, no.

This couldn't be happening. This wasn't happening.

"I…"

What had he asked me? I couldn't remember.

I looked up at him with my lips parted and my brain spinning and my gaze glued to his. Somehow, I'd managed to wind up with my back pressed against the wall, hands spread out behind me. And Rebel had moved to stand in front of me, blocking out the rest of the room. I could still hear everyone else talking, but I couldn't make out any words. All I heard was my brain telling me to move closer.

Just a little closer and you can touch him.

Shit, I needed to breathe.

I sucked in a breath, which made Rebel's eyes narrow for a split second before he took a step back.

"I think we're going to start. We should probably go join everyone else."

I blinked, my brain trying to reset. "Okay. Sure."

But he didn't move right away, and I thought, oh my god, does *he* want to kiss *me*?

Then he shifted to the side and waved me in front of him. I got my feet moving and made it across the room without totally embarrassing myself.

Rain gave me a look as I stopped next to her, but I smiled and turned to face Ms. Patricia.

The fifty-something former Alvin Ailey dancer had been born and raised in St. David before leaving for New York to join the dance company. She'd returned almost a decade ago and had opened her dance studio. Now she taught all ages, from toddlers to adults. And apparently, she gave ballroom dance lessons for wedding couples.

"All right, everyone." The instructor clapped once then raised long elegant hands into the air. "Please stand with your partner so I can see what I'm dealing with."

Patricia walked back and forth, long gauzy skirt swaying around her legs, dance shoes on her feet and a Minnie Mouse t-shirt, as everyone paired off. Even the Colonel and Miss Raffi had joined the class.

I swallowed as Rebel slid into place beside me, so close I felt the heat radiating off his body. I had the urge to close the gap between us to soak up a little of that warmth.

"All right, now everyone face-to-face."

"She could give my pop a run as a drill sergeant."

Rebel's unexpected comment startled me and made me laugh at the same time.

I glanced up at him as we turned to face each other.

"I heard she's wonderful with children."

"Rebel. Do you need something?"

Rebel's gaze slowly left mine. "No, Ms. Patricia. I'm good."

"You most certainly are not. Stand up straight, dear. No slouching on the dance floor."

Rebel straightened like he'd had a rod shoved up his back. Now he towered over me, and I had to tilt my head back to look at him.

"Hmm." Patricia stopped next to us, tapping a finger against her cheek as she looked us up and down. "You're wearing heels for the wedding, aren't you, Erin?"

Right now, I was wearing my trusty Chucks. "Yes."

"Four inches, at least. Can you do that?"

I smiled. "Piece of cake."

When I looked back at Rebel, his brows were arched, but he waited until Patricia had moved on to Rocky and Tiffany, before he spoke, just loud enough for me to hear.

"I never took you for a spiked-heel kind of girl."

"I have hidden talents."

Rebel's mouth quirked up at the corner.

"Okay, everyone, eyes on me." Patricia called from the center of the floor. "I'm going to demonstrate. Raffi, you don't mind if I borrow your husband, do you?"

"Of course not. But I reserve the right to dance with Ronald at the wedding."

Patricia laughed, her voice low and rich. "You know my

husband will *not* have a problem with that. And neither will I. Music, please."

Instrumental music poured out of the speakers, and the Colonel and the dance instructor proceeded to show off their moves.

My mouth dropped open as Rebel's dad led Patricia around the floor with a smooth grace that left me dumbfounded. After a few seconds, I remembered to close my mouth and looked at Miss Raffi, who smiled as she watched her husband.

I snuck a glance at Rebel, grinning when I saw the same shock on his face that was mirrored on his brothers' and sister's faces.

"Music off."

Stunned silenced for all off two seconds before the clapping started. Somebody whooped, probably Rowdy. Patricia held up her hands and the crowd fell silent.

"Now, everyone, do what we just did."

We all laughed, before she pulled Rowdy and Tressy into the middle of the floor. We watched as she showed them the proper hold, telling everyone to watch and learn. Which we did.

But they made it look easy. Rowdy, especially, but Tressy had a natural grace. Together, they just looked...right. And when they smiled at each other, I gave a little sigh, hopefully not loud enough for Rebel to hear.

A second later, Rebel leaned closer, and my heart pounded a little faster. "I think Rowdy's been practicing secretly," Rebel voice slid into my ear like liquid. "No way he's a natural at this. Bastard."

I giggled. That's the only way to describe the sound that came out of my mouth, which I quickly covered with my hand.

"You're just jealous."

"No, but I am competitive. We're going to look fucking amazing, even if it kills me."

Trying to hide my smile, I whispered back, "We are *not* going to upstage your brother at his wedding. Besides, you don't know if I can dance."

"I've watched you walk. We'll be fine."

My brain chewed on that for a few seconds. He watched me walk? What did that mean? But I couldn't ask him because Patricia walked over to us.

"All right, you two. Let's see your hold."

We turned to face each other again. I steeled myself against the heart-flutter of staring into his eyes and instead chose to stare at his shoulder, where my left hand came to rest. My lungs contracted when he took my right hand and put his right hand on my back. I had to move closer so we could get into the proper position, which left very little space between us. And very little air.

"All right now. We're going to do a simple waltz."

With my eyes on Rebel's, we moved together in a square, following Patricia's directions, though I didn't really need any. Dance had been a required subject in prep. A lot of the other students had been children of royalty or diplomats or came from insanely rich families who attended actual balls.

I'd used my training several times in the past, mostly at school dances. And it must have shown. Rebel's eyes narrowed as we executed several turns.

"I have a feeling you've had training," he said. "You're a secret weapon, aren't you?"

I was secretly pleased and knew I shouldn't be. "I am not going to help you look better than your brother at his wedding."

"You already make me look better."

My cheeks flamed, but I couldn't look away. There was something about the way Rebel looked at me that locked my gaze on his.

"Dance was mandatory at my prep school."

Crap. Why did I say that? But Rebel didn't look surprised.

"Where'd you go?"

"Choate Rosemary."

"Know a couple players who went there."

The music stopped and so did we. Since I was facing a wall, I couldn't see anyone but Rebel. And he was looking only at me. I waited for more questions, but he just stood there, until I finally had to ask.

"You don't seem surprised."

He shrugged. "Your parents paid for you to go to a fancy school. It happens. Mine built a hockey franchise so their kids would have somewhere to play. And now they're paying for us to learn how to dance for my brother's wedding. I hope we don't have to go through this again when Rain gets married."

The music started again, and we began to dance. I realized we'd never let go of each other.

My brain grasped for a topic of conversation. "You think Rain and Brian are going to be next?"

"Well, it's not going to be me or Rocky. Unless he's got a secret girlfriend. And if that girl tries any harder to pick him up, he's going to run in the opposite direction."

I looked over my shoulder and bit my lip against a grin. Tiffany was talking and definitely flirting. Rocky looked like he wanted to be anywhere but here.

"Guess I lucked out." Rebel's voice barely rose over the music.

I wasn't thinking when I asked, "How so?"

"I was originally supposed to dance with Tiffany."

I'd forgotten. "Lesser of two evils, huh?"

"I don't think you're the lesser of anything."

Why did that tone in his voice make it hard for me to breathe? Rationally, I knew Rebel was handsome. Maybe more than handsome. And maybe I'd noticed that a little more than I normally did lately. But he wasn't my type.

Yeah, your type worked out so well for you before.

But Rebel didn't like me.

Except the past couple of weeks, it had seemed—

Nope. No, it hadn't seemed like anything. Stop it right now.

I smiled, hoping I didn't look like a complete idiot. "Thanks."

"All right, let's go one more time," Patricia said, "and I'll be by to give each couple some tips."

The music started again, but we didn't. I couldn't seem to get my feet to move. My brain kept repeating Rebel's words. And he kept staring at me.

"I can't exactly give you any tips if you're not going to dance."

I startled to hear Patricia's voice so close. Rebel, of course, must have seen her coming. His hands tightened around mine, though not in a threatening way. It felt more like he was keeping me close.

"I think we're good," Rebel said.

Patricia's brows rose into arches and her lips twitched like she wanted to laugh. "So there's no room for improvement?"

"There's always room for improvement. But I'm not sure I'm going to get any better. And Erin doesn't need any help. She's already too damn good for me."

"We already knew that," Rocky yelled from across the room.

Everyone laughed, then Rowdy tossed a dig at Rocky's two left feet, and Rain made a joke about Rowdy's inability to count to two without his feet, and Rocky said something about Rowdy that made everyone laugh.

But my brain wasn't processing words. All my attention was focused on Rebel, who continued to stare at me. I knew eventually someone would notice the way we were staring at each other, and I knew I should look away. I didn't know why I kept staring. Except we weren't fighting.

And I liked that.

"Why don't we take a break for a few minutes." Patricia's voice broke through the fog, and I took a step back from Rebel. "Everyone get some water, and we'll do another round."

Could I fake a heart attack? A panic attack? A burst appendix?

"I need to talk to my brother." Rebel's gaze finally released mine, and he glanced over my shoulder. "I'll be back."

He was gone before I could respond.

Leaving me flustered and wondering what the hell had just happened.

CHAPTER THIRTEEN

ebel

I REACHED *out and wrapped my hand around her neck, the braid containing her bright hair brushing against my skin. Electricity sparked up my arm and throughout the rest of my body. Pulling her against me, I sucked in air at the crush of her breasts against my chest.*

So fucking soft. I wanted to put my hands all over her. Wanted to run them up and down her body and feel her naked skin, warm against mine.

She gasped, and her lips parted, and I couldn't pass up the chance to taste her.

She must have seen the intent on my face. Her blue eyes widened even more than they already were, her hands tightening on my shoulders. As I bent my head, her eyes closed and—

.   .   .

SHOOTING STRAIGHT UP IN BED, I woke from the dream with a hard on, lungs hungry for air and skin full of goosebumps.

Fuck.

Throwing my legs over the side of the mattress, I sat with my elbows on my knees and my head in my hands, trying to will my erection away and not having much luck with that.

What the actual *fuck*? There was no fucking way in hell I should be having sex dreams about Erin.

Sure, we'd kind of buried the hatchet the past couple of weeks. And last night we'd reassured everyone around us that we weren't going to ruin the wedding with our bickering.

But this ...

Maybe it was something I'd eaten.

Forcing the dream to the back of my mind, I headed for the kitchen, remembering at the last second not to walk out of my room naked. I grabbed a pair of gym shorts, pulled them on and headed to the kitchen. The sun had barely cleared the horizon, as I stood at the floor to ceiling window and looked out at the woods.

I loved waking up to this view, had missed it badly when I'd been away all those months.

Con No. 1: Missing this view.

Pro No. 1:

I'd have to think about it.

Since I'd always been an early riser, and I knew Ian was not, I was surprised to see him emerge from my spare room about half an hour later. He looked like he'd had a rough night.

Join the club, kid.

"Coffee?"

Yawning and running a hand through his bed head, he nodded and shuffled over to the counter where the coffee maker sat. Then he just stood there as he realized he didn't know where the mugs were.

Looking over his shoulder, Ian's brows rose in a question, and I pointed to the cabinet in front of him. Of course, he managed to pick the wrong cabinet the first time. I smiled as I watched him pause, his hand frozen in midair for several seconds before he shut the door and opened the correct one.

It took him at least a full minute after he poured himself a cup of coffee, drank it then poured another before he turned back to me, leaning back against the counter and looking at me through barely open eyes.

"You're gonna stunt your growth drinking that much coffee."

Holding my gaze, he lifted the mug and took another healthy smile while he gave me the finger with his free hand.

This is why we got along so well.

"Wanna get some ice time in this morning?"

His brows arched, mug halted halfway to his lips as excitement sparked in his eyes.

"Really?"

"Yeah. I could use the exercise."

Especially after that dream, which I definitely didn't want to think about.

"Must be nice to have ice whenever you want."

I didn't hear an ounce of jealousy or envy in his voice. Just that big-puppy energy, ready to bound out the door and put on his skates. And he was right. It was great. I'd grown up privileged, and it hadn't occurred to me until I was nearly a teenager that other kids didn't have what I have.

Not that my parents would let any of their kids think they were better than anyone else. I'd had a job at the arena by the time I was thirteen. And so had my brothers and sister.

I nodded. "It is. The arena doesn't have anything booked this week so we should have the place to ourselves. Most of the guys take the month off, and my family's pretty preoccupied with the wedding, so…"

"Absolutely. When do you wanna leave?"

"How about we get dressed, get some food and then head out?"

Ian paused for a second. "Is Erin's bakery open? Can we stop there?"

For a second, I had the stupid thought that Ian knew about my dream. Then I came to my senses and realized the kid had a crush on her. My jaw locked for a split second against an absolutely ridiculous surge of possessiveness.

What the actual actual *fuck?*

First the dream, now this. I had Erin on the brain. But if I said no, Ian would want to know why I didn't want to go to Erin's place for breakfast, and I didn't have an answer. At least, not a good one.

"Sure. No problem."

Which is how I found myself walking into Erin's bakery at seven in the morning. Ian wore a huge grin, which would probably make this all worth it. I still didn't know what had happened to blow up his plans. I was hoping he'd have told me by now, but I also knew if I just kept my mouth shut, eventually he'd spill. He knew I was safe here.

"Erin. Hey."

She caught sight of Ian before she saw me, and her smile did stupid things to my blood pressure. I knew what was going on. I just didn't know why. Why, after knowing her for all this time, was she making me fucking *dream* about her? Maybe I really did need to get laid. I just knew it wasn't going to be her. We didn't even like each other.

Not true.

"Hey, Rebel, you're getting food, too, right?"

I snapped back to reality, where Ian was staring at me, confused, and Erin watched me with an expression I couldn't read. I stepped closer to the counter, her gaze stuck to mine. Ian must have already ordered.

"What can I get you, Rebel?"

She smiled, but it didn't quite reach her eyes, which were guarded. Why? I thought last night had gone well. Actually, I thought the last couple of weeks we'd managed to declare a truce.

What the hell had changed since last night?

I ordered what I always did, her cherry almond scones, watched her nod and retreat to the kitchen.

At the moment, we were the only customers, though I knew the café did a pretty decent business most mornings.

"Grab a table," I said to Ian. "I'll be back in a second."

Not waiting for him to respond, I headed into the kitchen. "Erin?"

She stood at the large table in the center of the room, with her back to me, throwing what I assumed was dough on the surface and kneading it like she had a vendetta against it.

"What did the dough do to piss you off?"

She let out a little scream and spun around with a little jerk.

"Rebel! What the hell are you doing back here?"

Pink flushed her cheeks, and she had a smudge of white on her chin that looked like flour. Her blue eyes flashed even brighter than normal, her lips parted as she breathed in heavily. I couldn't help but notice the rise and fall of her chest, and the dream I'd had this morning replayed itself in my head with every detail in full color.

Jerking my gaze back to her face, I noticed how the freckles on her nose stood out just a little more. And how her hair seemed to be trying to escape her braid. My fingers curled into my palms. I wanted to set it free.

I had to swallow before I answered.

"Are you okay?"

She blinked at me. "What?"

"You seem…upset."

"I—You—What are you talking about?"

She looked genuinely puzzled, like she had no idea what I was saying. And maybe I was reading the situation completely wrong. Maybe she just hadn't wanted to see me this morning.

Then I saw her gaze slip to my mouth before snapping back up to meet my eyes.

I knew I should turn around and walk out. I also knew I wasn't going to.

"Did I do something to piss you off last night?"

Now she looked at me like I'd just asked her to make me a peanut butter sandwich with pickles and dirt.

"No. Of course not. I just have a lot on my mind."

That made sense. Especially with the wedding now less than two weeks away.

Still…

"Do you need help?"

"I think I can make a few breakfast sandwiches."

The small barbs in her tone felt like familiar territory. But they hit a little harder today for some reason.

"I meant, do you need help with the wedding? I know it's a lot—"

"What?" Her lower lip stuck out, and I had the absolutely insane urge to want to lick it. "You don't think I can do it?"

"Not what I said." My arms crossed over my chest, what I

was beginning to realize was an automatic response when she said something I didn't like. "I just don't want you to not ask for help if you need it."

"I've got it under control. Thank you."

Those last two words seemed like an afterthought, but they also sounded a little softer. "Good."

I didn't move right away, and she nibbled on that bottom lip before she said, "Is that all you wanted? I need to get your food together."

No, that wasn't all I wanted. I just didn't know what I wanted. Or why I'd followed her back here.

Bullshit.

"Yeah. Sure. Make it to go. Ian and I are heading over to the arena for some ice time."

Her expression softened when I mentioned Ian. "Sure. It'll be ready in a few minutes."

That was my cue to leave. And I took it before I did something really stupid.

CHAPTER FOURTEEN

A FEW HOURS AFTER THE WEDDING

Erin

"Rowdy and Tressy would now like to ask the bridal party to join them on the dance floor."

The wedding had gone off without a hitch. Literally nothing had gone even the slightest bit wrong.

Puffy white clouds that looked like they'd been painted by a master's hand hung in the bright blue sky. The humidity that'd been plaguing St. David for the past week had broken two days ago with a thunderstorm that had dumped just enough water to make the grass and the gardens glisten.

The late June sun shone brightly but the temperature was already dipping into the seventies.

I mean, really. Who has that kind of luck? Apparently, the Lawrences did.

And it must have rubbed off on me because everything I'd

touched had come together exactly as I'd planned. Every roll, every appetizer, every crudité tray… All of it, perfect.

Earlier this week, I'd thought I wasn't going to be able to pull it together. I'd had an issue with one of my burners. The pilot wouldn't stay lit, and I'd just about had a panic attack. The only electrician in town was out on a call at the local vet clinic and wasn't expected back for at least three hours.

After a frantic call to Rain, Rebel had shown up with a tool kit. While I gaped at him, he fixed the problem in under an hour. I hadn't even had time to thank him before I'd been back to work with my extra staff, otherwise known as the Angels dance team, measuring and kneading and rolling and cutting and chopping and prepping the hell out of everything so we could have it ready.

Then I'd taken a deep breath yesterday and just did the work. I didn't think about it. I just did it. I'd made enough small bites for five hundred people.

And I'd managed to make it to the bachelorette party Thursday night and the rehearsal dinner last night without having any issues.

But these past few minutes, as I'd watched Rowdy and Tressy dance, this was the first time I think I'd taken a deep breath in the past week.

Tressy and Rowdy made a beautiful couple. Tressy in her stunningly simple gown with a simple wreath of flowers on her head and Rowdy in a tux that had to have been made for him. He'd even gotten his hair cut. Not short, but just short enough to make him appear even more handsome than normal.

Krista had nearly stolen the show as the flower girl and ring bearer in her absolutely adorable white dress and custom-beaded high-top sneakers.

And the bridal party... Well, we cleaned up pretty well, or so Granddad had said.

The men all looked like they'd stepped off a magazine shoot in their blue suits and white shirts with matching ties. And each bridesmaid wore a unique dress in the same shade of muted aqua, which was the only color that looked good on all of us. Because of me, of course. The redhead.

But I thought I looked pretty damn good, if I did say so myself. My hair had been tamed into a neat knot at the back of my neck with little curls at the side of my face. Ian had given me a thumbs up as I'd walked down the aisle after Krista. But it was the look on Rebel's face that had almost made me stumble.

Standing next to Rowdy under the arch in the back garden of the Lawrences' home, Rebel looked even better than a model. He looked *real*. And really freaking *hot*.

As soon as I'd realized we'd locked eyes, I'd pulled my gaze away. I didn't want to turn bright red. I'd looked at Rowdy, whose broad grin made me smile. He looked like he'd won the lottery. And he absolutely had. Tressy was an amazing woman, and he was lucky to have her.

Of course, he wasn't so bad himself.

But he's not as handsome as Rebel.

I'd cut that thought off immediately, but it was still floating around in my head when Rebel stepped in front of me and offered me his arm to lead me onto the dance floor.

Don't stare. Don't stare. Don't stare.

"You look beautiful."

It was a good thing I already had hold of his arm. I nearly stumbled, which would have been totally humiliating. I'd managed to keep my cool all day. No running at the mouth.

No rushing. But now, I felt like a warm noodle, loose and jiggly.

I blindly followed Rebel out onto the floor. Had he actually said what I thought he'd said? Maybe I was hallucinating?

Rebel stopped, guiding me into place in front of him, taking my left hand in his. My other hand automatically reached for his shoulder, and I jolted when his large hand settled on my hip, warmth immediately seeping from him to me. Staring down at me, his lips barely curved, but I knew he was smiling.

The band started to play an instrumental version of "In Your Eyes," and we began to move. Perfectly in sync.

"Did you…"

No, I couldn't even ask. It was a stupid question. What if I'd misheard him? I didn't want to make things awkward.

He bent forward so he could speak into my ear. His warm breath brushed against the bare skin of my neck, making my lungs contract as all the air left them.

"Yes. I did. You look beautiful."

Now I could barely breathe, and goosebumps covered my arms. Something had changed between us in the last couple of weeks. I wasn't sure what had happened or why, but my body had decided to throw rationality overboard, while my brain started to whisper ridiculous things.

I looked up at him and found his lips closer than expected. Just for a second, I wondered what he'd do if I kissed him.

Somewhere inside my brain, I realized I wanted to.

Oh my god. That was *so* not going to happen.

His eyes narrowed, almost as if he was reading my mind. Or maybe it was just written all over my face. I directed my gaze to a point on his shoulder.

"Thank you." I cleared my throat. "You look very handsome."

His head retreated, giving me more room, and I barely heard his huff of laughter.

"Damned by faint praise."

My gaze shot to his again, and I had the urge to stick my tongue out at him. But the photographer was lurking on the dance floor and that would probably be the shot she took of me.

"You look amazing, and you know it."

He looked like he was going to smile but didn't want to give me the satisfaction.

"You should, too."

Heat drenched me from head to toe. It literally started at my scalp and made its way down my body like a wave. A tsunami. Or the blast from a preheated oven.

He watched me so intensely, I swore I could feel his gaze on my skin. I swallowed hard as we moved around the floor. Time to change the subject.

"The wedding was perfect."

For a few, long seconds, I wasn't sure he was going to let me off the hook. I didn't have a clue what was going on in his head. He'd never been the kind of guy who teased or made fun of anyone. Hell, he barely spoke. To anyone, but least of all to me. And now he said I was beautiful.

My brain was definitely not cut out to handle him like this. Like he was a normal guy.

"It was. I swear my mom decided it was going to be a beautiful day, and Mother Nature got right on that for her."

I grinned and glanced back up at him. "I can't imagine anyone telling your mother no."

"Not when it comes to her kids."

"She loves you all very much."

I found Miss Raffi on the floor, dancing in the Colonel's arms, smiling up at him like they were teenagers in love. And while the Colonel's smile wasn't as noticeable, you could tell it was there. He looked at her with so much adoration. I looked at Rowdy and Tressy, Rowdy wearing the same smile as his mother. I saw Rain and Brian on the other side of the dance floor, smiling at each other like they were in their own little world and there was no one else in the room.

It was sweet, but honestly, it made me a little sad. And I hated that. I hated being sad at a wedding. Especially for such good friends who deserved all the happiness in the world.

"What's wrong?"

Rebel's quiet question made my smile automatically reappear. When I glanced up at him, he scowled down at me. Hell, even that made me hot. How long was this song anyway?

"Nothing's wrong."

"Hmm."

I wonder if he did that deliberately. Made me want to step on his toes with my four-inch heels. And even with the heels, I still wasn't eye-to-eye with him.

Before I could say anything else, though, the music stopped. But Rebel didn't release me immediately, like I thought he would. He held on, just a second longer than I expected him to. He looked into my eyes until there was no one else around us and then he blinked and released me, before sticking out his elbow for me to take so we could leave the floor.

Walking back to the table, I smiled at everyone and waved to Granddad, who was sitting at a table with several of the older members of the community. But when Rebel returned me to the table where the bridal party was sitting, I felt like I could finally breathe again.

Except now I couldn't stop looking at him. He was right across the table from me. And staring back at me.

I needed a drink.

———

I DROPPED the chair next to Brian as Rain fell into his lap, both of us laughing as we kicked off our shoes after dancing for most of the night.

Dinner had come and gone, the cake had been cut and consumed. And I swore everyone in the room had come up to me to personally say how good it was. Every compliment made my smile wider. Damn it, I had wanted it to be magnificent. And it was.

Rowdy and Tressy had raved, and Krista probably had eaten a little too much of her special cake. She'd crashed out in her grandmother's arms about an hour ago.

I'd also had a few people tell me they'd stop by the shop this week to talk about upcoming events, which made me giddy.

That probably also had a little something to do with the amount of alcohol I'd had. I was feeling no pain after ten o'clock. Many of the older guests had made their way home already, but the true party was just getting started.

"No, no, no, that's not what happened. Bonesaw was the first one to take off his clothes and skate around the rink. Then of course, Rowdy had to follow."

Rain shook her head and waved one of her hands in the air, her other around Brian's neck as she sat in his lap and told everyone about the time one of the players had had to get stitches in his ass because they'd been skating naked at midnight. After a few drinks.

Rain and I had been on the dance floor for… I honestly didn't know how long. We'd danced with the guys and the girls and the kids. I'd even gotten the Colonel to join me for a dance, and damn, the man still had moves. I totally understood why Miss Raffi still looked at him like they'd just fallen in love.

My parents had never looked that way at each other. Come to think of it, neither did my sister and her husband. My brother didn't have a wife, just a revolving set of interchangeable dates. And since I didn't have anyone to look at…

Ugh. Sad. Didn't want to be sad. Not now.

Instead, I looked around the table. All of the Devils, along with the Angels and the rest of the friends' group who weren't part of either team, had pulled chairs over to the bridal party table. The band was taking a break before its final set, and only the piano player and the violinist were left on stage to provide music.

Several couples still floated around the dance floor, including the Colonel and Miss Raffi and Patricia and her husband, who'd swapped partners and were laughing and smiling. Which made me smile.

"And don't forget the time we made the rookies climb the fire tower in their jocks," Rebel added. "Fun times."

It was the first time he'd added to the conversation, and of course, I turned to look at him. He was smiling at someone, that wicked little half-smile that made me want to lick it off his lips like frosting off the beaters.

Whoa.

I couldn't remember exactly how many glasses of very

good champagne I'd had, but I think it must have been a lot. I was contemplating licking Rebel.

Why was the man so damn handsome?

"Hey, I was one of those rookies," somebody said. "I was pulling splinters out of my thighs for weeks."

"That's because you were so drunk you decided you were gonna slide up on your ass. On wooden steps."

Rebel had to raise his voice slightly to be heard as all the other guys around the table added something to the story. He was still grinning when he caught my gaze across the table.

A weird fizzy feeling started in my head and continued down my body, making my skin bubble with goosebumps, and my stomach feel squishy and wobbly.

Why was Rebel looking at me like he wanted to lick me, too?

Okay, wow. I must have drank much more than I thought I had. I totally must be reading him wrong. Except, I felt pleasantly buzzed, not outright sloppy drunk. The few times I'd drunk way too much hadn't felt like this. Then I'd felt icky and gross and sick to my stomach. Now, I felt giggly and light. Not icky at all.

"All right, everyone," the band's female singer announced from the stage, where the rest of the band was retaking their positions, "We're gonna start this set slow. Let's have those newlyweds back on the dance floor for another song."

Every guy there began to whoop and bang the table, while the girls raised their glasses and tapped them with spoons or their nails. And we whooped, too.

Rowdy stood and bowed to the table then held out his hand to Tressy with the sweetest smile. I'm pretty sure I wasn't the only one who sighed and wished I had someone who looked at me like that.

Shaking my head, my gaze somehow found Rebel again. Staring back at me.

It proved harder to pull my gaze away this time. That connection I'd felt all night now almost a physical tether pulling me closer to him. I wanted to stand, walk over to him and ask him to dance with me.

Wanted him to forget that he didn't really like me. Wanted him to want to dance with me. Wanted him to hold me against that broad chest and put his heavy arms around me and make me feel safe and wanted. Maybe even desired.

Okay, a girl could fantasize. Especially about a guy she never had a chance with. But I also had to be realistic and know it wasn't gonna happen.

I turned to say something to Rain, but Brian was lifting her off his lap and onto her feet then steering her toward the dance floor. Kade, who'd been sitting next to me, held out his hand to Olivia, the Angel sitting next to him. Everyone else had paired off, and I had a flashback to prep. Senior formal, watching my so-called date dance with everyone else in the room except me.

He was the son of one of my dad's business partners and was attending another school in the area. I'd thought he'd liked me. Instead, he'd used me to meet the other girls in my class.

I'd pleaded a headache and left as soon as I'd realized what was happening. Which hadn't been soon enough. The looks I'd gotten all week after the dance had been so humiliating, I'd considered lying to the nurse and pleading debilitating migraines to spend the week in the hospital. Anything would've been better than the looks I was getting from the other students.

Stop feeling sorry for yourself. This situation is nothing like that.

"Dance with me."

The hand in front of my face was huge and scarred and attached to Rebel. I'd barely been able to hear him over the band, but I'd heard enough to know it wasn't an invitation. It was a demand.

I took a deep breath and looked into his eyes. He had that look on his face again. The one that made heat flash through my body.

I grabbed the champagne flute in front of me, downed the rest of it and took his hand. His completely engulfed mine as he waited for me to get to my feet. I'd kicked off my heels a while ago and exchanged them for the fluffy mules Tressy and Rowdy had gifted to their friends for the after party. They'd also had recovery sandals to choose from, but most of the guys still wore their shoes. Rebel had gone a different route. His feet were bare.

I found that sexy as hell.

As he led me out onto the dance floor, we got a few looks from people, especially one from Rain that I knew I'd have to answer later, but most everyone else was more interested in their own partners.

I'd had enough alcohol that I was over the line, but not enough to be sloppy. Maybe just enough to allow me to enjoy being held in Rebel's arms. And maybe he'd had more than he usually drank because he looked happy for me to be there.

We didn't say anything as we swayed to the music, staring at each other. The music wrapped around us like a web, keeping us close, ensnaring us in its mellow melody. I inched closer with every turn until we were pressed together from chest to thighs. Heat tingled from my fingertips to my toes. And all places in between.

Oh my god, I'm hot for Rebel!

My face flushed, and I watched his gaze drop to my cheeks. And lower. My lips parted, my brain glitching and my lungs needing more air.

Did I want him to kiss me? Did he want to kiss me? If I lifted onto my toes, would he get the hint?

His eyes narrowed, and I wondered if he'd read my mind.

Would he—

The song ended with a sweep of the drum, and silence held for a second before the singer said, "Now, let's get those hearts pumping again. We've still got a lot of time to party!"

The male singer's voice jarred me back to real life, and I took a step away from Rebel. At first, I wasn't sure he'd release me. His hand tightened around mine and the one on my hip squeezed just a little tighter. His jaw shifted, and his gaze narrowed, locking me in.

A second later, he released me, and I swayed. His hands landed on my shoulders, steadying me. I'd definitely had way too much to drink. I wanted to snuggle up against that broad chest, lay my head above his heart and let his arms pull me in even closer. And that, my friends, was the road to Crazytown.

"Uh… Yeah."

I turned and headed for the other side of the room.

CHAPTER FIFTEEN

ERIN HURRIED ACROSS THE FLOOR, practically running by the time she got to the opposite side of the room. Away from me.

If I was smart, I'd do the same in the opposite direction. Instead, I stood there and watched her. The band had ramped up the party vibe again and everyone on the floor had taken places for a line dance.

"Hey, bro. You gonna join in or just glare across the room?"

Erin disappeared into the hall that led to the bathrooms.

I glanced at Rocky, his cheeks flushed and his glasses sitting awkwardly on his nose. Sleeves rolled up and tie nowhere in sight, he looked like a professor who'd had one too many at a faculty gathering. His huge grin made me smile, but a little voice in my brain kept telling me to follow Erin.

"I'll leave the dancing to you. I need to—"

"You were dancing with Erin. I thought you two had a hate-hate relationship."

My smile disappeared in a flash. "Who told you that?"

Rocky didn't notice the sharp edge on my tone, his interest somewhere on the dance floor. Little brother loved to dance. Must have inherited that gene from Mom.

"No one had to tell me. It's been common knowledge for years." He shrugged. "You don't get along. Hey, I'm gonna…" He pointed toward the dance floor, his feet already moving in that direction.

"Don't let me stop you." I waved him back onto the floor, taking a few steps back so I wasn't in the flow of things.

Rocky headed into the fray without a backward glance. I watched him for a few seconds as he wove his way into the crowd, winding up beside Tressy, who let him grab her hand and twirl her around before joining in on the dance like he knew exactly what he was doing. Maybe he did.

I didn't have a clue. And honestly, I didn't care. My entire attention was focused on the hall where Erin had disappeared.

Almost everyone left at the wedding was on the floor or hanging out at the bar on the other side of the room. The band must have turned up the volume, the floor vibrating beneath my bare feet.

I started walking, skirting the crowd, sticking to the wall. My gaze focused on that hallway. She still hadn't emerged. No one stopped me. Hell, I don't think anyone even noticed me. Everyone was having too much fun on the dance floor. They bounced and laughed and shook like crazy people.

Good. I didn't want to answer to anyone. Didn't want to talk to anyone. I had one goal in mind.

Inside the hallway, the music became a little muffled. Still loud but not as overpowering as it had been in the great room. The air was also a little cooler here. I'd ditched my jacket hours ago, rolled up my sleeves, and I had no idea where I'd put my tie. I'd left my socks tucked in my shoes under the table.

Still, I felt like I was in a sauna, but the heat was coming from inside of me.

What are you doing?

Hell, I knew exactly what I was doing. I wasn't being affected by the amount of alcohol I'd drank, though I'm sure that had helped bring down my walls. Those walls were in pieces right now, and I didn't even want to build them back up.

She'd gotten under my skin. I didn't know how. I just knew it'd been building, and I needed to do something about it, or it'd drive me crazy.

She wasn't there.

I stopped before the end of the hallway, looking everywhere. I even walked back to the end of the hall and looked out over the dance floor to see if I'd missed her. She wasn't anywhere to be seen.

Was she still in the bathroom? Was she okay? Had something happened to her?

Had she left?

I was on my way back to the ballroom to ask Rain if Erin had said goodbye when I saw the shadows shift at the end of the hallway. And I remembered that there was a door that led into the garden.

Maybe I'd had more to drink than I realized. Or maybe I just had one thing on my mind, and it wasn't the layout of my parents' house.

I should leave, and I didn't mean follow her. I should go home, because what I wanted to do was stupid. I didn't do stupid things. And I tried my damnedest not to do really stupid things that would cause issues I couldn't fix.

And I still walked to the door and opened it.

She sat on a lounger at the edge of the gardens, looking away from the door. She must not have heard me. She didn't turn, the music from the party covering my approach. I couldn't see her face, but she had her legs drawn up to her chest with her arms wrapped around them. I couldn't believe she was cold. The temperature had only lowered to about 75 degrees.

Then again, her dress left her shoulders and the lower half of her legs bare. That dress had made me question things about myself I'd never questioned before. Like why, until these past few weeks, had I never been attracted to her.

And I don't just mean attracted. I meant, I wanted to kiss my way up her legs until I had that dress around her waist and had my mouth on her—

I shut down the X-rated image in my head before it could go farther. Even though I'd been dreaming about the woman for the past couple of weeks. I wanted more than dreams.

Was it just the alcohol talking?

I stopped and gave it a few seconds.

No.

The alcohol let me jump the wall I'd built around the feelings I'd developed for Erin. Now I was going to do something about them before I decided it was a really bad idea.

I walked over, stopping just behind and to the side of her chair. I didn't want to startle her or let her think I was sneaking up on her. I wanted her to know I was there. I wanted her to know *why* I was there.

It took a couple of seconds, but finally she turned her head and looked up at me. I couldn't believe at one time I'd thought those wide eyes looked at the world with a skewed vision. Now I knew she just had a different way of looking at things. A sweeter way. A way I couldn't. And I wanted her to look at me that way.

I'd seen glimpses of it during the past couple of weeks. And maybe more, if I was honest. And right now, that's all I wanted. Honesty.

She stared up at me, and I swore I saw stars reflected in her eyes. Her head tilted slightly to the side, her teeth digging into her lower lip as her arms tightened around her legs. I wanted to reach for her, pull her up against me. Instead, I forced my arms to hang at my sides, hands loose as I waited for her to make a move.

Another couple of seconds passed before she reached for one of my hands. She looked down as she laced our fingers together, as if it was the most interesting thing she'd ever done. I watched her because she was the most beautiful woman I'd ever seen.

She'd loosened her hair from the fancy style it'd been in for the wedding. I liked it better this way. I wouldn't feel bad when I ran my fingers through it. Some women didn't like to get their hair mussed. I don't think I've ever seen Erin when it wasn't. Except for today.

Swinging her legs over the side of the lounge, she left space next to her. I took the hint and lowered myself down, adjusting our hands so they weren't at an awkward angle. But I didn't let her go.

We sat there for a few seconds, the darkness cut only by the low-voltage lighting in the garden. Otherwise, it reminded me of a movie set. Kind of magical.

I turned to look at her and found her turning to look at me. I didn't stop to think. I leaned down and kissed her. She was already on her way to meet me, and our lips crashed together.

Heat exploded and lust ignited with an almost vicious twist in my gut.

The fact that she seemed to be just as overcome as I was amped my desire. I couldn't get enough air, but I didn't want to stop kissing her. Some part of me thought, if I stopped, she'd realize what was going on and leave.

Hell, I wasn't even sure what was going on. I only knew I didn't want to stop. I wanted to press her back into the lounge cushions and let my mouth roam her body. Wanted to stroke over her bare skin and find every soft part of her.

My mouth released hers for a split second so I could breathe, and the little sound she made shot straight to my cock. I was already stiff and aching, but some part of my brain still resisted.

Until I opened my eyes and looked into hers. I heard her heavy breathing over the music, felt my own lungs working to pull in air. But it was the look in her eyes that made me realize this was going to happen.

I saw no hesitation, no question. Just an overwhelming desire.

Standing, I grabbed her hand and tugged her to her feet then led her through the garden, brushing past the roses Pop spent so much time on because my mom loved them and the bed of all white flowers that glowed in the moonlight.

Erin tightened her grip on my hand when we made it across the stone patio to the door into the now-dark kitchen.

I thought about stealing her back to my place but that would take too long, and my brain kept urging me to go faster. I knew she was staying in a room here, and I even knew which one it was. Rain had told me.

I could do this walk in my sleep. Hell, I'd done it half-lit more times than I cared to admit as a teenager. Winding our way up the back staircase and through the hall to the second floor, we finally reached the door to her room. I opened it just as she said, "Careful."

I nearly tripped over something that sat just inside the door. I kicked it out of the way, pulled her through and shut the door behind her.

In the moonlight coming through the open windows, I saw her lips part, like she was going to say something, then shut as if she decided against it. Then she put her hands on my cheeks and pulled me back down to kiss her.

She tasted like the fruity sweet cocktails most of the women had been drinking all night. I had no idea what was in them. I'd been tossing back the bourbon that had made my dad's family's fortune.

Had I had too much? No.

Had I had just enough? Yes, I had.

She kissed me like she wanted to inhale me, our mouths sealed shut, tongues dueling. My arms wrapped around her waist and dragged her fully against me. Her body melded into mine, soft curves flattening. My hands ran from her waist up the sides of her body, my thumbs brushing against the sides of her breasts.

She made a little noise and wriggled closer, and my fingers somehow found the zipper of her dress and yanked it down. I barely heard the sound it made. She did some little shimmy thing with her body while we continued to kiss, and the dress slid to the floor like magic.

I didn't have time to think about that, though. She'd started in on the buttons of my shirt. I had no idea how she managed to get them undone so fast. Hell, I don't think I could've managed it right now. But she had the shirt off my shoulders in seconds, her hands following it down my arms to push it to the floor. Then she stuck a finger in my chest and pushed me backward. And when I say pushed, she put some effort into it. Not that I wouldn't have given her anything she wanted right then.

I opened my mouth to tell her that, but the back of my legs hit the bed and my knees bent. My ass hit the mattress at the same time my brain registered the fact that she was practically naked. I had about four seconds to openly gaze at the splendor of her nearly naked body. Breasts overflowing a strapless bra that seemed to defy gravity to stay in place. Flat stomach. Curved hips covered only by the tiniest straps of a bikini that matched the bra.

I blinked, and she had her hands on the button of my pants. The woman had some serious skill with buttons. The next thing I knew, she was pulling down my zipper with one hand and pushing me back onto the mattress with the other, and I wasn't about to say no.

When my back hit the mattress, she straddled my hips, her hands landing on either side of my head and her lips falling back on mine.

Holy fuck.

Electricity sizzled at the contact. My hips arched, cock wanting in on the action. My hands found their way to her hips, her skin soft and silky. I dragged my palms down her thighs then up again, this time my thumbs catching in the little strings of her panties. Her hips rocked side to side, her tongue licking along mine.

When I did nothing more than let them snap back into place, she made a little sound in her throat and tried to pull back. But I was on a mission. I needed more of those sounds.

I put one hand on her neck to hold her in place and used the other to open her bra, surprised as shit when it actually worked. The surprise turned to hunger when I tossed it somewhere and cupped one of her breasts in my hand.

She made one of those sounds again, the kind that made my dick throb and the heat in my gut boil over. With a move I hadn't been sure I'd be able to pull off, I flipped our positions, this time getting a little squeak from her.

Her eyes were half-lidded and her lips kiss-puffy. And naked breasts...

"So fucking pretty."

I didn't realize I'd spoken aloud until she smiled. I'd never seen her smile like that at me. I liked it. Why didn't she smile at me like that all the time?

Because you don't get along.

Fuck that shit. We were getting along just fine now.

I dropped my mouth on hers again and sealed our lips together. I didn't want to talk. Didn't want words to ruin the mood. Not that I hadn't meant every damn word. I had. This just wasn't the time for words. Not when she let me kiss her until I could barely breathe and run my hands up her perfect body until I cupped her breasts in both hands and squeezed.

She sighed into my mouth and arched into my hands, her hands finding their way to my shoulders and stroking down my arms, fingers wrapping around mine and urging me to squeeze her tighter.

When I did, she made another sound that revved my desire into another level. A desperate level. I wanted to rush to get naked and inside her, but I also wanted to take my time. Draw things out. Make this moment out of time last.

Desperation won. Especially when her hands shoved down my pants and boxer briefs, freeing my cock. I didn't need her hands on my cock to make me any more ready. I could hit pucks with the damn thing now.

Still, her warm hands felt so fucking good when they wrapped around my dick and cupped my balls.

"Damn, that feels amazing."

I heard her suck in air, waited for her to say something. Then…silence. I lifted my head and opened my eyes. Hers opened, and our gazes locked. And I wanted her to say something. Anything.

Instead, she watched me, sucking in ragged breaths as she stroked, tight and slow then loose and fast. I wasn't going to last much longer if she kept that up. And she seemed intent on doing just that. I wanted to be inside her when I came.

"Erin."

I spoke her name deliberately, watched her expression visibly brighten when I did. As if she liked to hear me say her name.

Then she nodded, and I knew she was answering the question of whether or not she wanted to have sex with me. I mean, it felt kind of obvious, but I still needed to know.

"Hold that thought."

She nodded again, and I rolled to the side, shoved my pants and boxers off my legs and grabbed my wallet out of my back pocket. I hadn't sex in more than a year, but I was prepared. I slid the condom out of the wallet and set it on the bed next to her.

Then I went onto my knees so I could strip the last bit of clothing from her body. All that was left was her panties. And when I dropped them over the side of the bed, I let my gaze eat her up for a few seconds.

Erin was no stick figure. She had beautiful curves that I

planned to explore more. But later. Right now, I wanted something more.

I spread out beside her so I could kiss her again, wrapping one hand around neck for several seconds, my thumb resting against the pulse throbbing beneath her skin. Her head tilted back, neck arching into my hand. Giving herself up.

I had no idea how hot that would make me until just that second.

Needing another kiss, I sealed my mouth over hers, my hand sliding across her shoulder then down to cup her breast, tightening on her flesh before using my thumb and forefinger to pinch the nipple.

Apparently, Erin liked it hard. I could give her that. We were more evenly matched than I'd ever considered. And until recently, I hadn't given the notion any thought. And now I couldn't stop thinking about it.

What other areas would we be compatible in?

I dragged my mouth from hers, following the path my hand had taken. But my patience was running out. I sucked a nipple into my mouth, running my teeth over the tip and biting down, just for a second. She made that sound again, in the back of her throat, and heat pulsed through my body.

My hand slid into the curls on her mound, tugging them for a second, feeling her hips arch as my hand slipped between her legs. I groaned at the slickness, dipping my head to rest it between her breasts for a second.

"Fuck, Erin. You're wet."

"Don't stop."

"No fucking way."

I realized it was the first time she'd spoken since we'd come up here to the bedroom. And I wanted to hear her say my name. I lifted my head and looked her in the eyes.

"When I make you come, I want you to say my name."

Her eyes got wide, and her mouth formed a stunned circle. But still, she didn't say anything.

"Understood?"

She nodded slowly. I guess I'd have to make do with that. Now I needed to come through on my end of the deal.

I dipped two fingers into the slit of her sex, but just barely, getting them wet then pulling them up to her clit. Circling the hard little nub, I watched her face to see what she liked. I hadn't been wrong that she liked it a little rough. Her breath came hard and heavy as I petted her clit, but she moaned only when I pressed my thumb against it and sank one finger between her labia.

She arched again, and I nipped at the breast I hadn't paid attention to yet. Her hands cupped my head, fingers weaving into my hair and tugging.

Yes. I liked that. I wanted her to do it harder, but I also wanted to make her moan again, so I kept my mouth on her breast and worked my finger deeper inside her. I sucked hard, licking a path between her breasts as I gave attention to both breasts. Her body moved against mine, hands clenching harder at my hair.

That was more like it.

The tension in her body ratcheted higher, her hips lifting, trying to get me to go deeper. Instead, I pulled almost all the way out, ground my mouth down on hers then added a finger and slid back in until they couldn't go any farther. I got the response I wanted. Another, louder moan filled the room, her tongue flicking against mine with more demand.

My brain latched onto that sound, wanting more. Wanting everything she could give me. Obsessed now with her pleasure, I pulled back to watch her face as I sank deeper, curling my fingers and stroking her inner walls.

Her eyes didn't open, as if she was focused inward. Good. That's what I wanted…for her to be out of her head.

I watched her bite hard on her bottom lip, watched her neck arch as she bowed up into me again and again, while I fucked her with my fingers. She clenched around me, tight and hot. I held out as long as I could, wanted her right on the edge.

I put my mouth to her ear and bit the lobe, just hard enough to make her moan again.

"Grab the condom, Erin."

I deliberately said her name. I suspected she had the same reaction I did to her saying my name.

Her eyes fluttered open slowly as I continued to work my fingers inside her. I had a flash of apprehension that she'd change her mind. And I'd get out of bed and walk away. But damn, I really hope she didn't. I'd never wanted another woman more than I wanted her. And I wasn't going to examine that now.

She looked over her shoulder at the table and reached for the packet.

Sliding my fingers free as she breathed out a heavy sigh, I let my fingers trail up her body, still sticky with her moisture. I traced a circle around one nipple then moved to the other, her flesh pebbling.

Lust surged again, twisting low in my gut.

"Put it on."

I barely recognized my own voice, and she shivered. I rolled onto my back, and she rose up onto her knees beside me. In a second, she had the condom open and rolled it down my cock. Sensation rocked me to my core, electricity searing my nerve endings. My hips arched, a groan rumbling in my chest. Her eyes flicked up to mine, her lips curving in a smile.

And still, she didn't say a word. It just made me want to hear her voice even more.

Her hand lingered on my cock as she swung one leg over my waist, fingers dancing along the length. Her smile widened, a tease in the curve. I lifted my hands to grip her hips. I didn't try to guide her, just held on, flexing my fingers into the soft flesh.

I let myself enjoy the view, gaze sweeping down her body from her breasts to her thighs then back up to meet her eyes.

"Beautiful."

Her smile widened, that hint of wickedness being overtaken by that sunny brightness she never seemed to be without, except around me. But not now.

I felt like I'd been granted a penalty shot. Or like a peasant who'd been smiled at by the princess.

She looked like a fucking queen as she maneuvered into position, holding my cock in place so she could slide onto it. Her eyes fluttered shut as she took me in, but I forced mine to stay open. I wanted to watch her. Needed to watch. She took her time sliding down my length, the tight glove of her sex gripping me, sucking me in. I had to fight against the urge to move, wanted her to control this. At least for now.

When she finally bottomed out, she paused, took a deep breath and opened her eyes.

"Move. Make me come."

Goddamn, her voice did dirty things to my body and my mind. So many different urges hit me at once, but she still hadn't said my name. And I knew that was deliberate. Baiting me.

Gripping her a little more tightly, I rolled her hips, biting back a groan at the sensation flooding my system. Part of me wanted to roll her over and fuck her hard, but then I wouldn't be able to watch her face. And right now, I needed to watch.

I wanted to see her when I began to thrust. Shallow at first, her breasts bouncing with every motion, mesmerizing. I thought I'd be able to make this last, but my body had other plans. Desire rose up in a furious wave, fingers digging into her hips as I lifted her then let her slide back down.

Our rhythm increased with every frantic breath, her hands coming to rest on my chest as she moved with me. After a time, she tried to take over the pace, her hair falling over her face as she bent lower, changing the angle.

Without warning, I lifted her off and flipped her onto her back. She gasped, her arms falling onto the bed at her sides, but I moved over her a second later. I thrust inside as her legs wrapped around my waist, my hands planted on either side of her head.

Now I moved with more purpose. I had a goal. My name leaving her lips as she came. I thrust harder, her legs tightening around me, her hands grabbing at my shoulders. She was so hot, so slick, and we matched each other's pace perfectly.

I felt the warning in the base of my cock, groaning. It was too soon. But then she made another little noise, a new little noise, and I changed the angle of my hips, just enough, and felt her suck in air.

Almost there.

"Come on, Erin." I thrust, shallow and fast. "Come with me."

But she was already there.

"Rebel. Oh my god."

Fuck yes. That's all I needed.

I sank deep and came, feeling her pulse around me as she gave me what I wanted.

CHAPTER SIXTEEN

THE NEXT MORNING

I STARED AT REBEL, my shock slowly turning to panic.

With one hand on my slightly aching head and the other holding the sheet up to my naked breasts, I scrambled onto my butt and tried to form words other than profanities, but all my mouth kept forming was "Oh my god."

Rebel's expression was unreadable. He didn't look shocked, but he did look kind of sick. Like waking up with me had turned his stomach.

Back at you, buddy.

My stomach definitely felt like I'd ridden a roller coaster for the past eight hours.

That's not what you were doing for the past eight hours.

Images from last night flooded my brain like I'd accidently opened a porn site, and they were playing clips from our greatest hits. Vivid and shocking and…hot. So very, very hot.

Heat swamped my body, from my hair to my toes. And everywhere in between. I realized I was biting my lip only when his gaze dropped and his jaw clenched. For some reason, my gaze dropped to his lap. Oh, for fuck's sake, yes, I was looking at his cock and, yes, there was definite movement under the sheet covering him from the waist down. Very low on his waist.

I remembered trailing my fingers down those defined abs, petting the silky dark hair that arrowed from his belly to his balls. Remembered cupping him in my hand and hearing him groan. Remembered—

I dragged my gaze away and turned to sit on the edge of the bed. But of course, now he could see my naked back. And probably my butt and—

What did it matter? He'd seen everything last night.

I swallowed hard.

I didn't have to think very hard about what had happened last night. While parts of it were fuzzy, I hadn't been blackout drunk. No, I'd drunk just enough to let some otherwise hidden desires come to the surface.

And then I'd acted on those desires. With the secret object of those desires.

"Erin."

I made a sound when he spoke, a squeak or a hiss or just a breath that didn't go down right. His voice saying my name scrambled my insides like a whisk scrambled eggs. It made me light-headed and brought up lots of other memories of him saying my name last night. Like when he made me—

"Erin, you okay?"

I took a deep breath. And then one more just to make sure I could.

"Yes." I spoke to the wall in front of me. "Yes, I'm fine."

"Good. I guess that makes one of us."

He sounded like he always did and yet... he didn't. Rebel didn't normally sound unsure of himself. He always seemed like he had his shit together. Even if I thought he was wrong about something, he knew he was right and didn't care what other people thought.

Right now, though, he sounded confused.

I turned my head so I could just see him out of the corner of my eye. The bed wobbled as he pulled a few pillows behind his back and propped himself up. His chest remained on full display, and I couldn't help myself. I turned a little more just be sure I could see it probably.

I think I saw nail marks. From where I'd raked the acrylic tips that I'd had done specifically for the wedding since my nails were shit from all the dishwashing and kneading. I had an appointment to have them removed Monday morning. They'd get in the way—

Holy shit. I'd left marks on him.

My head snapped back around to stare at the wall again.

"Do you feel okay?" I forced myself to ask.

Maybe he was too drunk to remember anything. Maybe he would—

No, I didn't want that because then he hadn't really wanted me last night. It'd just been the alcohol.

Maybe that was for the best?

Shit.

"Except for the fact that you're ready to jump out of bed and run screaming? Yeah, I'm fine."

I scrambled around on the bed, tugging on the sheet so I didn't uncover anything I didn't want him to see—again—and gaped at him.

"What? Like you're not trying to figure out how you can climb out the window to get away from me?"

His mouth twitched, like he wanted to smile but wouldn't allow it. "I've climbed in and out of that window more times than I can remember. If I wanted out of here, I'd be gone."

My brain pinged with all sorts of new information and questions. Then I looked around the room. Hockey stuff all over the built-in bookshelves on the other side of the room. A desk covered with pucks, some of them wrapped in tape. Hockey jerseys in acrylic boxes on the walls, some with the name Lawrence and some with Jedi. Jedi was Rebel's nickname with the Devils. Hockey sticks in a little teepee shape in the corner.

"Oh. This is your room."

"Used to be, yeah."

"Oh." I swallowed hard, my mind churning. But I had one question I needed answered right now. "How drunk were you last night?"

I heard him sigh out a hard breath. "Not that drunk."

My heart started to pound, and I bit my bottom lip until it hurt. "What does that mean?"

His gaze pinned me in place. "It means I remember everything. It also means I knew exactly what I was doing last night."

My mouth dropped open before I could stop it. "Oh."

I dropped his gaze because I couldn't hold it.

"Yeah. Oh." A little of his sarcasm crept back into his tone, making me feel a little better surprisingly. "So... How drunk were *you*? Did *you* know what you were doing last night?"

He was giving me an exit strategy, a chance to pretend I'd had no idea what had happened so I could slink out of here and never look back.

Did I want to take it?

Maybe?

Coward.

Yeah, but I also knew we weren't going to have a meaningful conversation about this right now. I couldn't stop wondering if he had matching marks down his back.

With an effort, I forced myself to look directly at him so he knew I meant my words. "Yes, I knew."

After a couple of more seconds, I had to drop my gaze or ask him to turn around so I could check his back. Instead, I pointed to a door on the wall to the right of the entrance.

"Is there a bathroom through that door?"

He didn't bother to look where I was pointing. "Yeah."

"Can I…?"

"Yeah. I'll…ah…let me find you something to wear."

"Oh shit. My bag's in one of the guest rooms."

"I'll go get it."

Ridiculous panic bubbled up. "What if someone sees you?"

He looked like he wanted to say something in response to that, something I wouldn't like, but then he thought better of it. I don't know if I'd wanted him to actually fight me about it or what.

"I don't think anyone else is up yet. My parents' room is on the first floor now, and I haven't heard anyone walking around. Rain gave you the empty room next to her old room, but I'm pretty sure she and Brian aren't going to notice if I go in there to get your stuff. Neither of them are going to be up this early."

I took a second before nodding, not knowing what else to do. I didn't want to do a walk of shame down the hall and risk getting caught. At least if Rebel got caught, he'd have an excuse for coming out of his room.

Although, maybe I should just make a run for it, if the room wasn't that far. My bladder made the final decision. I really needed to pee.

I nodded. "Okay."

He shrugged. "Okay."

Then he grabbed the comforter covering his waist and all the interesting bits below, and I made another one of those embarrassing squeaks and turned away as he threw the comforter off. Which was ridiculous. I'd seen it all last night. Touched almost every inch of him. And enjoyed every second.

Hell, we'd had sex last night. More than once.

And I wanted him again.

I was being ridiculous, but then everything about this situation was ridiculous. The bed shifted as he got up, then I heard drawers open and clothing rustle.

"It's safe to look."

Humor laced his tone, and my cheeks flushed.

"Be right back," he said and was out the door a second later. I only got a glimpse of his ass in a pair of gym shorts before the door closed behind him.

I scrambled off the bed and ran for the bathroom. Two minutes later, I came back into the bedroom, trying not to trip over the sheet I'd wound back around my body. I froze when the doorknob turned, my heart pounding at the thought that we'd been caught.

Then he walked in, like we hadn't just spent the night together and, if anyone found out...

Honestly, I think if anyone found out, they wouldn't believe it.

Rebel watched me as he set my overnighter on the bed.

I was reaching for it when he said, "You wanna talk now or later?"

My hands froze halfway to the bag, but I forced myself to grab the tab and open the zipper, keeping my gaze firmly away from him.

"I don't think talking about last night is going to change it."

"Who said I wanted to change it?"

My gaze snapped back to his as he settled back onto the bed, hands laced behind his head. My mouth dried at the sight of his six-pack abs, on full display. His shorts hung low on his hips, and the broad chest and the trimmed stubble on his cheeks and chin. I'd thought he might shave it completely for the wedding. I'm so glad he hadn't. I could still feel his whiskers on my skin. I probably had patches of whisker burn on my thighs.

Then his words sank in.

"I don't... What?"

"Why do you think I want to change what happened?"

I blinked at him. "Because... Well, I guess—"

His gaze narrowed. "Do you want to forget it happened?"

I didn't know what to say, couldn't find the words I wanted to use. And that was a shock. I was never at a loss for words. This is what he did to me.

When I didn't answer, he leaned forward, grabbed the bag and pulled it toward him. Since I still had my hand on the zipper, I started to lean forward, until I had to catch myself with my other hand on the bed. Which meant I released the sheet.

It loosened, and the front gaped, making me gasp and release the bag while I grabbed at the sheet and scrambled off the bed. Rebel's gaze slipped to my chest and lingered there, lust transforming his expression into one I'd only ever seen last night.

Rebel wanted me. I mean, I knew he'd wanted me last

night. He's been *hard*. I can't believe he still did this morning, though. It just didn't make sense.

We hated each other.

Except, no, we didn't.

When his gaze finally lifted, I thought I might combust. It felt like tiny fires flamed under my skin. The heat in his eyes scorched, matching the intensity of last night. I couldn't breathe.

"Erin. We need to talk about this."

I knew one thing. I didn't want to talk about it now.

I wondered if anyone would see me streaking for my car in a sheet. Maybe no one was up yet. I gauged the distance to the door. Knowing me, I'd trip over the sheet and end up sprawled in the front hall with my ass naked for the world to see.

"I need to get dressed."

His brows rose. "Maybe we should do this naked."

My mouth dropped open, but not at the suggestion. No, it was at the images flooding my brain. Of Rebel. Naked. Last night.

"I..." wanted to see him naked again. "That's not happening."

He stood and walked around the bed, as my hand tightened on the sheet.

"I can live with that. For now. Go ahead and get dressed. Then we'll talk. Later."

He turned, opened a drawer in a dresser and grabbed a t-shirt before he walked out the door.

CHAPTER SEVENTEEN

I KNEW Erin wanted to make a run for it, and I didn't want to torture her now, so I gave her an out.

I saw the glances she kept making at the door and the deer-in-the-headlights expression. She had no filter, never had, and I read her every thought plainly on her face.

And honestly, I wasn't sure I wanted to do a post-mortem now either.

Erin and I had had sex. Really fucking great sex.

I was still trying to wrap my head around all the implications of that, which wouldn't mean a damn thing if she didn't want to talk to me ever again. The house was still silent as I walked through the second-floor hall to the back stairs and took them to the kitchen. The sun had barely risen, and I didn't hear anyone else moving around. Not a floorboard creaked in the whole place.

Only the bridal party, family and a few close friends had stayed in the house overnight, which meant there were probably fifty or so people in rooms around the building, not including the bride and groom who'd escaped to their home just a mile or so away.

I'd planned to go back to my place last night, but obviously that hadn't happened.

I'd had sex with Erin. Really great sex. And not just once.

And in my childhood bedroom, no less.

Shaking my head, I went straight for the coffeemaker, which someone had thoughtfully set to start brewing at six a.m. I poured a mug, sat at the counter, gazing out the back window into the garden, where Erin and I had first kissed.

Would she sneak out? Try to leave before everyone else got up?

Or would she come down and act like nothing had happened last night?

I didn't think she'd skip out. I know her bakery had platters and stuff they needed to pick up. Mom had hired a cleaning crew for today, but I knew Erin well enough to know she'd want to handle her own stuff.

So I waited. About fifteen minutes later, I heard shuffling on the floor.

"Good morning, sweetheart. Did you have a good time last night?"

Mom strolled in wearing an oversized t-shirt and a pair of pajama pants with cups of coffee all over them. She had her hair pulled up in a messy bun and wore the black-rimmed glasses she rarely ever used because she had contacts.

"Yep." Didn't have to lie about that. "We didn't keep you and Pop awake, did we?"

She made a shooing motion as she sipped her coffee. "I

thought I told you we were spending the night in the guest house. We could still hear the music, but it didn't keep us awake."

The guest house was on the other side of the building from the ballroom, set a little back into the trees.

"Good. The band was good, but they were loud. I'm surprised we didn't get noise complaints from town."

Mom made an amused sound. "Who would've called? All the neighbors were here. What time did the party finally wrap up?"

Tricky question. I didn't exactly know.

"I guess I went up around midnight? Maybe one. Not sure."

Mom gave me a funny look. "Well, we paid the band until one. So if they were still playing, you didn't make it to the end. I hope everyone had a good time."

Mom put two mugs of coffee on a tray she pulled from a cabinet then opened the fridge and pulled out a tray of breakfast food. Muffins, croissants, donuts, pastries, breads. When I realized that wasn't the only tray, I got off my ass and gave her a hand. How the hell all this food fit in there was a mystery. It was like someone with a degree in Tetris had packed it in.

"Erin outdid herself with all of this." She paused as we put the trays on the counter then fussed with them for a few seconds before piling a plate high with muffins and pastries and adding that to her tray. "You two seem to have put aside your differences these past couple of weeks. I know your sister appreciates it."

It took a little effort not to smile at my mom's comment. I know she was fishing for information, but I had no reason to think she knew what Erin and I had gotten up to last night.

"I think we understand each other a little better now."

Mom smiled, her gaze intent for long seconds. Then she picked up her tray. "That's good to hear. Do me a favor and fill that carafe next to the coffeemaker, and then make another pot, okay? I think I hear people stirring. Dad and I plan to be lazy this morning, but Erin said she'd be here to help with breakfast. See you later, hon."

I followed Mom's directions, realizing Erin couldn't just cut and run. I swallowed more coffee and let that sink in. There was a very small part of my brain that was telling me to get the hell out while I could. That if we were in the same room when my sister or Brian or my brother or, hell, anyone who knew us came in and saw us together, they'd know immediately what we'd done last night.

Instead, I kept one eye on the entrance to the back stairs, watching for her to show.

I'd just taken a bite of one of her cherry almond scones when quiet footsteps on the stairs announced another arrival a few minutes later. When they paused before continuing into the kitchen, I knew it was Erin.

My heart actually began to thump a little harder in anticipation. I told myself it was the coffee kicking in.

When she stepped into the room, our eyes met and held. That stupid saying about the world stopping when we looked at each other... not exactly true. The world kept spinning, but maybe it slowed a little. And it got a little harder to breathe.

Then her gaze slid away as she walked into the kitchen and headed straight for the coffee. After she'd poured herself a mug and taken a long sip, her back straightened, and she turned to face me with an expression that reminded me of a kid facing the principal.

Then Rain shuffled into the room.

"Hey—" my sister yawned, long and loud and ruffled her

hair, which was a mess and made me smile. "Ugh, why am I up this early? I mean, seriously. Brian's still asleep, but my eyes popped open, like, fifteen minutes ago, and I couldn't fall back to sleep. Probably because I smelled coffee. I love coffee, but damn, I don't want to be up right now."

"Good morning to you, too."

Rain held up an index finger while she lifted a mug to her mouth and swallowed at least four times. Erin took the opportunity to make herself busy with the trays of food, moving them around on the island, grabbing plates from a bag I hadn't noticed sitting in a corner on the other side of the room.

She took the plates out of the plastic wrap and set them on the counter, reached into the bag and brought out plastic utensils, reached in again and brought out insulated cups for coffee and plastic juice cups. The utensils went in holders, also in the bag. I began to wonder if that bag had a little Mary Poppin's magic. I wasn't going to be surprised if she pulled out a sink.

But no, the bag got folded and stashed under the counter somewhere. Apparently she knew this kitchen better than I did. And I'd grown up in the damn house.

Then she went about setting up a breakfast spread that rivaled any bed and breakfast. She even told the radio to play something called "Breakfast playlist" and soft instrumental music filled in the empty spaces in the room.

Rain had finally put down her mug and was giving Erin a hand when Ian wandered in, yawning and scratching his head. His face had sleep lines all over that made him look even younger than he was.

"Coffee's over there," I told him, grinning when he didn't

even look at me but made an immediate U-turn, eyes barely open. Open enough to see Erin, though.

"Hey."

Her smile at my younger teammate hit like a punch in the gut. It wasn't jealousy. I didn't want to punch the kid for looking at her or talking to her. No, it was the feeling I got when she smiled.

"You have a good night, big brother?"

Rain stood by my side. She'd gotten so close without me seeing her, but somehow, she'd maneuvered herself next to me without me noticing. And the way she was staring at me…

I returned her look, taking another slow sip of my quickly cooling coffee.

"It was a great party. You have a good time?"

"I did." She continued to stare at me with a look I recognized. And rightly feared. "You know, I don't remember seeing you at the send-off. You go up to bed early?"

Metaphorical red lights flashed in my brain. "Yeah. I'd had enough socializing."

Except for the naked socializing I'd done with one other person, who was slipping Rain and I little glances from across the room as she fussed with the coffeemakers.

Her brows arched. "Little too much to drink?"

"No, actually. Just had enough of the party."

She nodded, her gaze sliding away. Straight to Erin.

"Erin must've gone to bed early, too. I don't remember her at the send-off either."

"How was it?"

"How was what?"

I wanted to grunt at her. "The send-off. Rowdy and Tressy get out the door okay? I mean, they didn't trip and fall down the walk? Make for an awkward wedding night if someone got hurt."

I never saw her arm swing out until she smacked me across the chest.

I rubbed my chest, grinning. "Hey! What the hell was that for?"

Rain's gaze narrowed. "I'm not sure yet, but I know you did something."

Had she seen us leave? No, she couldn't have. We hadn't left together.

"I think your radar might still be a little drunk."

"My radar isn't drunk, and neither am I. Though I *was* feeling no pain last night. Erin, everything looks amazing. Doesn't it, Reb?"

I got another glance from Rain, this one even more pointed. And longer.

"Yeah. It looks great."

"And it tastes amazing." Ian's voice was muffled by the food in his mouth, which he realized too late was bad manners. His cheeks got red, and he swallowed hard before he said, "Sorry."

Everyone laughed or shook their head, and his grin returned, mostly directed at Erin, who returned his with a wide smile of her own. I wanted that smile for myself. I knew I was being greedy and ridiculous, but goddamn it, I wanted her to smile at me like that. And I wanted people to know she was smiling at me.

I wanted more of what I'd had last night. But when she looked at me now, I saw wariness and worry in her gaze. She didn't want our friends and family to know.

And that pissed me off.

She caught my eye just then and something in my expression must have tipped her off to what I was thinking. Her eyes widened, like she couldn't believe what she was seeing.

Hell, I couldn't believe what I was thinking. Didn't I have enough on my mind without wondering what I was going to do with these feelings for Erin?

Then again, I needed to do something with these feelings. Needed to figure out what to do with them. Do *about* them. I didn't want to forget them, didn't want to ignore them.

And, yeah, I wanted more of her.

I just needed a plan.

CHAPTER EIGHTEEN

"You feel all right this morning?"

The kitchen had filled up pretty quickly after Ian walked in. Surprisingly, by seven-thirty, there were at least fifteen people having breakfast.

I'd made more than enough baked goods for everyone who'd stayed overnight, including the tray I'd made for the newlyweds and delivered to their home yesterday. This week had been the busiest of my life and also the most fulfilling. I'd gotten it all done. Everything I'd needed to do. I'd had a schedule, and I'd stuck to it, and everything had gone to plan. Everything.

Except last night. Sleeping with Rebel had not been part of the plan.

I slid a quick glance at Rain, who'd plopped into the seat next to mine at the breakfast nook in the corner of the kitchen. Everyone else had gathered around the island where I'd laid out the food and the coffee, talking and laughing and talking about the wedding and the reception.

So far, no one had asked why I'd left before the end of the party. Or where Rebel had been.

I glanced at Rain, who'd sat beside me with a glass of orange juice and a croissant, which she was dipping straight into a Nutella jar.

"Yeah, I'm fine. Why?"

"You're kinda quiet."

Yeah, because I'd been holding a silent conversation with myself for much of the morning while I made sure the trays stayed full and the coffee was made, though Rain and Rebel made sure they pitched in.

"Guess I just don't have a lot to say this morning."

"Hmm. You didn't seem to have a lot to say yesterday either. Or last night. Something's definitely going on with you."

"You're seeing things that aren't there. Honestly, I'm just busy."

I didn't think Rain was going to let me off the hook. She had that look in her eyes. Yesterday had been all about the wedding. About making sure everything went off perfectly. Or at least as perfect as it could. We'd all been working toward a common goal, which was to make Rowdy and Tressy's wedding day the best it could possibly be.

"You don't need to be this busy. The tough part is over. Take a break. Especially since you've got so much on your plate in the coming weeks. Camp. Book club. And that wedding."

"You're doing another wedding?"

I jumped a little to hear Rebel's voice so close. I hadn't

heard him come up behind him, but now he slid into the chair next to Rain. He had a glass of milk and a cherry almond scone. I made those specifically because he always ordered them. His hair looked rumpled but not messy. And damn it, it just made him look sexier.

I dragged my gaze to somewhere over his shoulder and forced a smile that I hoped looked real enough.

"No, I'm not doing another wedding. My cousin's getting married in August, and I've got to make a command performance."

"Where's the wedding?"

Was he really interested? And why would he be? But he kept staring at me with those intense brown eyes, as if I was the only person in the room. My lungs got tight, and my gaze dropped to his lips. And I thought about last night again.

My body flamed all over, heat rushing beneath my skin and making me want to fan my cheeks. I'm pretty sure they'd just turned bright red. If Rain had been looking at me, she'd definitely know something had happened between me and her brother.

But she was staring at Rebel, her brows arched.

"You know, you should go with Erin."

My head whipped around, my mouth dropping open. Was she insane? What was she doing?

I thought for sure Rebel would immediately tell her off, tell her she was crazy. Why would she ever think he would want to go with me to a family wedding?

But all he said was, "And why should I do that?"

Now my head snapped to look at him. I was going to get whiplash.

"Because you won't take any shit and, if you're with her,

they won't say stupid shit to her. They'll take one look at you and run screaming in the other direction."

When she put it like that, I could see the reasoning. She was right. Most of my family would take one look at Rebel and decide giving me grief for my life choices would be a bad idea at that moment. Just to see the look on my mom's face if I showed up with him might be worth it. But there was no way he'd agree. I was insane to think he'd agree. I mean, it was stupid insane to think Rebel would go with me to my cousin's wedding. Why would he even consider it?

"Does your family say stupid shit to you a lot?"

My mouth dropped open, but I had no idea what to say to his question. Things between us were weird. Like, really fucking weird. Last night had made everything weird.

And yet I still wanted to answer.

"My family and I don't see eye to eye on a lot of things. We have different opinions on, well most everything."

"Like you living here."

"Yes."

"So, when's the wedding?"

Was he serious? Would he actually consider going with me?

"First weekend in August. In the Hamptons. But you'll be back at practice, won't you?"

He shrugged, looking like he was actually considering it. Which he couldn't be. "Not then, no."

"It's a little late in the season for a society wedding, but…" I shrugged and shook my head, my mouth feeling out of my control at the moment. "The McNamara family doesn't adhere to rules, at least, not anyone else's. Plus, I think she wants to nail him down before he changes his mind. Ooh, that sounded petty, didn't it? I'm not usually like that but—"

I snapped my mouth closed. Damn it, I was babbling. I'd been able to keep it under control for the past couple of weeks since I knew it annoyed Rebel. And I knew it shouldn't matter to me if I annoyed him or not, but I'd wanted Rowdy and Tressy's wedding to be stress free, and I certainly didn't want to be the cause of any stress if there was some. So, I'd purposely tried to be, well, not so chatty.

It'd helped that I'd been hyperaware of Rebel for the past few weeks.

And look where that got you. In bed with the man and secretly wanting more.

I couldn't look at him right now or everyone would know exactly what I was thinking. But I couldn't not look at him. I flashed a glance his way and, yeah, he was staring at me, his expression considering.

Considering what? Me?

Oh geez.

I got up from the table, nearly knocking my chair over in my effort to get away.

"You know, I'm just gonna make sure the trays are refilled. I'll be back…later."

Then I headed for the fridge but not before I heard Rain say, "What did you do to Erin?"

I moved a little faster so I didn't hear him lie.

CHAPTER NINETEEN

THE WEEK AFTER THE WEDDING

ebel

"Rebel, how are you? I hope your brother's wedding went well."

"Hey, Coach. The wedding was great. Thanks for asking."

Redtails coach Cory was on the other end of the line. Cory and I had known each other for years, though he was older than me by a decade. He'd never played for the Devils, but if you got paid to play hockey and you played in a certain area of the country for most of your life, you got to know the players no matter what league you were in.

It was how I'd gotten the call to play with the Redtails, even though I hadn't come up through the ECHL.

I didn't have a clue why he was calling, though.

"I'm glad to hear it. And look, I know this call is out of the blue, but I know you haven't signed your contract yet. And I know the deadline isn't until next week, but I wanted to touch base."

And shit. I really didn't want to have this conversation. I still didn't have a clue what I was going to do about that contract.

"I just want you to know how well you played last season and how much you added to the team."

It took me a couple seconds to respond. That's not what I'd been expecting to hear. Part of me had thought maybe they'd rescind the offer. Honestly, it would make it easier on me if they did. With everything leading up to Rowdy's wedding, I hadn't had time to think about what I was going to do.

Liar.

Okay, I hadn't wanted to think about what I was going to do.

"Thanks. That's...nice to hear."

"I know I might be out of line, but I feel there's some hesitancy on your part to coming back. I could be totally off base, and this is not me pressuring you. Hell, this isn't even me calling as your coach. This is just me telling you that you added value to the team last year, and I wanted you to know that."

Well, shit. "I appreciate it. And honestly, I'm not sure what I'm doing yet. I've got a lot to think about."

"You know I'm here to talk if you need a sounding board. Hey, tell your dad hi. And Reb? Make the decision that's right for you."

I was still thinking about what Cory had said the next day when I went to the arena to meet with the high school hockey coach and talk about the upcoming camp. Yeah, I was doing it. Of course I was.

The amount of times the coach thanked me was embarrassing, but the guy cared about his kids. Couldn't fault him for that.

"I'm just glad to be able to help out," I said as he finally stood and shook my hand. "I'm looking forward to it."

He reminded me of the coaches I'd had growing up, of all the camps I'd attended, that my parents had sent us to simply because my brothers and I loved the game. Rowdy and I had attended most of them together. I remembered them as some of the best times of my life. I wouldn't fuck that up for these kids.

I wasn't surprised to see my dad standing in the hall as I opened the door to let the coach out. He and I had met in Pop's office. They talked for a few minutes, making it clear they knew each other pretty well. I wasn't surprised. I swore Pop knew everyone in town, and if that was an exaggeration, it was only slight.

"You got a few minutes," Pop said after the coach disappeared down the stairs to the front lobby.

"Yep. Something up?"

Pop shook his head, and we headed back into the office, this time with Pop behind the desk. It was his office, after all. At least for a few more months.

I rubbed at the dull throb in my chest.

"Something wrong?" Pop's brows arched.

I put my hand down. "No." Except for the fact that he was retiring, and life was throwing me curveballs from every angle recently. "What's up?"

He settled back in his chair, a sign that I should get comfortable.

"You make up your mind about your contract yet?"

And that was Pop. No lead up. Just dive right in. That ache

in my chest migrated to my gut, tightening like a vise. I wondered if he'd read my mind or just had really fucking good instincts.

Shaking my head, I huffed out a laugh. "As a matter of fact, Coach Cary called yesterday."

Pop just nodded, like he'd already known. "And? You wanna talk about it?"

I leaned back in my chair and thought about it for a second. "I'm not sure."

Of course, Pop understood that those three words covered a hell of a lot of ground.

"Fair enough. Your mom said you're taking Krista out to dinner tonight. I love that little girl but, damn, she wears me out."

Rowdy and Tressy had left for their honeymoon to Greece two days ago, and Krista was staying with my parents for one of those weeks. She was spending the following week with Tressy's mom and sister in New York. Mom had called yesterday to ask if I'd take Krista to dinner one night while they were gone.

"She specifically asked if Uncle Rowdy could take her one a date," my mom had said. "She's a trip, that one."

I said I'd pick her up tonight at five. Mom had called me a sweetheart and said I should be there around quarter-of-five. Krista had to be up early to go to swim lessons.

Apparently, that would be the best date I'd have all week. Erin and I had exchanged exactly three texts since the wedding. I'd asked her Sunday night to meet me for dinner one day this week. She'd texted back that she'd have to check her calendar and let me know. She'd never gotten back to me.

I'd decided to give her a few days to process everything, also known as the night we'd spent fucking each other's brains out. Hell, I was still processing. And dreaming about it. Every time I fell asleep, I was back in my old bedroom with Erin naked and all over me. Yeah, I woke up with a hard on.

And that was definitely not what I should be thinking about. But my brain just would not stop bringing her up.

"Thought I'd take her for pizza. And a trip to the bookstore."

Pop nodded. "She'll love that. I think she might love books almost as much as Rain and Rowdy." He paused for a second. "Erin's done some good things for this town. Took her awhile to find her place here, but I think she's gotten her footing. She and your sister make good partners."

Was he fishing for information? I wouldn't put it past him, but there was no way he could know about Erin and me. If anyone in town had found out about us, Rain would've known by now. And I would've gotten my ass handed to me.

"They do."

"You two bury the hatchet? You seemed pretty civil at the wedding."

"Civil's my middle name."

Pop's laughter bellowed out, filling the empty spaces in the room and making me grin. My brothers and sister and I would make bets about who could make Pop laugh more. Usually it'd been Rowdy. Whenever I got him to laugh, it felt like I'd climbed a mountain. Probably because we were a lot alike.

"I don't know that I want to go back, Pop."

His lips still held a little curve. "There a reason for that?"

Yeah. Several. Some that had to do with him. I leaned forward, elbows on my knees and looked at the floor for a few seconds, trying to find the right words.

He was retiring from the team he'd built from the ground

up. I'd thought he'd be around forever. His retirement was a reminder that he wouldn't.

"I'm not sure…" I sighed, shaking my head. "I'm not sure I'm enjoying it enough."

Pop didn't say anything right away, his gaze laser-focused on me. As a kid, that look had made me go deer-in-the-headlights because I'd done something stupid that required a Pop talk. Stupid kid shit, like being out after curfew or cow-tipping or shooting targets at midnight in the woods.

This wasn't like any of those other times. This was more like the time he'd come to college when I'd crashed out. But I wasn't an anxiety ridden twenty-year-old anymore. I was a grown-ass adult with a major decision to make and no idea what I was going to do.

"Okay, so what do you enjoy about it?" Pop folded his hands over his stomach, his classic listening position.

I didn't have to give that much thought. "I like the level of play. It's a challenge. I like challenges."

Like Erin.

Nope, not what we're talking about.

Pop nodded. "Okay, what else?"

"I like the guys. I like the coach."

"All good things."

"Yeah."

"But…"

I took a deep breath. "It's not home. It doesn't feel like home. *This* is home."

Pop's expression didn't change. "You've been there less than a year."

"I know." I shoved a hand through my hair, trying not to look as frustrated as I felt. "I know I should give it more time. I don't want to feel like I'm giving up. I don't want to be that guy who had this great opportunity and was too afraid to take it."

"*Are* you afraid? There's a difference between being afraid and knowing what you want."

"That's the problem. I'm not sure I know what I want."

"I think you know what you want." Pop's smile was barely visible, but it was there. "But I think you've told yourself you should want something else for so long that you started to believe it. I know it might seem like you don't know what you want, but it's not true. Rebel, you have always known what you wanted. And you went after it, even when it was the most difficult thing in the world for you to do."

"I've fucked up a lot."

He slashed a hand through the air. "Hell, kid, everyone fucks up. You hit a rough patch in college, but you didn't let it define you. You fought back and look at you now."

I snorted. "Sitting here bitching to you about attaining a goal so many other guys would sacrifice their first born for."

Got another laugh from Pop for that one. I enjoyed the hell out of it.

"I don't think they'd go that far but, yeah, you got a break. But it was a break you've busted your ass to get. You earned it, Reb. You've got skill, sure, but you also have drive. It's made you a damn good hockey player. But you know that's not all there is to life."

That's all there'd been in my life. I mean, I had my family, but there'd been no woman for a long time. Yeah, there'd been dates and one-night stands, but I hadn't found one woman who either wanted to put up with me or who I saw myself spending my life with. If I was going to have a relationship with a woman, I wasn't just looking for companionship. I wanted what my parents had. I wanted long-term. I wanted forever. And I hadn't found anyone who came close to being that person.

Until now.

The thought sat in my brain like an itch I couldn't scratch. Was I really going to go there with Erin? And if I did, what did that mean for my career? I wasn't looking to do long-distance. And Erin was tied here.

All the more reason not to start something, to write off the wedding night as a fluke, a moment out of time.

But I didn't want to. Even now, sitting here talking to my dad, I wanted to be with her. I wanted to know why I couldn't stop thinking about her. Wanted to know what had changed between us. When that change had happened.

And what the hell we were going to do with it now.

"Something else on your mind, kid?"

Grinning, I shook my head. "Nothing I need your help with."

"Then I probably don't want to know."

"Probably not."

He nodded and I thought he'd drop it.

"You know, sometimes you can miss a good thing standing right in front of you."

I chose to believe he was not talking about Erin. I couldn't believe he knew anything about that night.

I nodded and stood, ready to leave. I had prep work I needed to do for camp, and I didn't have a whole lot of time to do it. Pop remained behind the desk.

"Thanks again for taking the camp. I think you'll have fun. Just...give yourself some grace on the other shit, kid. You got at least a couple weeks before you have to make a decision. Whatever it is, it'll be the right one for you."

CHAPTER TWENTY

SIX DAYS AFTER THE WEDDING

"AND I LOVE books with princesses who have swords. Mommy read this one where the princess has to save her kingdom, and her parents were turned into trees, and her brother was an annoying bird who never knew what was going on. I don't think I ever want a little brother. They're so much work."

"Sounds like you got it all figured out."

I looked up from the laptop where I was ordering books for the store and immediately started to overheat. I knew that voice.

Rebel and Krista had just walked through the door. I hadn't seen him since last Saturday, when we'd woken up in bed together after spending the night having amazing sex.

I hadn't texted him back. I'd had no idea what to say.

I straightened as our gazes met and held, and heat spread

through my body with sizzling flashes. That heat remained, even when he looked away, his attention focused on Krista, who continued to chatter. She held onto his hand as she skipped beside him, and his expression... The man actually grinned.

I'd only ever seen him give that smile to Krista. I might have been a little jealous. But I certainly couldn't stay jealous at an eight-year-old. Especially not one as adorable as Krista.

"Miss Erin! Miss Erin!" She broke free from Rebel and ran to the desk. "Uncle Rebel said we're gonna look at all the books."

"Hi, Krista. That sounds like fun. We just got a whole lot of books, and they're all on the shelves in the Book Forest. I think Miss Abby is back there now, and she can show you where all the new ones are."

Krista's smile could light the entire town. "Come on, Uncle Rowdy."

"I'll be right there, Krista. Just gotta talk to Miss Erin for a minute."

Behind me, I heard Abby say, "Krista? Come back and join us for a story. We're just starting."

I'd actually forgotten there were other children in the store. I'd been working on inventory for the past two hours. It normally wouldn't take that long but I kept getting distracted. I had bread in the ovens for tomorrow and had to keep an eye on that, and the store was busy.

We offered children ninety minutes of fully supervised activities every last Thursday of the month so parents could get something to eat at one of the local restaurants or do a little shopping of their own at the other stores on Main Street. We hired a couple of local teenagers to help Abby, and so far, it'd been a huge draw. It was one of our biggest nights outside of book clubs. I was actually thinking about opening the café for a few hours on those nights, but then I'd have to hire more people and just thinking about that made me twitch.

"Go ahead." Rebel smiled at Krista. "I'll be right here."

"Okay, bye!"

Rebel watched her take off at a run through the store before she disappeared into the entrance to the children's section, his smile widening as he watched.

Then he turned to me and that smile became something else as he walked forward and leaned on the counter.

I took a deep breath. "Krista looks—"

"You haven't answered my texts."

Okay, guess we were going to jump right in.

I looked around to see if anyone had heard him, but there was no one in the vicinity. I wondered if he'd be able to catch me if I made a run for it. Which was stupid. It was my store. And I couldn't stop staring at the man.

His beard was trimmed, his hair perfect. He wore a short-sleeve henley with two buttons undone that perfectly molded to his upper body and khaki shorts that I'm sure made his ass look great. And I would totally be looking at that when he turned around.

But right now, he watched me intently, looking like every suburban mom's dream son-in-law candidate. But then he always looked like he put in a little effort to look good. And he really, *really* did.

I breathed deep and released it on a sigh. I could stare at the man all day. But then my brain started to throw out images of when he didn't look so put together. When he'd looked a little rumpled and…gloriously naked.

"I've been busy?"

Why did I make that sound like a question? Ugh, I was ridiculous.

He nodded. "Makes me think you don't want to talk to me. And we need to talk."

I knew that. At least, rationally, I knew we needed to discuss what had happened like two adults. However, there was another part of me who wanted him to just show up at my door one night, walk into my home and throw me on the couch and ravage me.

I'd never been ravaged. I mean, like, full banging up against doors and pushing things off tables and making the headboard bounce off the wall. I'd never thought I wanted that. Sex with my fiancé had been nice. And yeah, I know how that sounds. And you'd be right in thinking you know exactly what I mean. I did mean exactly that.

Sex with Rebel had not been nice.

It'd been amazing.

"Maybe I don't want to talk."

His jaw tightened, and he was probably biting his tongue. I couldn't tell if he was upset that I didn't want to talk or if he'd read my mind and knew what I wanted to do instead of talk. It's not that I didn't want to be with him. It's that I didn't want to talk while I was with him.

But I knew he couldn't read my mind, and he probably took my words at face value, which meant we were going to have to talk.

"But you're right," I added. "We need to sit down and have a …discussion."

His expression didn't change, but his gaze swept over my face, probably noting the hot spots on my cheeks and the way my lips parted when I drew in air. It was hard to breathe around him. But when I did, I smelled the clean, oceany scent of his bodywash.

My gaze fell from his eyes to his lips, which I could still feel on the inside of my thighs when I closed my eyes at night, then to his throat where his pulse beat hard enough for me to notice.

What would he do if I leaned over the counter and put my lips on that pulse? Would he let me? Would he wind his fingers in my hair like he'd done Saturday night and hold me steady so he could kiss me like he was starving for me?

Was he starving for me like I was starving for him? The craving got worse every day. And yet... How had we gotten here? I needed to know. So...

"Are you going to be at the arena tomorrow getting ready for camp?"

His gaze narrowed for a second, before he nodded.

"Why don't we plan to meet there around two-thirty? The lunch rush will be over, and I can get away for a couple of hours. We can talk about the arrangements for the camp lunches. And, um, whatever else we need to talk about."

He didn't say anything, just looked at me for a few, very long seconds. Those dark eyes held mine like we were alone in the room. Or back in his childhood bedroom. The arena would be neutral ground but somewhere we could talk alone. Without our neighbors and friends knowing we were getting together and blabbing it to the rest of our world.

"Sure. Tomorrow. We'll talk."

Then he turned and headed for the children's section.

And yeah, his ass looked great in those shorts.

———

I DECIDED to walk to the arena Thursday. It was a beautiful summer day. The sky looked like someone had colored it with a blue crayon and the few fluffy clouds floating in all that blue looked painted there.

Yeah, it was almost eighty-five degrees, but the humidity was low, and a nice little breeze blew across my skin and cooled the heat of the sun. The trees sparkled like emeralds on the surrounding hills, and the streets were practically deserted as I set out from the bakery. Rain staffed the bookstore today, so I knew she wouldn't be at the arena.

The walk was just over a mile, but I didn't mind. It gave me a chance to clear my head before I had to face Rebel. We did need to talk about the lunch plan for the camp kids. I wanted his input before I ordered supplies.

I just didn't know why we needed to talk about the wedding night. Except for the fact that every time I thought about it, I got hot all over, and I wanted to push Rebel against a wall and climb him like a tree.

I'd never wanted to do that to another person. And it was a huge change from wanting to stick my finger in his chest and tell him to lighten up. I'm not sure I wanted him to lighten up anymore. I think…I might like him just the way he was.

Turning that over in my head as I walked, I made it to the arena in twenty minutes, with ten minutes to spare. I peeked around the corner into the parking lot and saw only Rebel's truck there.

Good. That was good. We could talk and no one would be listening in or watching us and spreading rumors about how we suddenly seemed a lot closer than we had before the wedding.

I knew the front doors wouldn't be open, so I headed for the side doors that led into the lower level where the locker rooms and the other meeting and utility rooms were. Just as I was about to open the door, my phone rang.

I glanced at the number and felt my stomach dip.

I debated not picking up, but I knew my mom. She'd just keep calling until I answered. And since I was early, I could get this out of the way before I talked to Rebel.

"Hey, Mom. What's up?"

"Hello, dear. I just wanted to let you know that I'm planning a short visit to St. David's next week."

My mouth dropped open, but I couldn't find the words to respond. My mom hadn't visited since I'd told her I was staying. She'd told me then that I was making a huge mistake and throwing away my life. She'd never understood that I didn't want her life. And I loved the life I'd made here. My granddad was here. My friends lived here. The businesses I'd created.

Only one word finally came to mind.

"Why?"

I knew it was the wrong thing to say as soon as the word left my mouth, but it was the only question I had. Then she laughed and confused me all to hell.

"Apparently, my daughter owns several businesses in town, and my father owns a newspaper. I think that's enough reason to make a detour on my way to Chicago for a board meeting."

I let out a sigh of relief, careful not to let her hear me.

"So, you'll only be here a few hours?"

"Yes, dear. Don't worry. I don't plan to interrupt your day for more than that."

There was an edge in my mom's voice, and I could tell I'd finally pissed her off.

"I'm sorry, of course I'll be happy to see you. I've just got a lot on my plate next week. The bakery is doing the lunches for the hockey camp, and we've got to prepare for book club, and I've got another event next weekend that I need to work ahead on."

Her mom paused. "Sounds like you have your hands full."

The snarky voice in my head wanted me to ask her what she thought I did here. Did she think I just played at being a business owner? That I didn't bust my ass to make everything work? That I was like my brother's revolving door of girl-friends, who played at having jobs when really, they lived off their parents' money and constantly traveled?

Ooh, that was bitchy. But true.

"I do. But of course, I'll have time to spend with you while you're here."

"I'm glad to hear it. I have something I'd like to discuss with you."

My heart leaped into my throat. When my mom said she wanted to discuss something, my anxiety spiked. I hated that she made me feel like this, but it'd been happening since I was a kid, and I hadn't managed to control it yet. Not sure I ever would.

"Sure, Mom. I'll see you then."

"I'll text you my details. Talk to you soon. Love you."

The call disconnected, and I took a deep breath and then another one, trying to get my heart back into a natural rhythm. I opened the door and walked inside, heading for the room where Rebel had told me to meet him.

I knew my way around the arena, having been friends with Rain for years. My feet headed in the right direction, my brain still chewing over my mother's impending visit, even though I kept trying to change my focus. My therapist had given me some tools to make sure I didn't fall down the rabbit hole, but

I still couldn't catch my breath when I reached my destination.

Until I saw Rebel, leaning against a well-worn wooden table, scanning a sheet of paper in his hands. He hadn't seen me yet and turned away to pick up another paper from the table. I could see his profile now, and my heart beat in a different rhythm, one that came with heat low in my body.

My mother's call drifted out of my head, replaced by images from that night. That night I'd been dreaming about every night since. I knew I shouldn't. I knew it'd been a moment out of time, a blip in his life that he wanted to put behind him.

Of course, I should probably want the same thing. To just move on and mark it down to too much really good alcohol. But I couldn't. It wouldn't be true. No, I'd had just enough. I'd had the best freaking night of my life in bed with a man who, up until a couple of weeks ago had seemed to hate me. No, that was too strong. He just really, really didn't like me.

His head lifted and our gazes connected. And for a second, I thought I saw heat in his eyes. Heat for me. My body answered with a wave of achy longing that made me want to hug myself tight.

"Hey. Sorry." He blinked and the heat was gone. "I didn't see you there."

"I didn't mean to sneak up on you. If you're busy, I can—"

"No, come in." He waved me into the room. "I'm just going over the daily schedules."

I sat in one of the chairs at the table, trying to get comfortable and not squirm. "Looks like you're not impressed."

He took one of the chairs opposite me, leaning back a little, hands spread out on the table in front of him. I couldn't help myself. I had to look, remembering where those hands had been and what they'd done to me. It was all I could do to drag my gaze away and aim it over his shoulder.

"They're good. I want to make them better."

Wait, what were we talking about? Oh, hockey camp. That's why I was here. Not to stare at his hands. Or want to sink my fingers in his thick dark hair. I blinked and redirected my gaze to his shoulder.

"I'm sure the kids will love whatever you come up with."

I absolutely believed that. Rebel was nothing if not dedicated to the game. He loved it. You could see it when he played. He put his whole heart and soul into it.

"What's wrong?"

The question came out of the blue, leaving me scrambling to catch up. "What? Nothing."

His gaze narrowed. "Did something happen?"

Jeez, was it written on my face that my mom's call had flustered the hell out of me?

"Nothing happened. I'm fine." I think I might have grimaced. "I mean, my mom called to tell me she's visiting next week but..."

"Does she do that often?"

He had to know she didn't. Then again, he didn't really know me.

Except for all the things he'd learned about me the night we'd spent together.

"No, she doesn't."

"Do you want to see her?"

Did he really want to know the answer to that question or was he just making small talk? His expression gave me absolutely no clues to what he was thinking. But he'd asked the question so...

I shrugged. "I have a lot on my plate next week. Including the players' lunches. Do you want to go over the menus?"

That seemed like a safe discussion, one that wasn't so… personal.

"Your plate always seems a little too full."

Did he actually sound concerned?

Now I did squirm, just a little. "I like to keep busy."

He leaned back and crossed his arms over his chest. "Are we going to talk about what happened after the reception or are we just going to keep ignoring that it happened?"

Now my jaw dropped. Holy hell, that had come out of the blue.

I almost couldn't believe he'd said anything at all. I honestly thought he'd want to forget it happened.

"Do *you* want to talk about it?"

His chin lifted slightly. "I think we probably should, yeah."

"I'm not sure what we have to talk about. I mean, we both know what happened. We probably both had a little too much to drink and—"

"I wasn't drunk. Not by a longshot."

Oh. "Umm…"

So that meant…what?

"Were you?" he asked.

Should I lie? That didn't seem fair, not when he seemed to be laying it all out there for me to see.

"No. I mean…" I sighed. "No, I wasn't."

I'd known exactly what I was doing. And exactly *who* I was doing. And I'd enjoyed every damn minute of it.

He nodded, like he'd known what I was going to say before I said it. And he probably had.

"So what now?"

"What do you mean?"

"What do we do now?"

He spoke calmly and enunciated every word clearly, and my heart thumped a little faster. It almost seemed—

No, I didn't want to get ahead of myself.

"What do you mean?"

"I mean, where do we go from here? Do you want us to go back to our respective corners and pretend it never happened?"

It sounded brutal when he said it that way, and my stomach immediately dropped at the thought. Is that what he wanted?

"Or do you want to see how much better we could be now?"

My stomach hollowed out, just before a fierce desire fired through my blood. I wanted that second option. His words hung between us like a promise.

"What do you want, Rebel?"

"I asked you first."

His response made me laugh. I knew he was joking. His face gave nothing away, but I heard it in his voice. I don't know how, but I just knew it was there.

His lips twitched, but the intensity in his eyes deepened, drawing me in. I almost felt a physical pull toward him. What would he do if I climbed on top of the table and slid into his lap? Would I shock him?

Hell, I'd shock myself. But I still wanted to do it.

I took a breath, my gaze holding his. After a lingering pause, he stood. I followed his every move as he walked around the table. Closer to me. His body loomed over me, and my mouth dried. My hands gripped the chair arms, making a conscious effort to remain seated.

Part of me wondered if this was actually going to happen.

Were we—

Yep, we were.

He reached for me, hands on my shoulders pulling me to my feet so he could kiss me. And when I mean kiss, I mean he kissed me with so much force, I had to reach for his shoulders and hold on.

I swore I felt every inch of his desire like a physical presence wrapped around me. I also felt the hard imprint of his erection against my stomach. His track pants hid absolutely nothing, and he was so very hard.

I lifted my hips into him, rubbing against that ridge, my own need getting more demanding. Every day since the wedding, it'd been growing, like a hungry little pit in my stomach. I'd tried to ignore it, but it just kept growing. And now he'd let it out of its cage.

I kissed him back with just as much passion, adding fuel to his fire.

Wrapping his arms around my waist, he lifted me off my feet and turned to set me on the table, not pausing our kiss for a second. I was impressed by his dexterity just before my hormones took over again and demanded more.

My hands slid down his back and under his shirt, seeking and finding warm skin beneath. That warmth seeped into my skin, shooting tingles up my arms and straight to my nipples and lower.

Every erogenous zone of my body said "Yes, more, please."

And because I thought Rebel could read my mind, he slid his hands from my hips up my sides and cupped my breasts. I moaned into his mouth, my hands sinking into his back, nails probably leaving marks.

He groaned, a rumble in his chest that made me yearn to feel even more of his skin against mine. His head tilted, deepening the kiss as his tongue teased mine. And then it was no longer teasing but demanding. I was willing to give him anything he wanted right now.

I was willing to let him take me right here on the table. Or up against the wall. Honestly, I didn't care so long as he filled this growing ache.

I pulled away, saw his eyes open, and his expression freeze. Like he was afraid of what I was going to say or do. He was afraid I wanted to stop. My stomach fizzed like I'd swallowed an entire box of those crackly candies.

"Door."

The tension drained from his face, and he smiled. Getting one of Rebel's smiles felt like I'd won the lottery. There'd been a time when I couldn't imagine him smiling at me. And I hadn't known then how much it would mean now.

Dangerous territory.

Fuck. That.

I hadn't felt this way about a man since my fiancé had dumped me. Now I was going to soak it all in, as much as I could take, and gorge myself on Rebel.

Reaching behind me, he snagged the edge of the door and gave it a shove. It closed with a loud bang. If anyone else had been in the building, they would've heard it and probably come to investigate. I didn't care. And, yeah, maybe the chance of being caught added a little extra thrill.

I didn't have time to think, though. He kissed me again. Deep and hard and completely without restraint.

His hands slid under my t-shirt, pushing it up until I lifted my arms over my head so he could take it off. Patting myself on the back for putting on a pretty lace bra today, I watched his gaze move down my body. When he looked back up into mine, his smile was gone but the heat burned even hotter.

"Did you wear this for me?"

What should I say? The truth was, yeah, probably. I'd chosen it. It made me feel sexy, and it looked good against my pale skin. And in some deep part of my brain, I'd had this little fantasy going of us doing exactly this. Hooking up. Except for me it wasn't just a hookup.

And when Rebel looked at me like that, it didn't feel like just anything to him, either. He looked deadly serious. Except for that tiny hint of a smile left on his lips.

Thrusting my hands into his hair, I tugged him back down so our lips could meld again, but he pulled back a few seconds later.

"Did you?"

Did I really want to answer that question? If I answered truthfully, he might think—What? That I was hot for him? Well, that should be obvious. And since he seemed to share the exact same feelings…it made me feel comfortable enough to reach for the hem of his shirt and tug it up and over his head.

He let it go without a fight, and I think I might have sighed like a lovesick Victorian lady in a movie. That expanse of muscled chest made all my girl parts clench and tighten and ache. In the bright light of day, or at least in the light of the overhead fixture, he looked like the hockey god he was. Hard, hot and ready for any action.

I leaned forward and pressed my lips right in the center of his chest. The heat of his skin made me want to taste him all over. My hands flattened on the ridges of his abdomen before sliding around to his back to sink my fingers into the hard muscle there.

He threaded his hands through my hair, holding my head steady as I kissed my way across and then up his neck to his lips. He took over the second our lips touched, and I was more than happy to let him. Damn, the man could kiss.

His lips worked their magic as his hands fell to my hips and began to gather up my skirt. My legs were already spread to make room for his, but when the cool air hit my thighs, I shivered. He pulled me closer, my skirt riding even higher, until I felt the brush of his track pants, and what lay hot and hard behind them, against my sex. Everything inside me fluttered and went liquid, ready for him.

I worked my hands back to the front of his pants and slid my fingers beneath the waistband. He pulled away, breathing heavily, his head dipped but his eyes open, watching me. I didn't have the patience to take it slow and shoved his pants down to his thighs, careful not to hurt any delicate parts of him. But his cock seemed more than sturdy enough to take a little rough handling. He'd absolutely liked my hands on him that night.

"What are you waiting for?"

I tipped my head back to look up at him.

"Nothing. I don't want to wait."

"Good. Because I don't have a lot of patience right now."

"Me either."

He wore dark boxer briefs that I took a second to admire before I shoved them down, too. And laid my eyes on the true star of the show.

God, he was gorgeous. I sighed and looked up at him, but he was staring at my breasts, just before he cupped them in his hands. He squeezed, eliciting a moan from me, the pressure and heat of his hands promising so much more pleasure.

Since neither of us wanted to take the time to go slow, he released my breasts and laid his hands flat on my thighs. They were already parted around his thighs, but he widened them even more, exposing my silky panties. Which were now in the way.

He took a step back and took my panties with him. My legs had to close to allow him to do that, but the second he stuffed them in his back pocket, he worked himself between my thighs again, spreading them even wider than before. The cool air played against my aching folds, tormenting. My clit ached and my sex clenched, and I grabbed his hips to bring him even closer.

His cock brushed against my mound, but I realized then that the height of the table wasn't going to cut it. He must have realized the same thing at the same time.

"Condom. In my wallet. Put it on."

I quivered all over at the sound of his voice… and at the command, said in a voice so growly, I wanted to squeak with excitement.

Instead, I reached around to grab his wallet out of his back pocket, took out the condom and tossed his wallet on the desk behind me.

As I rolled the condom down his shaft, I knew he watche my every move, his gaze a hot brand on my skin.

"Hang on."

I understood the assignment. I wrapped my arms around his shoulders as he picked me up, turning until my back was against the door.

I held his gaze as he positioned himself then thrust home. My eyes closed as he filled me, my arms tightening around his neck and my head falling forward to rest against his. His heavy breath brushed against my cheek just before I felt his lips brush my forehead.

His arms held me tight, my legs wrapped around his waist as he took it slow at first, stealing my breath with each movement. With both hands on my hips, he controlled the rhythm. He controlled my response. And I liked it. I liked all of it. I liked the feel of him moving inside me. I liked the sense of being held and letting go.

I loved...this. Being close to him and feeling him move inside me. The friction gave me tingles, then shudders as my sex clenched around him, pulling him deeper.

Rebel groaned as he thrust harder and then held, stretching me wide.

"Fuck, Erin."

My arms tightened, pulling our bodies closer together until there was no space between us. My chin rested against his shoulder as he picked up the pace, his hands flexing in concert with his thrusts.

"You feel amazing."

His voice slid into my ear and straight to my clit, which needed just a little more friction for me to come. I arched just a little and...

Oh, god, yes. That was it.

I came hard, my body convulsing around him. I turned my head and let my teeth sink into his neck. With a groan, his hips snapped harder, losing his rhythm as he came.

"So, what happens now?"

My question fell into the silence like a tiny warning gong.

He'd gone quiet as we put our clothing back together, and I tried to tell myself that was just Rebel. He didn't run his mouth like other guys. When he had something to say, he said it. Maybe he just didn't have anything to say right now.

And maybe he had a lot to say but didn't know how.

But that wasn't Rebel, either. He knew how and when to use his words. If he wasn't talking now—

"Now you tell me what you want to happen."

Surprise that he'd actually spoken made my heart skip a few beats.

He wanted to know what I wanted? That was easy. I wanted him.

But it just wasn't that easy, was it?

I mean, sure, we could announce to everyone we were dating and have them all look at us like we were crazy. Up until a couple of weeks ago, we couldn't be in the same room together without wanting to strangle each other. Then they'd all go on with life as usual and everything would be fine. Except… he was going to leave. His life wasn't here in St. David anymore. It was in Reading with his new team.

Not that Reading was that far away. It wasn't. But—

"Erin." The low rumble in his voice made me want to sigh. "Stop overthinking. Just tell me. What do you want to happen here? With us?"

I shook my head. And stuttered out a reply. "I'm not sure. I mean, I wanted this to happen. Of course, I did. I just…" I stopped on a huff. "What do you want, Rebel?"

He sat on the edge of the table where we'd just had amazing sex, hands braced on either side of his hips. My gaze caught and held on his forearms. On the tendons I wanted to trace with my fingertips.

"I want to keep seeing you."

"You mean…like friends with benefits? I mean, are we even friends?"

His jaw did that little clench-and-release thing that fascinated me. And made my thighs clench.

"I don't think we have to classify our relationship. We're

explosive together in bed...and on tables, apparently. I don't think that's something we should ignore just. I know we haven't exactly been close until now. If we're both having fun, why not continue?"

My brain spun those words around in my head like plates on sticks.

Classify. Relationship. Explosive. Fun.

I tried to pick up any kind of clue as to what he wanted. But then I realized. He'd just told me. He wanted to have fun. He didn't want to classify what was going on. Reading between the lines, I understood that he didn't want anyone to know what we were doing.

I got it. I was friends with his sister. We owned a business together. Our lives were tangled together in ways that could seriously affect our relationships. And yet...

There was part of me that wanted more. And I needed to decide if I'd be okay with not having it.

"I think I need a little time to decide if this is what I want."

He didn't respond right away, but he didn't look angry or upset, and finally he nodded.

"If that's what you want."

Oh hell, I didn't know what I wanted, but I did know I wasn't ready to give him an answer right this minute. Honestly, I didn't know what I should do.

"You know what?" I said, "I think we should meet tomorrow at the café to go over the menus. If that's okay?"

I wasn't sure I could think straight now. My underwear rubbed against my clit, an achy little reminder of what we'd been up to. Before I could change my mind—or lay him out on the table this time—I turned and headed out the door.

He didn't follow and just before I turned to walk down the

hall, I turned and caught a quick glimpse of him, head down, hands clenched on the edge of the table.

It made my lungs clench and my steps falter. But I knew if I went back in there, I'd give him what he wanted. I'd been there and done that with another man, and he'd broken my heart. I'd tried to be the person my former fiancé had wanted but, in the end, that person hadn't been me.

I just didn't know if I could be the person he wanted me to be.

Even though I knew he could be the man I needed.

*Rebel*

"Hey Coach? Um, I, um, I got a problem."

Day four of camp, and I was pretty pleased with how it was going. The kids were eager to learn and happy to be here. Well, except for Baylor Cunningham. He showed up every day ready to train, but he lost focus often, and it'd been a struggle keeping him in line. He had a comeback to everything, but it was starting to affect the rest of the team.

I hadn't figured out yet if he was being deliberately disruptive or if there was something else going on.

"What's up, Cunningham?"

I tried not to let the edge show in my voice. I had plans to corner Erin tonight. I knew she had book club, and I planned to be there. And no, I hadn't read the damn book, and I didn't care.

She couldn't avoid me if there were other people around,

and I was tired of waiting for her to come to me. I knew she was busy, knew she had way too much on her plate, but the ache in the pit of my stomach kept growing. I wanted to see her. Wanted to spend time with her. And if some of that time was naked, all the better.

And if she told me she didn't want to spend time with me, well, at least I'd know for sure. For all that she liked to talk, she'd avoided talking to me for the past week. Even though I saw her every day, there never seemed to be time to discuss what had happened.

But I couldn't head out until all of the kids had been picked up.

"Um, my dad's not answering his phone, and my mom can't get away from work. Do you, uh, do you think I could get a ride to the library. Mom said she'd pick me up there when she's done."

The kid had my full attention now. I'd read all the campers' info before we'd started and, though I hadn't memorized all the facts, I knew Bay was one of the youngest here. His bright copper hair and blue eyes set him apart. So did his skill. The kid could skate, and he was a damn good defenseman. But I'd noticed his gear was well used, verging on unusable.

I'd already decided to get the kid a couple new sticks and pads, though I'd wanted to talk to his parents first. The problem was, I hadn't met them yet. He'd gotten a ride with one of the other kids every day.

"What time's your mom get off from work?"

"Uh, not sure."

"You want me to drive you home?"

Now the kid flushed bright red. "We live pretty far out. And…" his shoulders lifted and lowered awkwardly. "I don't like being there alone. I'd rather wait for my mom at the library. I could walk, but I—"

"Hell, no. You got too much stuff." A whole list of questions began to tick off in my mind, but I wasn't going to ask them now. The kid seemed embarrassed, and I wasn't going to rub salt in a wound I couldn't see. "I'm headed into town for dinner anyway. Hey, you wanna get some food? I could use the company."

His head popped up and his eyes widened. "Really? Yeah, sure. I mean, if you really don't mind?"

"I don't. You'd be doing me a favor. I won't look so pathetic."

"Thanks, Coach."

I snagged the kid's bag off the floor while he grabbed his stick and trailed after me out the door. Where we found Ian, trying to start his deathtrap of a truck. He looked ready to start banging his head against the steering wheel until he caught sight of me. Then his face flamed bright red. Christ, the kid didn't need to be embarrassed because he couldn't pay to get his damn car fixed. I knew now that he was sending money to his sister in college so she didn't have to work during school. But it left him short. I made a mental note to increase his salary for helping out at camp so he could fix the damn truck.

I stopped at the driver's side and bent forward as he rolled down the window.

"Hey, Bay and I are heading into town for some dinner. You wanna come?"

I'd never had to live from one paycheck to the next, but my parents had raised us to believe it wasn't the amount of money in your bank account that mattered. Only your character mattered. And Ian was one of the best people I knew.

"I can't get the truck started."

He looked so fucking frustrated and ashamed that I wanted to buy him a new fucking truck on the spot. But I knew that wasn't the way to handle the situation. It's not the way Pop would handle it.

"Lock it up and leave it. We'll come back tomorrow and get it working or get it towed back to the house so we can take a look at it. Actually, Pop's pretty good with engines. I'll call him. He loves to fu—uh, play around with engines. It's a hobby."

And if Pop couldn't fix it, then we'd figure it out.

The relief on his face told me I'd handled it the right way, and after Ian locked up his truck, the three of us headed into town in my truck to get something to eat. Ian and I had kept up a steady stream of conversation, mostly talking about hockey and Ian's truck, which apparently held a lot of senti-mental value since it came from his granddad.

Which meant I wouldn't just be able to help him buy a new car.

"So, my dad works on old cars a lot." Bay had been quiet since we got in the car, which was unusual for him, but he leaned forward to speak from the back seat. "He might be able to help with that."

"I thought your dad worked at the lumber yard." I glanced in the rearview to see Bay nod. "Yeah, but cars are his hobby. He likes to fix them up."

And it probably pulled in extra money, which helped with a daughter in college. There was a local garage and a chain lube-oil business in town, but this was the first I'd heard about another mechanic.

"Sounds good. Ian, you can give him a call tomorrow."

I glanced over to see Ian doing calculations in his head with his bank account.

"Sure, I can do that."

But I heard the tone in his voice, and I knew the calculations weren't in his favor. Shit.

We decided to go to Paolo's for pizza. Bay had called his mom and told her what was going on. She'd wanted to talk to me, too, apologizing profusely for not being able to get Bay on time. I'd assured her it wasn't a problem, and we were going to grab some food.

She released a quiet sigh. "Thank you, Rebel. I'll put some money on his card—"

"That's not necessary. But I do have a favor to ask. Bay said your husband works on older model engines, and our assistant coach is having an issue with his truck. Would your husband—"

"Oh, of course! Daniel was planning to take Bay to camp tomorrow. He could take a look at it then. Daniel loves to tinker, and he hasn't had a new project lately. He'll be thrilled."

I thanked Mrs. Cunningham and handed the phone back to Bay, who looked a hell of a lot happier now. Even Ian's expression looked a little lighter. And maybe I felt a little pleased with myself for solving the situation.

Dinner with Bay and Ian was the most relaxed I'd been in days. Talking hockey with them eased some of that tight knot in my chest, though not all. The situation with Erin still weighed on my mind.

The way she'd left the arena the other day... My back teeth ground together. I'd wrestled with the way we'd left it the other day, but I wasn't sure how to fix it. And yeah, I knew I was the one who had the problem.

She'd needed something from me, something more than I'd been willing to give. Hell, I still didn't know what I wanted.

The only thing I knew for sure was that I wanted her. We had off-the-chart chemistry. I'd never wanted another woman the way I craved her. But I hadn't seen her or heard from her since last week. I'd met her at the bakery to go over the menus, like she'd asked, but it'd been all business. We'd talked food since we'd had an audience. The two women who worked in the bakery for Erin were in and out of the kitchen, along with a few customers who straggled in throughout the entire hour I was there. There'd been absolutely no time to discuss our situation.

And I'm not sure she would've wanted to. I'd pissed her off or upset her, and I didn't know what to do to make it better. I didn't know what she wanted.

"Hey, Reb, you finished?"

My attention snapped back, and I gave the server a nod. "Yeah, sorry."

"Everything okay?" Ian asked, giving me a questioning look.

"Just zoned out for a second."

"Are you stoked to get back to your team?"

Bay's wide-eyed look of excitement made me cover a wince. I really had to make up my mind.

"I'm stoked to get back to playing hockey."

Ian took the ball and ran with it, telling Bay about training camp and meeting new teammates and being excited to see the old ones. Bay asked a few questions, but mainly Ian rambled.

But there was something in Ian's voice that clued me in to the fact that he had some reservations going on, too. Something we were gonna need to talk about. I was fast coming to the realization that I didn't want to resign with the Redtails.

Instead of letting Ian twist himself into a pretzel trying to convince himself he was excited to go back, I asked Bay about camp. Bay had a lot to say about that, all of it and an hour and a half later we stopped only because Bay's mom hurried through the door, apologized profusely for not being able to pick him up on time and thanking me several times before hustling him out the door, with the promise that her husband would drop Bay off tomorrow morning and take a look at Ian's truck.

After I paid the bill, telling Ian I was going to write it off as a business expense, I had an idea. Kind of a sneaky one, but still.

"Hey, you mind taking my truck home. I need to talk to Erin about…something."

Ian's lips curved before he caught back a true smile. But I could still see it shining in his eyes.

"Sure, but I could just hang around if you want."

"No. That's okay. Not sure how long I'll be."

Ian's smile grew, but surprisingly, he didn't say anything snarky.

"I won't wait up for you."

Okay, he didn't say anything too snarky. Shaking my head, we walked out of the restaurant. He headed for my truck while I headed for the bookstore. It was only a couple of blocks away, and the night was beautiful. Yeah, it was hot, but there was a breeze, and the sun had fallen behind the hills so it wasn't oppressive.

Several shops remained open late on Thursdays, main street windows glittering from the inside lights and the remaining sunlight. I stopped in front of the bookstore, looking inside. There seemed to be a lot of people for a weekday night at six-thirty, but then I realized it was teen book-club night, which explained all the teenagers in the store.

Several groups of girls sat in clusters around the store, sipping from thermal cups. Eight boys, a few I recognized from camp, sat at a table, playing a game with cards.

Finally, I saw Erin on her knees in front of a little boy who couldn't be more than five, who looked ready to cry. She held his hands and looked into his eyes. I didn't recognize the kid. But I knew that look on Erin's face. She listened with her whole body to what he was saying, nodding as he said spoke. She didn't say anything until it was clear the little boy was finished, then she said something and, whatever it was, it had a calming effect.

And when she was done, and the boy hitched one last big breath, she smiled and so did he.

God damn, she took my breath away. I mean, literally, I felt like all the air got sucked out of my lungs. Of course, as she got to her feet, she glanced out the window and saw me, staring at her like her own personal stalker.

Neither of us moved, our gazes locked, until she looked down, her attention snagged by the little boy, who tugged on her hand, wanting her to follow him. With a quick smile for me, she turned away and followed the kid to the back of the store.

Since I couldn't just stand there looking through the window without people staring at me funny, I opened the door and walked in.

The first thing that hit me was the noise. Usually the bookstore was an oasis of calm, kind of like a library. Tonight, the music was a little louder and definitely for the younger crowd. The boys at the table talked over each other as they slapped cards on the table. High-pitched teen girls chattered in about twenty different conversations. It all seemed a little chaotic. And perfectly Erin.

Walking farther into the store, I caught sight of her near the back, the little boy she'd been talking to holding her hand while munching a cookie. I followed, knowing I should leave. She was working. And yet I couldn't make myself go. I wondered if I was good, would I get a cookie?

Grinning, I turned around a bookshelf and ran into the object of my desire.

She "oofed," and I grabbed for her shoulders to make sure she didn't go down.

"Whoa, sorry." I kept my hands on her shoulders for longer than necessary and only released her when she looked up at me with arched brows. "You okay?"

Her brows arched higher. "I'm fine. Not the first time I've run into you."

As soon as the final word left her mouth, she flushed bright red. My grin widened, and her gaze dropped to my lips before sliding somewhere around my shoulder.

I couldn't take my eyes off her. She didn't look any different than she had when she'd dropped off lunch today. She wore pink overalls with a white t-shirt, her rose-gold hair braided in her normal style. And yet, something had changed. With me.

It seemed every day my feelings for her intensified, my desire for her smoldering in my gut. I clamped down hard on that. I wore track shorts, for chrissake, and there were teenagers with sharp eyes all over the damn place.

I had the unusual urge to tease her, but again... Kids.

"Looks like you have your hands full tonight."

"Teen night is always busy. But I love having them here."

Her smile did a number on my nerves. I swallowed hard.

"Noisier than normal."

She laughed, the sound running up my spine like fingernails.

"You should be used to that. I've been to your hockey games."

"True."

"Miss Erin, did you read that new book we told you about yet? You said we could talk about it this week."

The girl, who looked familiar, called to Erin from one of the nearby tables.

"I'll be there in a few seconds, Amelia."

The girl looked over at me, sharp eyes not missing a thing.

"Sorry, didn't realize you'd be so busy. I should let you get back to the kids."

"Did you need something, Rebel?"

Yeah, I just wasn't sure I should. I felt like my life was on hold, that I had too many life decisions to make. And yet, she was the one thing I knew without any doubt that I wanted.

"I do."

I let that hang there for a few seconds, watched her lips part and her eyes widen slightly, waiting for me. Until finally, she huffed.

"And are you going to tell me what that is?"

"No."

Now, her lips curved, and her eyes shone with laughter. How was that even a thing?

"I actually think you're teasing me, but I can't be sure."

"Happy to be a man of mystery."

She laughed, and damn, if I didn't want to pat myself on the back. Or pat her ass, which was probably a sexist thing to say, but she had a great ass, and I appreciated the hell out of it.

Fuck, I needed to get out of here before I embarrassed the hell out of myself and her.

"Hey, Coach, you wanna play?" One of the boys I recognized from camp called to me from the table.

"Hang on, guys, I'll be over in a second."

"Miss Erin," another teenage girl walked over, "we're ready to start book club when you are."

Erin looked at me and shrugged.

"Sorry."

I nodded. "You're busy. I'll let you get back to work."

I could tell she wanted to say something else, but it was there and gone in a split second. Her smile dimmed a little as she looked back at me.

"I guess I'll see you around then."

Absolutely. I just needed to get my shit together and figure out what I was going to do with her.

"I'll see you soon."

CHAPTER TWENTY-TWO

SECOND WEEK OF CAMP

I SPENT the next few days replaying Thursday night and the minute I'd spent talking to Rebel.

I hadn't seen him since then, at least not to talk.

I'd dropped off lunch Friday at the arena, but I'd been running late. Rebel had still been working with one of the kids when I'd left. The bakery had been mobbed Saturday, and I was exhausted by the time I cleaned up and left for the night. When I got home, I considered texting him but fell asleep on the couch and didn't wake up until midnight and went to bed.

And dreamed about Rebel.

I woke up sweaty and horny. I considered texting him Sunday to ask if he wanted to get together. But I didn't want that dream to influence any decisions I might make. And every time I was around Rebel, my brain felt like some had stuck a whisk in there and scrambled it around.

Since I'd lived most of my life with my brain stuck in a whirlwind, I knew this was different. I *liked* Rebel. I more than liked Rebel. And that was a problem. I wasn't sure how he felt about me.

Ugh. I felt like the awkward teenager I'd been fifteen years ago. And it was only going to get worse. My mom would be here in half an hour.

Yay.

Not.

Now the guilty hit. I should be happy to see my mom. And I was. I just knew I'd be exhausted by the time she left, no matter how long she stayed.

"Top me off, kiddo. Need a little more caffeine to deal with my daughter."

Granddad sat at a table in the bakery, waiting for my mom to make her appearance. Most of the breakfast rush had come through already and only a few tables were taken. Great. Something else for Mom to comment on.

Okay, get a grip.

I gave the refrigerated case another swipe with glass cleaner to make sure it gleamed, then turned around to make sure all the tables were clean and there was nothing on the floor.

"Sweetheart, take a load off. The place looks great. There's nothing to criticize."

I snorted. "Have you met my mom?"

Wincing, I walked over to give my granddad a hug. "Sorry. I don't mean to—"

"Oh, honey, no need to apologize." He hugged me back. "Just remember your mom loves you. She's just..." he rolled his eyes, "a little demanding."

I was about to respond when the door opened, and Rebel walked through.

My mouth dropped open.

"What are you doing here? Why aren't you at camp?"

He didn't answer right away. Nodding to Granddad, he walked up to the counter, dressed for camp in track pants and a dark t-shirt with the Devil's logo that molded lovingly to his chest. My attention stuck on how good he looked in that shirt, and when he got to the counter, he leaned against the counter, his gaze holding mine.

"I need coffee. And a cherry almond scone."

Words wouldn't come, my brain trying to make sense out of what he'd said.

"Coffee? You have coffee at the arena." I shook my head, like I was trying to make the words, out of the corner of my eye, I saw my granddad shake his head and turn to the side, but not before I glimpsed his smile. What was going on?

Then I caught sight of the other customers, all of whom were regulars, staring at us and grinning. If Rebel saw any of this, he either didn't care or... well, he probably just didn't care.

Wait, did they know what had happened the night of the wedding?

No. No way. No one knew about that. I hadn't told anyone, and I know Rebel wouldn't have told anyone.

Oh my god, maybe someone had seen us at the arena? No, that was even more unlikely—

"Erin. Coffee. Black, please."

I refocused on Rebel, eyes narrowed as I tried to figure out what was going on. Did I have something on my face? Was my skirt ripped and my ass was showing? What the hell was going on?

With a huff, I turned to the coffee machines, grabbed an extra-large cup, because that's all he ever ordered, and filled it to the brim. I reached for a lid, figuring he'd take it and go, but he said, "Don't bother. I'll drink it here."

Okay, now I knew something was up. I set the cup in front of him and crossed my arms over my chest, staring at him like I could get him to tell me what was going on with only the power of my gaze.

He stared back, his lips puckering to blow on the steaming coffee. Damn the man for having lips I wanted to bite—and feel on the inside of my thighs. Heat started at the top of my head and worked its way down my body, right to my core.

Shit, shit, shit.

I absolutely did not need this now. Not when my mom's Town Car pulled up to the curb outside the bakery. I sucked in air, my desire for Rebel combining with the anxiety of my mom's visit, making me a complete flaming idiot.

Until Rebel put his hand over the fist I was making with my left hand. I hadn't even known I was doing it, but the warmth of his grip made me relax, just enough to take a deep breath.

"I'd really like that scone to go with the coffee."

His soft rumble drew my attention away from the window, where the driver was getting out of the car and walking around to back passenger door. His dark gaze held mine, reminding me of the time we'd spent together lately. Naked. And a little of that anxiety about my mom leached away.

There were so many reasons that shouldn't be possible. And yet, Rebel made it so. Our secret affair (how that word fit into my life right now was crazy) gave me something else to obsess—no, to focus on. Having Rebel here helped ground me.

I hadn't even noticed my mom get out of the car, but the

door to the bakery opened, the little antique bell tinkling as it did, and my mom walked through. Before I could watch her dissect my pride and joy with her critical mind, I turned to get a plate so I could get Rebel his scone.

Behind me, I heard my granddad say, "Hello, Pammie. How are you, sweetheart?"

I heard my mom's slightly annoyed, slightly amused sigh at the nickname, the one only her father was allowed call her. And then she hugged him.

"Daddy, it's good to see you. All this country air you keep talking about must have magical properties. You look… better."

Now she had my full attention. My mom didn't give out compliments often. And even though that might sound like a back-handed one to some people, I heard actual emotion in her voice.

In my mind, I heard my therapist's voice say, *Just because your mother doesn't act like you doesn't mean she doesn't have feelings. She just expresses them differently than you do.*

But then she turned to me, and I felt myself put on that fake smile I always used around her.

In my peripheral vision, I saw Rebel's gaze narrow, like he knew I was faking it. I watched him turn from the counter, walk over to Granddad's table and set his coffee and plate down.

"Pammie," Granddad said, "I want you to meet Rebel Lawrence. Rebel, my daughter, Pamela Wright."

My mom turned to Rebel, in his t-shirt and track pants, and I braced for her to dismiss him with barely a look. Instead, she took his hand.

"Reston Lawrence's son, yes?"

Oh my god. Rebel smiled at her. Like, flat-out smiled, and

it was glorious. I had the insane urge to tell my mom that I'd slept with him, twice, as if that might give me a little more standing in her eyes.

"Yes, Ma'am."

Jesus, you need to get a grip.

The world felt out of whack today. Rebel wasn't supposed to be here. He wasn't supposed to be talking to my mom. I still didn't know why he wasn't at practice. Had something happened?

And my mom was here, and she and Granddad had hugged. Actually embraced. I couldn't remember the last time they'd done that. Then again, I couldn't remember the last time they'd been in the same room together since I'd moved here almost five years ago.

Okay, that was an exaggeration. Granddad and I had gone home to the Hamptons for Christmas last year. And he and Mom had seemed on much better terms then, though I hadn't really noticed. I'd been caught up in my own drama. Like always.

"Erin, honey, your bakery looks charming." Now the world tilted on its side. My mom had just given me a compliment. "Is it a slow time?"

She looked around, assessing everything, and I wanted to rush to tell her that it wasn't always this quiet, that she'd just missed the morning rush and lunch rush wouldn't start for another hour and a half. I felt the need to justify everything.

Instead, I took a deep breath and nodded. "Yes, it is."

"Good. Then you have time to talk."

I didn't really. I needed to get started on to-go sandwiches, and I had rolls and bread in the ovens.

"Actually, I have some things to do in the back. You can come with me, if you want."

Her brows arched, the only outward sign of her surprise. "Of course. I'd love to see the kitchen."

Since I couldn't tell if she was being sarcastic or sincere, I nodded and turned to lead her into the back.

"I've got to prep for lunch, so we can talk back here."

Checking the bread, I pulled it out just before the buzzer was ready to do off. My mom walked over to the racks where I stored the bread and drew in a deep breath.

"Oh, that smells amazing. I'd love to try some, but gluten doesn't agree with me anymore."

Since she sounded sincere, I pushed down the hurt that she didn't want to try my bread and asked, "I'm sorry. Is that a new issue?"

She hummed an acknowledgement. "I was diagnosed as gluten intolerant about a year ago. It's definitely taken some getting used to."

I froze. "I didn't know that."

Mom looked me in the eye. "You haven't been around to tell."

While I looked at her with my mouth hanging open, she strolled around the room, looking at everything. The ovens were well used, and the outside could do with a little polish, but everything was clean. Sure, there were crumbs everywhere and my decorating tools sat in the sink to be washed along with several muffin tins and cake pans. The hockey camp lunches lay unconstructed but ready to be put together on the prep table on the far side of the room.

"How are you making out with your businesses?" she said. "Are they doing well? The town seems pretty small to support both."

Like my therapist suggested, I took a few seconds to think about my response, to not react out of hurt or anger. Mom hadn't really said anything that I hadn't considered myself, hadn't questioned my judgement. She'd asked a question.

"Actually, we're doing well. The bakery is growing every month, and we just hired a full-time employee at the bookstore."

"Do you work here alone? Seems like too much for one person to handle alone."

Another breath. "This is our slow time, so the staff usually take a couple of hours before the lunch rush."

Mom nodded, still walking around the room until she stood next to me.

In her heels, she stood a couple of inches taller than me. Her hair remained its natural blonde with some chemical help, but she still looked…perfect. Her makeup looked professionally done, even though I knew she did it herself every morning. She never went anywhere without it, but she didn't wear a lot. She had that old-money look you couldn't get from makeup alone. You had to be born into it.

My sister looked a lot like my mom. Blonde and blue-eyed. Straight nose and perfect cheekbones. She'd had the ice princess thing down from the moment she could walk. Our brother took after our dad. Tall, fair hair, handsome.

None of them expressed emotion well. And not one of them had a problem with it.

I looked like my great-grandmother on my mom's side. Actually, if you looked at pictures of us side-by-side through the years, it'd be hard to tell us apart, except for the fact that my teeth were perfectly straight thanks to braces.

My grandmother had been an immigrant who'd fallen for her employer's son. That story had had a happy ending, thankfully. My parents had married because their parents had decided they'd make a perfect match. They did.

I just didn't seem to fit.

"You look tired." My mom's gaze swept me up and down, and I felt the old resentment and hurt bubbling up. "You need to take better care of yourself. I worry about you here all alone, taking care of your grandfather alone. You both should be back in New York, where your family can help."

You know she means well. You know she means well. You know she means well.

"Granddad and I have each other. We're fine. We're happy here."

I wish that hadn't come out as defensive as it sounded. I winced when my mom's brows arched again.

Two brow arches already. Wow, you're killing it today.

She took another look around the kitchen, as if it could tell her more than my words.

"You've made a good start here," she said, before giving me a brief smile. "If you need us, you know your father and I will be ready to help you with whatever you need."

I knew that. I just wish I didn't feel like she thought I couldn't handle this one on my own. Hurt twined around my heart, but I refused to let it take root. I had the sense that she meant well, and I tried to focus on that.

"I…Thanks, Mom. I'm really glad you had time to stop by. I'm just sorry I don't have more time to spend with you. I've got to get these lunches made for the hockey campers."

She didn't say anything for several seconds, before nodding and giving me a slight smile. Then she shocked the hell out of me by stepping up to give me a hug. She wrapped her arms around my shoulders and pulled me close.

My mom wasn't a hugger. She was a cheek kisser, never really comfortable with PDA as I got older. And it wasn't just me. My brother and sister got the same treatment. They never seemed to mind. As I'd gotten older, I'd realized it was a Her problem and not a Me problem.

My arms wrapped around her, and I hugged her back, a happy little smile curving my lips. Then she pulled back and patted my cheek before she turned to walk out of the kitchen.

I couldn't help myself. I followed, watched her lean down to kiss my granddad and pat him on the shoulder.

"Don't be a stranger, Daddy. You know James and I would love to have you visit. And you know there's always room for you in our home." Then she turned to Rebel. "It was nice to meet you, Mr. Lawrence."

Before she walked out the door, she turned to look at me once more. "See you at the wedding, dear."

I faked a smile and nodded, watching until she got in her car and drove away. My head spinning, I turned and headed back to the kitchen, way too much swimming through my brain at the moment. I took a few deep breaths before I grabbed a knife and started slicing the rolls so I could make the sandwiches.

After a few seconds, I saw movement in the doorway and looked up to see Rebel push through the swinging door. He didn't speak as he leaned against the wall, arms crossed over his chest.

Emotions swirled inside of me, so many I couldn't pick them apart. Surprise. Shock. A little guilt.

And now Rebel stood there, staring at me.

Finally, I couldn't take it anymore. I pointed the knife at Rebel.

"If you're here for the lunches, they're not ready yet."

His lips quirked in what passed for a smile from him.

"You going to carve me up and put me in the sandwiches? I don't think I'd taste too good, although after leaving them with Bonesaw and Ian for the morning, the kids might appreciate seeing me carved up."

It was such a bad joke that I really shouldn't laugh. But I did. It almost sounded like a bark, and my hand shot up to my mouth to cover it. Luckily, it wasn't the one holding the knife.

He waited a beat before he said, "You okay?"

Was I crazy to think he actually cared? Or was I seeing what I wanted to see and not what was truly there? But if he didn't care, why was he here?

I shook my head, though that wasn't my answer to his question. "I just feel like I'm never enough for her."

Well, shit. That was way more than I'd wanted to reveal. And probably more than he'd wanted to know. But he was here, and I needed to talk. No, I *wanted* to talk to him. I wanted him to tell me everything was going to be okay. That was so ridiculous, I should be ashamed of myself.

"Why do you think that?"

I rolled my eyes. "Just forget I said that."

"Not gonna happen."

"Don't you need to get back to camp?"

He shrugged. "Ian and Bonesaw have it covered."

"Rebel, I need some space."

"Is that why you've been avoiding me?"

Grr, this wasn't the conversation I wanted to be having now. I didn't want to be having any conversation now. Not with him.

Liar.

"I haven't been avoiding you." *Yes, you have.* "I've been busy."

His gaze dropped to my lips, and the by-now familiar heat rolling through my body in waves. I wanted to kiss him. Or I wanted him to kiss me. I didn't really care which way that went, but I had no idea where we stood, what was going to happen with us. He was leaving—

"Erin."

"Yes."

That was definitely an answer to a question he hadn't asked. If he was asking me if he could kiss me, that was my answer. If he was asking me to leave with him and get naked, that was also my answer.

He pushed away from the wall and closed the distance between us. My heart pounded harder with every step he took until it was in my throat when he stood only inches away from me.

"We need to talk. You can't avoid me forever. And you're fucking amazing. Don't forget that. Don't let her make you feel less than. Because you're fucking not."

While I struggled to breathe, he turned and walked out of the kitchen.

Well, damn.

I just fell completely in love.

Oh, man, I was so screwed.

CHAPTER TWENTY-THREE

Wednesday afternoon after camp, my sister stalked into the room I was using as an office in the arena and shoved the door shut behind her.

I needed to finish these developmental reports for the kids, giving them suggestions for areas they should focus on before their season started. It'd taken me longer than it should have. My mind kept wandering.

I had to give the Redtails my answer next week, and I still wasn't sure what it was going to be. And if I wasn't chewing that over, I was thinking about Erin. Namely, about what we'd done the last time she's been in this building.

I covered a wince at the sound of the door hitting the frame and threw my pencil on the table.

"What the *hell* did you do to Erin? Her mom shows up in a freaking Town Car, does I-don't-know-what to upset Erin and then you follow her into the kitchen, and you both disappear for, oh, between five minutes and half an hour, according to certain sources. Then you walk out, don't say a word to anyone, and Erin isn't talking. What gives?"

Good question. Leaning my elbows on the desk, I watched her drop into the chair across from mine and glare at me.

"Hello to you, too."

Rain's brows arched. "I'm not kidding, Reb. What'd you say to Erin? She's been quiet, and that's not like her."

Damn it. Yeah, it probably was my fault. She'd sent someone else with the lunches today, and I figured I wouldn't see her tomorrow either.

What did you expect, asshole? You'd told her she was amazing and walked out the door. Of course, she wasn't talking. You confused the fuck out of her.

"Your sources tell you her mom is a fricking ice cube? That woman could freeze the balls off a reindeer."

My sister's mouth opened and closed twice before she shook her head, amazed at my skill with words, probably. Then she started to laugh. And laugh. She continued for at least half a minute, and I wasn't sure she was going to stop any time soon. By the time she did, she had to wipe her leaking eyes.

"Oh, my god. What the hell does that even mean? No." She held up her hand, trying to catch her breath. "Don't explain. I think I might have a stroke if you do. Just...give me a minute."

It took her at least another fifteen seconds before she calmed down enough to continue.

"Damn, Reb, you gotta warn a person when you're going to be funny. It's not like you. And yeah, I know her mom's not exactly warm and fuzzy. But I don't think that's all she's upset about. What did you say to her?"

Should I tell her? "Your source didn't tell you?"

Her nose wrinkled. "No. They weren't close enough to hear anything."

I paused for a few seconds. "I told her she shouldn't let her mom get to her."

"And…"

"And what?"

"What else did you say?" She enunciated each word perfectly and slowly. "I know that's not all that happened."

I paused, considered, and decided fuck it. I wanted to know what Rain had to say. "I told her she was fucking amazing."

I don't know what I'd expected Rain to do with that, but it wasn't grin like the fucking Grinch, and not the three-sizes-too-big Grinch. No, it was the evil Grinch grin, the one who was planning to steal Christmas.

She shrugged. "Okay. You're not as stupid as I thought you might be."

I frowned even harder. "What the hell does that mean?"

She looked way too innocent. "I'm not sure what you're asking?"

This was a trap. I'd already told her more than I should have. And yet…

"You're a menace."

"Not the first time you've called me that."

"Won't be the last."

"Aw, there's the grumpy older brother I know and love." She studied me for a second. "Are you going to take her to that wedding?"

"You're a pain in my ass."

She burst out laughing again, nearly doubling over. When

she finally got herself under control again, she said, "Rebel, you like her, right?"

Actually, I more than liked Erin, but I wasn't going to give my sister any more ammunition than she already had. So, I glared her until she calmed down enough to speak again.

"You know I love you," she shook her head, "but you're an idiot."

Now, I glared at her and, when that didn't work, I sighed and studied the wall behind her.

"I've got to finish these reports—"

"You know you could just ask her out, right?"

Of course I could just ask her out, but...

"What happens if I go back to Reading?"

Her eyes shot wide, and I realized what I'd said.

"What do you mean 'if'? Are you seriously thinking about turning down the contract? Is everything okay? Did something happen?"

"Everything's fine. Nothing happened. And would it be the end of the world if I turned down the contract."

She shook her head. "No, not at all. Sorry, that's not... I didn't mean it like..." She huffed out a sigh. "Look, don't take my head off when I say this, but I never really thought you were going to be a good fit with the Redtails."

Biting her bottom lip, she looked at me like I was an unarmed land mine that could go off at any time.

Instead, I just shook my head. "Why didn't you say that before I signed?"

"Oh please. You got what all the guys want. You got *asked* to play up. *They* came to you, which meant they think you're good. Isn't that what everyone wants? To be recognized for their skill?"

When I didn't say anything, she heaved a huge, exaggerated sigh.

"Reb, come on. You're not stupid. You know you're a damn good player. And if you don't, maybe you are an idiot." She pulled a face. "Sometimes you are an idiot. Like this thing with Erin. Dude, we all know something's going on with the two of you—"

"What do you mean, 'we all'?" A pit opened up in my stomach.

"I mean, do you really think people don't see you two making eyes at each other every time you're together? Trust me, we do."

"I'm not making eyes at her."

"Uh huh. Keep telling yourself that. Just don't think we don't see it."

I bit my tongue, trying not to be that guy, the one who asks the juvenile question.

"I'm not sure she wants to deal with me."

She looked at the ceiling as if it might agree with her that I was an idiot. "Have you tried asking her?"

She said that like she was speaking to my younger self. The awkward teenager who barely knew how to talk to girls.

I sighed, shaking my head. "I've got reports to finish."

"Fine. I'll go and leave you to it." She stood and walked to the door, but I knew I wasn't getting off that easy. She turned as she opened it. "Don't be an idiot. And don't miss out on something that could be amazing just because you don't think you should want it."

―――

"HEY COACH, we got something for you."

It was the last day of camp, and the kids had had a blast scrimmaging against the Devils players who were still in the area for the summer and a few of the parents.

I'd just come off the ice after the handshake line and stood in the home bench as the adults left the ice.

Juli Petrovski stood on the ice, stick across her shoulders and hands on either end. One of the best forwards at camp, the sixteen-year-old grinned, eyes bright, brown ponytail hanging over her shoulder.

I glanced up and saw the kids gathered at center ice.

"What's up, Pets?"

Juli glanced over her shoulder and nodded toward the media booth above the penalty box on the other side of the ice. Music pumped out of the speakers, this season's Devils' theme song, making all the kids grin like demons.

Juli backskated to the group, and I laughed as I realized what they were doing.

I don't know when they'd managed it, but the kids had learned the Devil's victory dance. All of the teams in our league had a dance they performed at the end of every game they won. Ours was a line dance that involved a little Electric Slide, a little Hustle and something Rainy called "coordinated chaos."

The kids gave it their all, and honestly, they were a hell of a lot better than the Devils ever had been. The Devils players and the parents crowded into the box with me to watch the kids, shouting encouragement and pumping their fists in the air.

Halfway into the song, Juli came back to the bench, waving at me to join them.

I got a few pats on the back when I didn't move fast enough, but of course, I wouldn't turn down these kids. I'd had the best time with them these past two weeks, and I was going to miss seeing them every day.

My blades hit the ice, and the kids cheered as I got in line with them and finished the dance. It'd been a hell of a long time since I'd done this, and the steps didn't come back as easily as I thought they would. Probably because I was laughing my ass off. And so were the kids.

They circled around me and laughed and sang until the song was over and then they all waved their arms at whoever was in the media booth and the song played again.

This time, the Devils players and the parents hopped on the ice with us. Even though Ian didn't exactly know what was going on, he gave it his best shot, grinning like he'd never had so much fun in his life. Bonesaw had moves, and he and a few of the other kids got pushed into the center of the circle to show off.

I was happy to be back on the outer line, cheering them on. My face hurt from smiling by the time we'd gone through four full songs.

I didn't realize she was there until a few of the adults started to file off the ice, pleading bad knees, bad backs and general old age, which made the kids laugh even more. She stood at the doors to the Zamboni entrance, watching through the glass. Maybe she thought she wouldn't be seen. Maybe she wasn't trying to hide but had just stopped on her way out, curious about the music.

Our gazes met and held. And held. Until finally, I told the kids I'd see them after showers.

Skating over to the open gates, I stopped at the boards and said, "You busy tonight?"

Her eyes blinked open wide, and her lips parted. Then she blew out a short breath.

"I am." She didn't look happy about it, so that was something. "The bookstore's open until eight. Saturday's are always crazy, and Sunday, we have brunch and the bookstore's open until five. Monday, I need to make sure everything's set up before I leave on Wednesday for the wedding next weekend."

When she finally stopped to take a breath, I bit back a smile. "So how about next weekend?"

"Are you… Do you want… Wait. Are you saying you'll come to the wedding with me?"

She looked flustered and unsure, almost like she thought I might be punking her. Which kinda pissed me off.

"That's exactly what I'm saying."

Rapid blinking. I couldn't tell if she was trying not to cry, or she couldn't get her brain to compute. "Seriously? It's such late notice, and I'm sure you have other plans. I'm sorry we haven't spoken about what happened at the bakery. I know you meant well. It's just—"

"Erin. I was serious. Every word I said, I meant. And yes, I want to go to the wedding with you."

The visible relief on her face made something in my chest go soft, but I'd gotten kind of used to that happening around this woman. I think maybe she'd broken me.

No, that wasn't right. She'd fixed a part of me I didn't know was broken.

"Thank you. I just… Thank you." Then she took a breath, and I braced for whatever was coming next. "I have to leave Wednesday. The bridesmaids are having a bachelorette party Wednesday night I have to attend. Not that I want to, but it will look bad if I'm not there. I know it's a lot to ask, but the wedding is Friday night—"

"I'll be there."

She looked afraid to be hopeful. "Don't you start training next week?"

He shook his head. "It's informal. Camp doesn't start until September."

I didn't say which camp I was going to, because I needed to talk to a few people first. But after I did, she was next on the list.

And I hoped to hell it made a difference in the next phase of our relationship. Because, damn it, I wanted that next phase.

Her smile made my already fast-beating heart fill with a feeling I thought might be actual joy.

"Thank you, Rebel. I really appreciate you coming with me."

I wanted to kiss her. My hand itched to wrap around her neck and pull her close. But it wouldn't be fair to make a declaration like that publicly. At least, not yet.

I had to put things in place first. And I had a few people to talk to.

"Me, too. I'm looking forward to it."

———

SATURDAY MORNING, Ian ambled into the kitchen and grabbed the coffee pot like it was a lifeline. His hair looked like he'd stuck his finger in a socket, and he had lines on his face from the pillowcase.

I'd been staring out the back window in the woods for probably fifteen minutes, wrestling with myself. But I knew what I was going to do.

"Hey, you got a minute?" I said.

Ian gulped down two swallows of black coffee and nodded.

"What's up?"

I paused for a second, but I knew this was right.

"I'm not going back. To the Redtails."

The kid's expression went from barely awake to wide awake to miserable in the space of a couple seconds. Then he made a conscious effort to suck it up and smile.

"Hey, that's great for you. I mean, I know you've been thinking about it, and I know you missed home and... Yeah."

He petered out, like he couldn't think of anything more positive to say.

"I've got a question for you."

He nodded and shrugged at the same time, looking for all the world like I'd kicked his puppy.

"Are you happy in Reading?"

His head, which had been drooping, shook back and forth. Still didn't look up at me.

"You want to play here?"

Now his head popped up, eyes wide. "Seriously?"

"We're gonna have a couple of openings. I'm taking one. The other's yours if you want it."

He didn't answer immediately. Then he started to smile.

Closing the distance between us, he wrapped his arms around my shoulders and hugged the shit out of me. I hugged him back until he pulled away but kept a hand on his shoulder.

"I take it the answer is yes."

He nodded. "Yes. Thank you, Reb. Really. I just... Thank you. When my dad said he didn't want me to come home, I didn't know what I was gonna do. I didn't have anywhere else to go."

Tread carefully. "Is there a reason he didn't want you to come home?"

Ian's mouth flattened into a straight line. "It's complicated."

"Most father-son relationships are."

"Yours doesn't seem to be."

Again, I didn't hear jealousy, just sadness.

"My senior year in college, I thought I was going to flunk out. I have depression and anxiety issues I've been dealing forever."

Ian stared at me with wide eyes. "Seriously? You?"

"Yeah. But I only got help after I told my dad what was going on. I thought he'd be disappointed. I thought I was letting him down. It wasn't until we talked that I realized he only wanted to help."

Ian fell silent for several seconds.

"My dad's got early onset Parkinsons," he said. "He's only in this forties, and it's not too bad yet, but we know it's going to get worse. I wanted to spend the summer at home. He said he didn't want me wasting time mourning him while he was still alive."

I thought about that, rolled it over in my head. "I'm sorry about your dad. That's a tough situation."

"It really fucking sucks." Grief and anger interlaced in Ian's voice. "I know there's nothing I can do to change what's happening, but…"

"It kinda sounds like your dad doesn't want to burden you with his problems."

"I thought he'd be happy I wanted to spend the summer at home."

I suddenly realized why Ian's dad had told him to spend the summer like he normally would. Vacationing with friends.

Training. Development. Being a twenty-one-year-old. "He wants you to be happy and enjoy your life. I know it sounds harsh, but maybe he doesn't want you to see him struggling."

That's why I hadn't told my parents how badly I'd been struggling at college. I hadn't wanted them to see me like that. I'd been young and stupid, and I'd needed help.

Ian's dad probably thought this was the best for Ian.

"Have you talk to your dad since you've been here?"

Ian shook his head. "I've been too angry." He sighed. "Do you really think that's what's going on?"

"The only way you're going to know is if you call your dad. Talk to him. Tell him what's going on with you."

"And if he doesn't want to talk to me?"

Pretty sure that wasn't going to happen, but I didn't want to give the kid false hope if I wasn't right.

"Then we'll talk about that later and come up with a new plan. But don't worry about having a place to be. You're welcome here for as long as you want to stay."

Erin

I'D SURVIVED the past two nights in my parents' home. I'd survived the bachelorette party.

And so far, I hadn't broken my jaw gritting my teeth.

Everyone was just so damn polite. Mom treated me like I was made of glass. Everyone at the bachelor party had acted like I was crazy to have wanted to leave all of this behind and open a bakery and a bookstore in some backwater town in Pennsylvania, of all places. One woman had actually asked if I was talking about the plot of a movie.

A few of the women at the bachelorette party had given me fake smiles and said how sorry they were about my failed engagement. The one that had ended five years ago. I'd managed not to roll my eyes and had asked about their children.

Sue me for being petty, but none of them had kids and I

knew it. They'd looked highly offended that I would even think they looked like they'd been pregnant and made a fast retreat. My sister, who'd been standing by my side, had actually seemed impressed and given me a slight smile.

I'd seen my dad for a grand total of fifteen minutes so far. He was in the midst of a huge European deal and had stayed in the city until last night. He'd arrived home after I'd gone to bed, and he'd been in his office when I got up. He'd given me a distracted kiss on the cheek and a pat on the back when he'd come out for coffee a little while ago.

I'd made it to Friday, and Rebel would be here soon.

Butterflies danced in my stomach, but they were giant butterflies with huge wings, and I think they'd moved into my lungs, as well. It was hard to breathe.

And now, I was alone in the kitchen with my mom, staring at each other in the kitchen, holding mugs of tea.

"I never really asked how you like it in St. David," she said. "Are you happy there?"

Since she sounded sincerely interested, I didn't overthink my answer. I didn't have to.

"I love it there. It feels like home."

My mom's expression didn't change. "I'm not surprised. It seems like the right place for you."

Now, I was flustered. And a little pissy, which I didn't like.

"Really? Then why do you constantly make me feel like I should move home? Like you think I can't survive on my own?"

She actually looked puzzled. "That's never been my intention. I don't know why you would think that. I certainly don't think that."

"Well, I definitely get that feeling whenever we talk about it. So maybe we shouldn't."

I didn't want to do this now. Not when Rebel would be here any minute.

But my mom had a different idea. "Erin. I realize we don't have the best of relationships, but I have never thought you incapable of taking care of yourself. I simply think you take on too much at once. Your brother and sister are more focused." She held up a hand to stop the words that wanted to rush out of my mouth. "And that's not a slight against you. Don't jump to conclusions. Do I wish you had stayed in New York? Of course, I do. What parent doesn't want their children close to them? But you left. And you never came back."

My brain chewed through that information like a paper shredder. "My fiancé dumped me a week before our wedding. Everyone kept asking me what'd happened, what did I do. Like it was my fault he didn't want to marry me. I needed a fresh start. I rebuilt my life and started a business. I didn't do that to punish you. I couldn't stay here and have everyone look at me like I was some pitiful creature. I saw an opportunity to get away, and I took it."

"We understood why you wanted to leave. However, when months and then years passed and you didn't come back, we all felt like you'd turned your back on your family. That doesn't mean I'm not proud of you, Erin. I am. But you don't seem to know that."

Since she'd never said that to me before, I got this warm, fuzzy feeling in my chest that I didn't necessarily associate with my mom. My bottom lip tried to quiver a little.

There were so many things I could have said to that. I could've been angry or upset. But she wasn't wrong. I hadn't known they were proud of me. I did now only because she'd just told me.

I nodded and smiled, because that's all I could do. "Thank you, Mom. It's nice to hear."

"You're welcome." And we went back to staring at each other until she said, "You should probably go put on your dress. Your brother and sister will meet us at the chapel. I'll have to drag your father away from his office in half an hour so we can get there on time."

Just then, the doorbell rang, and I froze. I wanted to run to the door and throw my arms around Rebel's neck and hold him close. I wanted him to tell me he'd missed me. I wanted—

"Just friends, you said." My mom's voice held a hint of amusement, as if she knew exactly what I was thinking.

I wondered if she'd be impressed if I told her we were friends with benefits. I'm not even sure she'd know what that meant.

I nodded. "Just friends."

Her head tilted to the side, and I definitely saw amusement flicker in her eyes. "Mmm hmm. I'll be sure to tell anyone who asks."

Since I didn't have a response to the fact that my mom seemed to have made a joke, I got my feet moving and flung open the front door.

I had to suck in air so I didn't pass out.

"Rebel. I'm so…happy you're here."

That was absolutely not what I wanted to say. I wanted to tell him he looked good enough to eat. I wanted him to grab me and kiss me. I just wanted him.

His gaze traveled from my head to my toes, just as I realized I was still wearing my silk robe. My hair and makeup were done, but I hadn't put on my dress yet. Instinctively, I reached for the lapels and pulled them together.

His lips quirked in a sexy grin. "You look beautiful. But I

hope you're not wearing that to the wedding. I might have to defend your honor."

I smiled then laughed. I was just so damn happy to see him. Coupled with the days I'd spent avoiding him during camp, I felt like I'd been deprived of him for way too long.

I wanted to stand here and stare at him all day. But we had a wedding to go to. And we both needed to change.

"Come in. I just need to put on my dress, and we can leave for the church."

He walked into the house, glancing around at the grand entrance, a garment bag over his shoulder.

"Hello again, Mr. Lawrence."

My mom appeared at my side, startling me as she reached out to shake Rebel's hand.

"How are you, Mrs. Wright?"

"Honestly, I'm ready for the reception so I can have a drink." Her dry humor made Rebel smile and surprised the hell out of me. "Why don't you and Erin go upstairs to change. We need to leave for the church in half an hour."

Rebel looked back at me. "Lead the way."

My nerves made a return, twisting my stomach in a knot.

This was really happening. Rebel was here and would be my date for the wedding. I couldn't wait to show him off. And it wasn't because my ex was going to be there.

My ex and I hadn't talked since I'd left New York City and moved to St. David. Most people probably thought he was the reason I'd stayed away. And maybe that had been one of the reasons, at first. But I'd stayed because I'd grown to love the small town and the people who lived there. One, in particular.

I tilted my chin toward the staircase.

"Just up to the second floor. You can use the guest room."

Turning, I hurried up the stairs, knowing he followed,

knowing my mom watched from below. I was lucky I didn't trip.

The second we turned the corner to head down the hallway, Rebel wrapped his hand around my upper arm. I stopped as a zip of electricity shot through my blood.

"Hey, you okay?"

I wanted to melt into his arms and press my cheek against his chest, but it would mess up my makeup. His voice, so rough and deep, lit tiny fires low in my body.

"I'm fine."

I wanted to add, "Now that you're here," but I couldn't bring myself to do it. I couldn't be that vulnerable. Not until I knew why he'd agreed to come. And I couldn't bring myself to ask him that. I wasn't sure I wanted to know the answer.

What if it wasn't the answer I wanted to hear?

"Then let's do this."

He sounded so sure of himself, so confident. I really didn't want to go to the wedding, but I also couldn't wait to arrive with him. The other women would drool over him. And if they didn't, they were blind or stupid.

"Thank you."

His eyes glinted. "You can thank me later."

It got hard to breathe. I knew how he wanted to be thanked. And I had absolutely no qualms about giving him what he wanted.

"Now go get dressed before I mess up that lipstick."

It was such a male thing to say. I swear if he smacked my ass when I turned around to go to my room, I might spontaneously orgasm. I should return my feminist card now.

The man made a sound low in his throat. "If you keep looking at me like that, it's not going to be just your lipstick that's messed up."

Delighted, I smiled and batted my eyes at him. I wanted to flirt with him. I wanted him to know that I was flirting with him. "Is that a promise?"

He stared down at me with a look I couldn't decipher. I felt like he wanted to say something but then thought better of it.

"Yes. It is. Now go."

I grinned, happiness spreading like alcohol through my blood and making me tipsy. I flashed him what I hoped was a flirty look then turned and headed for my door, which was only a few feet down the hall.

"I'll be waiting," I heard him say just before I disappeared into my room.

THE CONFIDENCE I'd had when I'd walked out of my bedroom in my Chanel dress and heels had slowly seeped away.

Rebel had been waiting for me in the hall, leaning against the wall, looking like he'd walked out of a magazine ad. With his hair combed and his beard tightly trimmed, the man could pass for a movie star.

And the way he'd looked at me before we'd left had made me want to skip down the stairs. Probably would've tripped in the heels.

He'd managed a little small talk in the car with my dad, who actually seemed to make an effort to be engaged. He told me I looked pretty and kissed my mom's hand before helping her out of the car. My mom didn't even look surprised at the show of affection. Had I been way so long that I'd stepped back into an alternate reality?

Then his phone rang, just as we got to the church, and he

stepped aside to answer, while my mom, discreetly rolled her eyes and told us he'd catch up.

The wedding was staged perfectly. My cousin made a truly beautiful bride and her husband looked totally in love with her.

But the reception…

So many people. *So* many cliques and former acquaintances from boarding school—of course my cousin had gone to the same school. We were Wright heirs, after all.

Everyone wanted to meet Rebel. Of course they did. He was gorgeous. And mysterious. And he wasn't one of them, so they all wanted a piece of him.

My face hurt from fake smiling. But through it all, Rebel held my hand. And I don't mean figuratively. I mean, he never stopped touching me. And not in a creepy way. If he wasn't holding my hand, he had his hand low on my back. It felt possessive. I liked it. It felt right.

But when Meredith Huntebrinker approached me as I made my way to the restroom after dinner, I had the momentary urge to flee back to him. The smirk on her face let me know she'd read me as clearly as a billboard. She'd always been a bitch, the mean girl in high school who loved to pick on the younger girls and the less confident ones. Like me. She hadn't made it her mission in life to make mine miserable, but I hadn't been her only target. She'd had four grades of girls to torment.

But I wasn't that same insecure girl anymore.

"You turned into the dark horse, didn't you, Erin? You disappear off the face of the earth after your fiancé dumps you and reappear with the hottest piece of ass in the room. Where'd you find him? And how much did you pay him to come with you?"

We'd stopped in the darkened hallway outside the restrooms. I considered ignoring her. She didn't really deserve an answer. As a teenager, I would've put my head down and scurried away in the opposite direction.

Screw that. According to Meredith, I'd won the prize for the hottest date at the wedding, so yay me. Which meant I had something she wanted. And would never have.

I turned to face her, which she hadn't been expecting. Her brows rose in surprise, and she actually took a step back.

"Did you need something, Meredith? Perhaps a personality that isn't stuck in high school?"

Now, she looked impressed, her smile still as sharp as a knife.

"Ooh, the stray kitten grew claws. Good for you. I'd still like to know where you found that one. He's yummy."

Shock stuck my feet to the floor as she continued into the restroom. I followed a few feet behind and found her reapplying her lipstick in front of the mirror.

"Do you make it your mission in life to be a bitch?"

The words flew out of my mouth before I could even think about them, but Meredith just shrugged as she looked at me in the mirror.

"It works for me. But seriously, where'd you find him?"

It took me a second to realize she was dead serious and not at all ashamed of it. She was who she was and made no excuses. I could almost respect that if she hadn't made me and so many other girls' lives such hell in school.

Then again, I didn't really care what she thought anymore.

"St. David, Pennsylvania. Where I live now."

She mock-shuddered as she snapped her lipstick closed and stuck it back in her tiny bag. "Sounds horrid. Maybe I'll take a shot at him, anyway."

Then she walked out.

After I used the facilities, washed my hands and reapplied my makeup, I looked at my reflection in the mirror.

Oh hell, no, she would not take her shot.

He was mine.

I headed back to the dance floor, saw Meredith standing with Rebel. She looked sexy and flirty, and he looked like he wished the floor would swallow.

Meredith didn't stand a chance.

My gaze connected with his across the room, and his eyes lit up. He straightened a little and, when I started across the floor, he barely looked at Meredith as he said something and started walking toward me.

We met on the dance floor, the band mid-song. We came together like we'd been dancing together for years, and not just a couple of times.

"That's a viper. Thanks for saving me."

I threw back my head and laughed, drawing the attention of a few of the couples around us. Not one of them mattered more than him.

"I don't think you would've had any trouble brushing her off. You do grumpy so well."

"And yet here you are, in my arms."

"I am."

Come on, Rebel. Don't let me down.

It took him a couple of seconds, but he finally said, "Is this really where you want to be?"

Moment of truth. "Do you want me here?"

"Isn't it obvious? I want you, Erin. And I'll still want you when we get back to St. David."

"And when you leave?"

He went silent for a couple of seconds, and my heart began to squeeze painfully.

Then he reached up to cup my cheek with one hand. He'd never done anything like this in public, and it gave me hope.

"I had to spend some time away from St. David to realize that what I want is there. My family. My home. My friends. You."

Tears pricked at the corners of my eyes. "But you never liked me. What changed?"

"It wasn't you I didn't like. I was looking for something I couldn't find. I kept telling myself it wasn't there. And when I got the call from the Redtails, I thought, okay, this is it. This is what I've been looking for."

"Validation."

He shrugged. "Maybe. Or just the chance to prove to myself that I could do something more. Be something more. Rowdy and Rain were always going to run the team when Pop retired. I knew that. And I didn't think I wanted that. I just wanted to play. Then I got it in my head that I had to prove that hockey was all I needed. That contract with the Redtails… I wanted it. I did. But that's not home to me. Those guys…they're great, but they're not Bonesaw and Kat and Denny and Kookoo and Cudgel. They're not the guys I've grown up with and played with for years."

I smiled. "They could be your guys, if you gave them a chance."

"A quarter of them have already signed with another team. Another quarter'll be gone before midseason. That's not how I want to spend my career, moving from team to team. I know what I want."

"And what's that?"

"I want to be home. St. David is home." He paused, lifting a hand to brush a finger down my cheek to my throat, his gaze falling to my lips. "Home is where you are."

My smile was so wide, it practically hurt.

My hands rose to cup his face, his beard soft against my palms. "I love you, Rebel. You know that, right? I mean, I knew a couple of weeks ago, but I took one look at you when I first moved to St. David and fell a little bit then. I think that's why I used to babble around you so much. But you didn't want anything to do with me back then. And I'd just been dumped by my fiancé, and I'd moved to this little town where everyone knew each other, and I was outsider with all these plans to disrupt the peace."

He snorted, shaking his head. "But you won everyone over. Including me." He held me closer, my body pressed tightly against his, continued to hold my gaze. "I love you, Erin. All of you. I love the way you smile and the sound of your laugh. I love the way you see all my faults and still want me. And I really," he moved his lips closer to my ear, "really love those cherry almond scones."

My head tipped back, my laughter ringing out across the room, not completely covered by the sound of the band. When I brought my gaze level with his again, I smiled, so damn, happy, I thought I might be glowing. And I don't mean figuratively.

"I will bake them for you every day if you promise to dedicate your goal dance to me."

His smile melted certain parts of my body that shouldn't be melting in public.

"Every single one, babe. Every single one."

Then he kissed me. And it was amazing.

EPILOGUE

SIX MONTHS AFTER THE WEDDING

*ebel*

"WHAT THE HELL do you mean, I'm getting a penalty. That fucker tripped me."

The Devils were losing, unusual this season. We were on fire only two months in, but I'd just taken a bad penalty. No way in hell I was going to admit it, though. Especially not with the fans as fired up as they were.

I'd taken the bait from the Stag player, who'd checked Ian into the boards harder than he should have and made the kid limp back to the bench. Of course I'd gone after the bastard.

The crowd cheered and banged on the glass as I skated to the penalty box, plotting my revenge. And going over my dance.

My guys killed the penalty, and I skated back onto the ice, one thought in mind.

I made a beeline for the defensive blue line to the screams

267

of the crowd. I saw Max Butcher, who'd just gotten the puck, had picked me up. He made the pass of my dreams, straight at me and right on the tape, and I took off for the other end of the ice. The Stags defense got caught on the wrong side of their blue line.

And now it was just me and the goalie.

And then it was just me and the net.

The crowd roared as I nailed it home top right corner. My guys banged the hell out of my back as we skated to the bench for fist bumps.

Then the announcer called me out to center ice.

I found her in the stands, in the seats near the Devils' defensive zone. Erin liked to sit where she could see me play the most.

She wore a sweater with my number and name on the back, whooping and circling her arm in the air. She knew what was coming. It was my first goal of the season.

The music started. It'd taken me a few tries to come up with the perfect song for my goal dance, but I think I'd found it.

Bruce Springsteen's "Red-headed Woman."

It'd taken a little judicious editing to make the song family-friendly enough for our audience, and it was only thirty seconds, but I'd choreographed the hell out of those thirty seconds. For her.

I heard the crowd go wild, but I swore I could hear her voice over all of them.

And when we got back to my place that night after the game, I put on the song and performed it just for her.

I'd barely finished when she jumped into my arms and wrapped her legs around my waist. Her fingers combed through my still-wet hair, and she bumped her nose against mine.

"I love you, Rebel."

"I love you back."

After a kiss, I set her on her feet. And went to my knees.

If you don't know the song, go and listen to it. It's a good one.

Keep My Secrets

Rock My Heart

WICKED & CHARMING

Seducing Whitney

Claiming Ellie

Sharing Brianna

INDECENT

An Indecent Proposition

An Indecent Affair

An Indecent Arrangement

An Indecent Longing

An Indecent Desire

LOVERS UNDERCOVER

Lovers & Lies

Sinners & Secrets

Beauty & Brains

DARKLY ENCHANTED

Spell Bound

Moon Bound

Twice Bound

MOONLIGHT FANTASIES

Shadow Magic

Enchanted Magic

Dangerous Magic

MOONLIGHT LOVERS

Kiss of Moonlight

Visions of Moonlight

Edge of Moonlight

Temptation in Moonlight

Grace in Moonlight

Shades of Moonlight

DIVINE DESIRES

Dark Desires at Dawn

Rough Caress of Midnight

Double Fantasies at Twilight

Enchanting Temptations in Shadow

ABOUT THE AUTHOR

Stephanie Julian is a USA Today and New York Times best-selling author of contemporary and paranormal romance.

Visit her website at www.stephaniejulian.com for more information.

www.ingramcontent.com/pod-product-compliance
Lightning Source LLC
Chambersburg PA
CBHW050600190726
48283CB00007B/2218